"This is a cross-cultural, syncretic, folksy, razor-sharp narrative about the horrors of grief and the eternal debate over nature versus nurture. . . . *Monstrilio* packs in a lot, and the author pulls it off brilliantly. It is at once dark and tender, at times bleak, but balanced with humor that borders on slapstick. . . . For all the ground being broken in genre-bending horror, his is a distinctive, exciting new voice in fiction."

—GABINO IGLESIAS,
Los Angeles Times

"Bizarre and brilliant, *Monstrilio* is a sort of modern *Frankenstein*."

—LAUREN PUCKETT-POPE, *ELLE*

"How to explain my love of this bizarre book? It is grotesque, heavy, gut-wrenching, and painful, and I still loved it. . . . There is a lot in this story to unpack around death, self-acceptance, unconditional love, and challenging social norms."

—CHERI ANDERSON,
Boston Globe

"*Monstrilio* is full of surprises and delightfully messed up—at once precise and inscrutable and horrifying."

—PATRICK RAPA,
Philadelphia Inquirer

"This book is a slow-burning monster story incrementally creeping up on the unsuspecting reader . . . [and] a creative study on the process of mourning and the lengths people will extend themselves in order to preserve a loved one's spirit, presence, and essence."

—JIM PIECHOTA,
Bay Area Reporter

"An extraordinary act of imagination, an extended meditation that begins in grief, family, belonging, and moves past that, into a deeper discovery of the power of love—and the powerlessness of love, as well its strangeness. With *Monstrilio*, Sámano Córdova makes a remarkable, kaleidoscopic debut."
—ALEXANDER CHEE,
author of *How to Write an Autobiographical Novel*

"Simply exquisite. Easily one of my favorite reads this year."
—SARAH GAILEY,
bestselling author of *Just Like Home*
and *The Echo Wife*

"*Monstrilio* is unlike any other book I've read. Genuinely scary at times, it moved me with its humanity, made me laugh, and ultimately, made me cry. Gerardo Sámano Córdova has written a stunning exploration of grief, belonging, and familial love in prose so beautiful you won't want to rush through it—even as you need to know what happens next."
—ANA REYES,
author of *The House in the Pines*

"Haunting and often bleakly humorous, Gerardo Sámano Córdova's *Monstrilio* is a captivating tone poem of trauma, grief, and transformation. Córdova writes with the lyrical precision of a master surrealist and creates an uncompromising vision of literary horror that is so wholly unique and utterly his own."
—ERIC LAROCCA,
author of *Things Have Gotten Worse*
Since We Last Spoke and Other Misfortunes

"In Gerardo Sámano Córdova's spare, soulful, and singular *Monstrilio*, a mother's grief turns monstrous, literally taking on a life of its own. As tender and terrifying as its titular character, *Monstrilio* is just as likely to work its way into your heart as into your nightmares. Prepare to unhinge your jaw and devour it whole."
—MARIA ADELMANN,
author of *Girls of a Certain Age* and *How to Be Eaten*

"Gerardo Sámano Córdova's dark, soulful magic puts me in mind of Kelly Link or Carmen Maria Machado (and further back, Mary Shelley). The horror of grief has rarely been so viscerally or movingly evoked."

—PETER HO DAVIES,
author of *A Lie Someone Told You About Yourself*

"*Monstrilio* is the monster story about grief I've been craving. Bloody and full of longing, it gets under your skin and doesn't let you go. A thrilling and heartbreaking ride from Mexico City to NYC to Berlin, brilliantly capturing what it means to lose someone you love with ferocious tenderness. Gerardo Sámano Córdova is an international revelation and one of the boldest new voices writing today."

—AKIL KUMARASAMY,
author of *Meet Us by the Roaring Sea*

"Sámano Córdova's writing is piercing and intimate. Whether describing Monstrilio's first, vicious moments of life or the subtle, strained romance between Magos and her childhood friend Lena, Sámano Córdova keeps readers breathless. . . . His novel seeks to embody [grief], making this nameless, eternal pain something we can speak to and hold."

—ERIC PONCE,
BookPage, starred review

"Gerardo writes with the potency of a master, painting an image that takes feelings of genuine sadness and morphs it into a very disturbing situation. I read those first few pages with watery eyes and a grimace on my face, and from that moment on, I couldn't put the book down. This genre-bender takes an incredibly sad tale of loss and grief and coats it in surrealism and horror, and the result is one of the most original and fascinating novels you'll read this year. . . . An amazing read. Don't miss it."

—AKRAM HERRAK,
Independent Book Review, starred review

"Grief takes the shape of a monster in Sámano Córdova's disturbing yet touching literary horror debut. . . . Sámano Córdova creates complex characters who make difficult decisions that blur the lines between being human and being a monster. Fans of Eric LaRocca, Agustina Bazterrica, and Carmen Maria Machado will appreciate this unique take on the horror genre." —VERÓNICA N. RODRÍGUEZ, *Booklist*

"Sámano Córdova asks the reader to consider the limits of familial love and understanding. He provides no easy answers, and readers may find themselves touched and horrified in equal measure. . . . An enthralling debut that packs a heavy emotional punch. Fans of domestic horror like Zoje Stage's *Baby Teeth* or Ashley Audrain's *The Push* will find a lot to chew on here." —COLIN CHAPPELL, *Library Journal*

"Sámano Córdova's prose is beautiful. . . . He captures the heartbreak in aching detail, and the strangeness of the tale only adds to the power of emotions here. He also does a fantastic job of using setting to support the story without overpowering. Bloody and tender, *Monstrilio* is a singular novel, elevating both horror and family drama into something universal and unforgettable." —SARAH RACHEL EGELMAN, Bookreporter

"In this wicked debut novel, Sámano Córdova combines queer themes touching on identity, kink, and consent with Latin American mysticism for an unusually visceral coming-of-age tale. . . . There's no doubt there's nothing quite like it. A Promethean fable about reconstruction, reinvention, and the occasional human-sized snack." —*Kirkus Reviews*

"Sámano Córdova's work is as devastating as its premise is whimsical." —CARL LAVIGNE, *Ploughshares*

Monstrilio

GERARDO SÁMANO CÓRDOVA

zando

NEW YORK

Copyright © 2023 by Gerardo Sámano Córdova

Zando
zandoprojects.com

Originally published in hardcover by Zando, March 2023
First trade paperback edition, January 2024

Text design by Aubrey Khan, Neuwirth & Associates, Inc.
Cover design by Alex Merto
Cover image: detail from *The Nightmare* by Nicolai Abraham Abildgaard
(1743–1809) | Photo © Photo Josse / Bridgeman Images

Library of Congress Control Number: 2022945255

978-1-63893-160-7 (Paperback)
978-1-63893-037-2 (ebook)

10   9   8   7   6   5   4   3   2
Manufactured in the United States of America

A Papi, Mami y Pol,

You've been with me from the very beginning

and, for that, I am the luckiest.

Her son dies in a child-sized bed, big enough for him but barely enough to hold her and her husband who cling to the edges, folding themselves small so they fit one on each side of him. She savors the constant shifting and squirming needed to keep her in place.

Her son was alive and now he isn't. No thunder, no angels weeping, no cloaked Death, no grace; just his silent body, unbreathing, and the blunt realization that this is it.

How dull, she thinks. She could scream, get on her knees, pull out her hair, curse God. Take me, she could plead while beating her chest with her fist. She won't. She can't rally the drama she once imagined.

In her fantasies—is it too morbid to call them fantasies? She doesn't think so. In her fantasies, her son died in a shopping mall, one of the big ones in Mexico City, because in a mall there is an audience, and she wanted an audience but thought dying in the street was too sordid. At the mall, her son collapsed, and as she held his little body in her lap, mall-goers surrounded her in hushed awe of her sorrow, unimaginable to all, while she became a Pietà, marble and gorgeous. Tears, fat and clean, slid from her cheeks and pooled on her chin. When she imagined this, she cried along with her kneeling self.

And now, nothing. This is the moment—Death!—and not a tear. Perhaps she needs an audience, and her only audience in this room, this bright room, is her whimpering husband, and one whimpering man is no audience.

Her husband nuzzles their son in the space the boy's squat neck allows, as if her husband were the fawn and her son the doe. Her husband squeezes their son with his whole body: arms, legs, head, and chest. He grunts as he squeezes. His breaths are loud against their son's neck, smelling him hard. She squeezes their son too, tries what her husband tries because he seems to know how to grieve, and she doesn't. Her husband grabs her upper arm and pulls her toward the middle of the bed, toward their son. It seems her husband figures that if they push themselves hard enough, they might be able to bear him again. I bore him, she thinks. I won't bear him again. Her husband's blond hair falls on her son's face. She sweeps it away with the back of her hand, even when she realizes it can't tickle her son anymore. Her husband lets go of her. He makes no sounds. Maybe he has died too. She is too tired to check.

She is not too tired to leave the bed and open a window. A rush of cool air blows in. It's spring and the air is fresh, very undeath-like. Her hair is loose and because it's loose, she feels it flutter on her neck. A quick flutter, not enough to whip her fully awake. She hasn't slept. She will but not yet.

A CHILD'S DEATH IS THE WORST, they say, but she won't die of grief. Perhaps her husband can—he is romantic.

Their son's body will be taken away for cremation, then a funeral, black clothes, sad family, and sad friends. They are away from Mexico. In her fantasies his death was in Mexico. But instead, it happened in this middle-of-nowhere house they have secluded themselves in. She feels anger, a faint anger, only a lighter's flame of wanting to blame her husband, but her husband is too wretched to be blamed.

In this house in Upstate New York surrounded by trees, an owl hoots in the mornings thinking itself a rooster. Her son loved this morning owl, his tiny body wound in rapture. She listens for the owl, but perhaps it has already hooted and she has missed it. She mumbles a list in order to hear something—there are events that follow a death—and this reminds her of her friend Lena, always thinking steps ahead.

But what needs to come will not come yet. She is not done with her son, not yet ready to hand him away.

HER HUSBAND IS NOT DEAD, not sleeping, simply slack and raggy. She folds him. First, she folds his fingers into his palms, prying them from their son's pajamas. Then, from his wrists, she folds his fisted hands into his chest; his legs she pulls down off the bed. She enjoys his thick thighs and remains holding them for longer than she needs to, and he lets her, his muscles soft and heavy. His thighs are a comfort to her. Perhaps her touch is also a comfort to him. She swivels his head away from their boy, and her husband shuts his eyes, squeezing out tears. If she wanted, she could make her husband dance like a puppet, crawl him forward until he rolls down the stairs. But she won't do this. She holds his head close to her chest so he can muffle his sobs on her skin. She will let him lean on her as they walk out of the room, she holding more weight than she thinks is possible. When he stops and asks to be let back into the room to see his son, she shushes him, says he needs to sleep. She walks her husband to their bed, where he curls defeated.

Their son is only hers now.

She lies next to him and licks his ear, like an animal would.

He remains dead.

Her son wears cream-colored pajamas illustrated with silly dinosaurs in bright colors. He fits in them though they were meant for a younger boy. He loved these pajamas. They show thinning patches where the soft material has wearied. He would have worn them exclusively, roaring his way through the day, if she hadn't forced him to wash himself and change.

She wants to learn one last secret from her son. What part of a person's body is inextricably themselves? Not hair, though many people keep lockets of hair. Hair is too public and not a secret. His finger or his toe, these she knows well, how thin and long his fingers are, like her husband's, and how small and pudgy his toes, like hers. His tongue quick and lispy. His heart, a quiet, solitary heart engaged to her and her husband.

It has to be his lung. Her son, Santiago, has only one lung. This is it, this lung, the core of his Santiagoness. She loves and hates this lung, a mystery to her, a tiny lung that carried her son way past his expected life span. She wants to thank it, and also spit on it for not having carried him further. Mainly, she wants to see the lung and hold it.

Excavating one's child isn't a difficult task, if determined. First, she has to break skin, easy with a sharp knife, and her husband keeps their knives sharp. A sharp knife is essential for a good cook, her husband claims, and he is a great cook. She performs the first incision on her son's belly with the utmost care, lest Santiago wake up in a sudden rebirth.

He doesn't.

Her next cuts become bolder. Once he is open, she sneaks her hand under her son's ribs—she will not break them—to find the lung. She is no doctor. The procedure is messy. His heart does not pump anymore, so what oozes out is the blood his veins already carried.

Years ago, she saw a Lorca play produced at the UNAM. She remembers the girl who played the mother, a mother older than the girl could ever be. The girl was a stupendous actor. There was a wedding, and at one point, she can't remember why, this mother kneels on the floor and delivers a short monologue about what it means to see blood spilled on the ground, her son's blood. The girl in the play mimicked soaking her hands in blood, and when she licked them, palms and fingers, her tongue swiped every side of them. Because the blood is mine, the mother said.

There isn't enough blood for her to soak her hands. She smears and licks them with her tongue anyway. She savors her Santiago's blood, a taste of iron and warmth. She could suck more blood out of his veins, but she won't; she's not a vampire though now she understands the impulse—the craving to drink deep and thirsty in her bowels.

She finds his lung toward the right of his chest. Lighter and more inconsequential than she thought it would be. She wants to rip it out and keep it for herself. She pulls but not too hard, still thinking she can hurt her son. It won't detach.

The bed is a mess.

She whispers her son's name, like an apology. Though she made this lung the same way she made the rest of him, she decides her son should keep his lung. She'll only take a nugget. With a paring knife, she slices a piece, the downmost tip. This chunk is hers.

She takes the chunk of lung and places it in a clear jam jar her son used to keep pencils in. There's no lid, but she knows where to find one.

She wraps her long hair in a bun and fastens it with a pencil. As best she can, she puts her son back together. She unfolds the skin of her son's open belly, soaks a piece of sheet in her saliva and wipes dry blood off his body.

Her husband comes in and freezes, trying to make sense of what he has walked into. She planned on changing the sheets and wrapping Santiago in a clean set to spare her husband of seeing their son's maimed torso. She doesn't know whether he will scream, or hate her, or understand her.

"You've destroyed him," he says, and she finds the word *destroyed* curious. Has she really? No. She has destroyed nothing; nothing was left to destroy.

But she has made a mess.

"Magos." He says her name, as if it could summon an explanation.

"Joseph." She returns his name to let him know that she sees him standing there, gaunt and pale green.

MAGOS

LENA

JOSEPH

M

Joseph brought our cremated son home the day the dogwood filled up, its branches fat with flowers. I didn't know what the tree was called when I first saw it. Even when my husband called it *dogwood*, the name meant nothing to me. I understood the *wood* part, after all it was a tree, but the *dog* part was odd, as nothing in the tree resembled a dog. I had no name for it in Spanish and this made the tree seem even more otherworldly, because for things to become real, I must be able to name them in Spanish. I later learned the tree is called *cornejo florido*. *Florido* made sense—some dogwoods don't flower, and this one did, so one must specify—but the word *cornejo*, the true name of the tree, I didn't understand. I thought Cornejo was a last name. Like the *dog* in the English word, *cornejo* remained a mystery. I liked the tree's resistance to make sense.

The tree managed to enchant me right at first glance. I was baffled, as the tree had little to flaunt as extraordinary. Sure, it was leafy and extended its branches in a pleasing canopy, but lots of trees accomplish that. It wasn't even flowering when I first saw it, and all white, fat with flowers, is when it's at its most beautiful.

Perhaps I foresaw the dogwood's potential, that it would become white in spring and stand stark against the evergreens behind it.

That first day in Firgesan, the dogwood stood fully green at the farthest edge of the water as if floating on the large pond my son, Santiago, called a lake. We had moved from Mexico City to Upstate New York because of that house where the dogwood stood, because it was smack in the middle of nowhere, just woods and fresh air. Santiago needed a place to recuperate, like the sick people in English novels who went to the seashore.

The house was called Firgesan, and I got an aristocratic thrill knowing I would live in a house with a name. "A manor," my husband proudly explained to Santiago and me. "My ancestors built it in the late eighteenth century." It had started as a modest farm and had grown from there. From outside, his manor resembled a cube with a gable roof, not very large, white, and, in every way, unmemorable. But inside, it was grand with its high-ceilinged entrance hall, huge stained glass window, mulberry runner, and grandiose wooden banisters. Off to one side, through a dark corridor, there was a library with tall shelves and dusty books. Farther, at the very end, a sitting room with wood-framed windows along two of its walls, large couches, plush chairs, and tables with spindly legs, the way I imagined the word *parlor* to look: crowded, cozy, flowery, and comfortable. Santiago, like me, was in awe.

The grounds outside the house extended into fields that led to the woods that surrounded the property. The pond curved around the back part of the house, where a more contemporary deck had been built. The deck was outfitted with minimalist wooden garden furniture, its cushions upholstered in grays and dark teals. Joseph has excellent taste. He spent the month before Santiago and I arrived cleaning and arranging the house, a house kept but not inhabited in years. Joseph built the deck for me, so I had a space for myself to enjoy the house from.

The first day at Firgesan the sun shone with a shy light that softened all edges and made everything warmer. Joseph was lucky for that light, and the dogwood tree, and the flickering pond, and the breeze that blew as I sat on the deck, because it made it difficult to complain further, to question the move once more, to find fault with the house, to discover its loneliness. I was happy for our seclusion, then.

In winter, my first and only winter at Firgesan, the dogwood stripped down to its bare and feeble branches—it looked so skinny, a pauper a step away from death, fighting to survive the cold. My husband and son told me not to bother when during frosts I walked to it carrying steaming pots of hot water. "You'll kill it," Joseph said, and Santiago nodded behind him because he thought his father knew everything about everything. Still, I melted the snow and frost around my dogwood—I called it mine then. I knew I wasn't going to keep the tree from being cold, but I could offer it some comfort.

My dogwood bloomed in the spring, plump and gorgeous. "This dogwood has been on the property for more than a hundred years, Magos. It didn't need you to bloom again," Joseph said. By then, it didn't much matter that the dogwood had lived.

Our son died before the dogwood pushed out its first flower, a bloom so simple with four white petals and a burst of yellow-green in the center—a beginner's flower. I believed that flower was my son reincarnated. One believes the stupidest things in grief. I spoke to the flower and called it my son. And then I laughed because how ridiculous—how cruel, really—it would have been if my son was reincarnated as something so ephemeral, frail, and beautiful. I killed that first bloom with one swoop of my hand. Dead again, my son could become something else: the shell of a tortoise, strong and ancient, or a hideous fanged creature deep in the sea where he'd see wonders even he could've never imagined.

JOSEPH AND I HELD THE urn together and poured our son at the base of the dogwood. My son, turned to ash, flew, landing on the tree's trunk and on the grass and weeds that grew around it. When the weather was still kind, Santiago would sit under the dogwood and draw monsters. Perched on the deck, I would observe him, his colored pencils on a blue cloth case next to him, his knees folded up, notebook on his thighs. He would push one colored pencil in the case, making sure they stayed in their rainbow arrangement, before he used another.

As ash, everything Santiago touched now turned gray. Carried by the wind, some of him landed in the pond. In the pond, he became mud.

WITH SANTIAGO DEAD, Joseph and I had little to do in Firgesan. We didn't so much exist as much as we haunted, and with no one else to haunt, we haunted each other.

I grew observant and silent. I followed Joseph around, lurking through the house, in corners, behind doors, watching him like a scientist or a ghost. Joseph became fascinating to me, as if I were just then learning him. He cried. He stared blankly. He tried to draw, but he could only doodle little squares that overlapped each other. He'd go into a room, the library for example, and stand in the middle, among shelves of old books, lost and befuddled as if aliens had just beamed him there. I watched him shower. How tender he was with himself, with his hairy belly and chest, the slow way he scrubbed with soap, using both hands to lather. He massaged his thighs and passed the tip of the soap through the space between each of his toes. He stroked his penis clean.

I desired his body. I wanted to taste him, but the time I tried he took part without any spirit, without any of the hunger I felt, a deep, lustful hunger that needed him to squeeze me, bite me, push into me. So I gave his body up.

I watched him sleep, his hands tight in fists like Santiago's when he slept. One night, Joseph woke up to me staring by the side of his bed, screamed, and scampered away. In the same sentence he called me a monster and asked me to hold him. I watched Joseph not eat, fork his leftovers into the bin, rinse his plate, and set it in the dishwasher.

I can't remember if I ate or if I showered or if I slept.

I only remember him. Joseph. His hair grew opaque; it used to be luminous, multicolored, light blond, deep gold, and brownish depending on how the light hit. I had first fallen in love with his hair. And his forearms, thin and hairy, now thinner and balding. I pulled at the few remaining hairs. I pulled hard because I wanted to extract their brothers from where they'd hidden. He cried "Ow," but when I pulled harder, he let me.

If I spoke, I cannot remember my words, or the language in which I would have spoken them. I had lost language. I didn't need language; I was there to observe.

When Santiago used to grow bored of drawing or staring into the woods in his dinosaur pajamas, he would follow me around Firgesan, the way I now followed Joseph. He wouldn't speak, just observe me as if I were the most fascinating creature. It was annoying to have the kid follow me around, so small and so serious. Every task I did, even if it was folding sheets, became important. I didn't ask him to help me because I preferred him as a spectator. When he tried to help, he was clumsy.

Joseph demanded I do something else but follow him around. Joseph called me the worst shadow. A demon. He asked me to go away, but when he couldn't see me, he called for me. I was always around; I only had to come out from where I hid.

He did not mention how I had opened up our son, cut him, destroyed him, as he had claimed. I knew he hated me for it.

Did he? He wouldn't speak about it.

He asked me to cry with him, but his sadness was his and I couldn't steal it. He said we should go back to Mexico and that we should stay in Firgesan forever. He asked me what I thought, what I felt, what I proposed to do, but I thought and felt nothing. I had no proposal. Joseph wanted me to figure out what our new life would be, what it would smell like without Santiago's unbathed body's curdled smell marinating in those dinosaur pajamas, what it would sound like without his shuffling steps and his sudden rants, his "Did you know that . . . ," as if Joseph and I had been born at the same time as he and, like him, were just discovering the world. Santiago liked to make up explanations for the things he couldn't comprehend. He spoke of creatures that observed us and monsters that hid from us, and mixed with these fantasies he would talk of the way our cells renewed, making us entirely new human beings every so often.

At his best, Joseph became angry. He screamed insults at me so I would scream back at him. And I did, my voice loud and mean, but he gave up much too quickly. My fire was embers waiting to be fanned, while his was already dying. I saw my husband try to claw himself out of whatever dark, damp hole he was in. He huffed and slammed doors. He kicked walls. I observed him so that when he succeeded, when the day came that he finally pulled himself out— by anger, most likely—the day he did not seem doomed, I would know. Maybe he'd have a rope to throw me.

He did not succeed.

Instead I saw him decay. He didn't wash himself anymore. I missed watching his hands pass over his naked body, the hair subdued by suds and water. I missed desiring him. He didn't leave his bed for days at a time. He smelled, not in the pleasant way I remembered him smelling, but in a moldy way. He didn't attempt a doodle. Joseph grew boring. He wouldn't scream or plead anymore. He didn't call me a monster or ask me to hold him.

I smashed one of the vases which I was told, by him, had been in Firgesan for decades. I wanted him to snap, to finally and absolutely lose it. To break. He was withering. To wither is not the same as to break; to break is to have pieces to put back together, and to wither is to dry up, to wilt, to lose bone, to die, and death is the most boring. I needed to see pieces. So I broke the vase. He looked at me with bland pity, as if I were the one withering.

"What are you going to do?" I asked him, puffing myself up like a schoolyard bully.

I had forgotten my voice, how loud it could be, how much power it carried. I wished I had more to say. Joseph knelt on the hardwood floor. Each piece he collected he placed on his outstretched palm, a tiny clink each time. He threw the pieces of the vase away and I let him.

THE DOGWOOD WAS GREEN and bloomless when I left, some of its leaves already brown. I had seen my son and I knew the end. This was the end and so I left. I had life left in me. I also had a piece of lung.

I left Joseph. I left my ash-son too.

came back to Mexico City on an airplane with a ticket I can't remember buying. My friend Lena picked me up at the airport. I tried to understand how it was that she knew I would be coming. In a version of events, I called her beforehand. In another, the one I like to believe, she knew to be at the airport because she knows how to love me the best.

Lena did not cry or look solemn. She wore white sneakers, truly white, as if just bought, and a neon tracksuit. As usual, her hair was short and side parted. Lena did not say how sorry she was, no pésame, no wide eyes of pity. She was whole in a way I had forgotten a person could be. She gave me one hug, brief but tight. We were roughly the same height—short—and I cherished hugging someone who fit me so well. Lena let her head rest on my neck, her breath moist against me.

She hopped the tiniest amount with each step of her white sneakers, her glee perceptible only to me, lifting and swinging my suitcase as if it had weighed nothing. I was surprised to find I had only one suitcase. I should have had more, at least seven. Perhaps none at all. I was curious to learn what I had packed. The only thing I was sure I carried was the lung. Perhaps Joseph had packed the rest of the suitcase for me. Even though I suspected this couldn't be true, I hoped it was, that he and I were in cahoots planning my escape—a last joint effort in our lives.

I kissed the back of Lena's neck, where dark, thin, downy hairs grew, needy to love someone who wouldn't disintegrate. Startled, she turned to me, but I walked past her before she could blush or complain, her taste still delicious in my mouth.

Lena drove me to my mother's house, the big house in las Lomas with two jacarandas growing taller than the walls. I looked for sunglasses in my purse but found none. I couldn't remember wearing sunglasses since I sat on the terrace in Firgesan, months ago, before the winter, when I sipped lemonade and watched Santiago draw. I squinted at the light and held one hand up as a visor, the Mexico City sun suddenly a stranger to me.

CANELA, MY CHILDHOOD DOG, a reddish-brown Labrador, ran to greet me when we arrived, barking through the gate. Canela had been dead for years. This dog wasn't Canela. I couldn't remember its name, Canela's substitute, no Canela's substitute's substitute. Our dogs were always reddish-brown Labradors.

"Almendra!" My mother's call quieted the dog.

Though I had met this dog before, it took us a minute to recognize each other. She sniffed me. Then Almendra jumped on me, playful and happy, and I pet her.

"Hello, Lucía," Lena greeted my mother.

"Hi, Mami," I said.

"Magos," my mother whispered as she kissed each of my cheeks. My name from her mouth fell heavy, as heavy as heat.

"Jackie," she called to her housekeeper once inside.

Jackie brought a pitcher of lemonade into the living room, where I sat next to my mother. Lena sat in an armchair. Jackie looked exactly the same, her hair a frizzy perm barely held back by a thin blue hairband, her eyes large and eager. I wasn't sure exactly how old Jackie was, but if I was in my early thirties, she must have been in her late forties, maybe fifty. The thing with Jackie was her eyes were so alert, her demeanor so alive, that age in her seemed superfluous. I wondered if people thought the same of me. I stood up and Jackie hugged me. She said how sorry she was with tears in her eyes. She called me "Niña." Me, a child in her eyes. I cleaned her cheek with my thumb. Jackie wore black; this I remember because neither Lena, my mother, nor I did. I do not wear black.

"Are you hungry?" Jackie asked and I said no, but nevertheless my mother asked Jackie to heat up some tinga.

"How was your flight?" my mother asked. This wasn't truly the conversation she wanted us to have. She didn't enjoy small talk. Lena stood up and excused herself, saying she had to go back to the hospital. "Why?" my mother asked, and she tried to convince Lena to stay and eat something. I suspected she wanted Lena as a buffer between us. She loved Lena, not only because she was a surgeon whose success my mother couldn't help but partially award herself but also because Lena was a lot of what I wasn't. Thoughtful. Determined. Kind.

I wanted Lena to neither stay nor leave. I didn't want the days to go on: the questions, the inevitable events that would follow, the people I would have to see, the aunts and uncles and cousins, my friends. Except for Lena, I hated my friends. The looming days made me want to return to Firgesan, let myself wither with Joseph, dry up, become dust.

Lena left.

"Why didn't you come back sooner?" This was my mother's real question, the one itching.

"I came as soon as I could."

"Three months?"

"It wasn't three months ago," I said, but I had no idea.

It could've been years or minutes since Santiago's death, or three months like my mother said. I didn't know or care, but I wanted to argue, my voice a sturdy vibration I was pleased to exercise.

"I had to hear this from Lena. I'm your mother. You didn't even give me the chance to go see you. Be with you. With him." At this last pronouncement, my mother's voice cracked.

I only realized then that she had lost a grandchild. Her one grandchild. How bizarre that someone so far away as my mother then seemed, in this large, sunny house in Mexico, with its terra-cotta floors, arranged flowers, and paintings in gilded frames, so far away from my son's ashes, from the bed from which he never woke up, could feel his loss. Santiago was so mine, I could not fathom her feeling him gone.

I laughed.

My mother's lips became thin and tight. "Go rest," she said.

"I'm not tired."

I wanted her to keep questioning me, to prod, to fight with me, but she stood up and walked away. "Jackie, take Magos's food up to her room."

JACKIE CAME INTO MY ROOM with a tray of food: a glass of lemonade, tinga, and a woven basket with tortillas. She asked if she could help me unpack. I sat on the bed and ate while she arranged clothes in the closet.

"What's this?" she asked, turning the jar with the chunk of lung against the window, as though the afternoon sun would help her decipher it.

I grabbed the jar from her and stuffed it in a drawer full of childhood things that had once meant something to me. The drawer was old and wonky, smelled of childhood me, and wouldn't close all the way. Jackie stared as I jammed the drawer half-closed and then, giving up, as I pulled out a blouse from my suitcase and folded it against my chest.

"It looked like meat," she said.

"It's nothing."

"Is it a piece of Santiago? My grandma kept my grandpa's ear until it rotted, and she had to bury it behind the house." Jackie picked up a pair of pants from my suitcase—Joseph's. She folded and hung them. "Hair is more common, though. People keep teeth sometimes. Those don't rot."

Mine was a piece of lung, and so I didn't feel completely unoriginal. I took the jar out of the drawer and scooped the lung with my hand. The chunk was purplish-gray, the size of a strawberry and moist. Though not as moist as I remembered it being. I wondered how long my lung would keep; so far it didn't show any signs of rot. I showed it to Jackie, who inspected it, swiveling her head this way and that to get a good look at it. She held her hand open to indicate she wanted to hold it. I refused. I was afraid that if I let her touch it, it would disintegrate.

"It's part of his lung," I said.

I expected shock and repulsion, but I only got a nod.

"Have you fed it?" She pointed at the lung. "Feed it and it may grow."

"Grow into what?"

"I don't know." She laughed, but I didn't get the joke. "It's a story they tell in my town."

"Tell me."

Jackie ceremoniously folded a sweater, and once it was set neatly inside a drawer, she sat on my bed. I sat next to her.

"They say my great-grandmother's cousin, when she was young, many years ago, they say she wanted a daughter, but she didn't have a husband, not even a lover. Then, one day, a girl from the village died, a very kind girl, they say. My great-grandmother's cousin snuck into the wake, and when everybody slept, tired of crying, and the girl's body lay dead in the house, she cut her heart out." Jackie paused, and I thought she was waiting for an acknowledgment from me until I realized she had paused solely for effect. "She fed this heart. I'm not sure what she fed it, but she fed it. My great-grandmother's cousin was a really good cook. She believed this heart would grow into a daughter, you see, a girl just like the one the heart belonged to."

"It didn't?" I asked after another of Jackie's dramatic pauses.

"No. It became a man, a young man her age, a beautiful man who loved her deeply, more than any man has loved anyone. And she fell in love with him too."

"And then they had a child together," I said, hoping to predict the story's end. "The girl she always wanted."

"Yes, they did, but that's not the end of the story." Jackie leaned closer, like an older sister would do to regain the upper hand. "Someone stabbed my great-grandmother's cousin, right after she had the baby. They stabbed the pretty man too. He was so beautiful and she was so happy that my town had grown angry and jealous of their fortune. That girl's heart was not hers to take."

"How terrible."

Jackie shrugged.

"What happened to the baby?"

"She disappeared."

"She died?"

"Someone took her away. Some say she vanished like a ghost. Some that she never actually existed."

"Do you believe this story?"

"I saw photos of my great-grandmother's cousin and her man, and he was really too handsome to be real. He had these beautiful bones here." Jackie touched her cheekbones, hidden behind her fleshy cheeks, comparing them to mine, which jutted out like my mother's. "Like yours."

"So if I feed this lung, it won't become Santiago?" Through the jar, I peered at the lump of purplish-gray matter, as if in it I could find some resemblance to Santiago. Of course, I could find none; I only knew the lung was his because I had cut it from his body myself.

"No." Jackie looked at me with immense, lacerating pity. "No, mi niña. That's not Santiago. Santiago is dead." Jackie's voice was calm, her aura of hair springy. "What you have there is something else."

"What is it then?"

"A lump of flesh. It's no one. Just meat."

There's a way of believing where one believes and does not believe at the same time. For example, I believed Jackie's great-grandmother's cousin's lover was born out of a girl's heart. There was no reason I shouldn't believe it—extraordinary things happen everywhere and all the time, so why not in Jackie's town all those years ago? I just didn't believe I lived in the same world as that cousin.

"I know this is not Santiago," I said with a dumb giggle.

I knew. I knew this lump of flesh was not my son. This lump did not follow me around telling me about mushrooms that looked like aliens, and could very well be aliens, or drive me insane by refusing to speak except through growls. The lump did not suddenly hug me and breathe into my chest in panic, wordless and wheezing, hanging on to every bit of oxygen he could. It did not jump on my lap and ask me to massage him or squeal for no apparent reason except glee. It did not startle Joseph as he nodded off in front of some horror novel, making him jump in his chair and flail to regain balance.

This lump did not make me laugh.

Once, Santiago told me we couldn't know where electrons existed exactly, that we could only guess, a cloud of probability, and wasn't that fascinating because we were also made of electrons and maybe if he tried hard enough, he could be everywhere and nowhere at the same time, like electrons did? I told him to try. He shut his eyes tight and held his breath and said he couldn't do it yet. He said he needed to die first and then he would be jumping to another position, jumping, jumping, jumping, never to be reached but always present in a hazy cloud.

"I'll be a cloud, Mami." He undulated his arms unlike any cloud I had seen. I smacked him in his forehead.

"You're here now," I said. "I know exactly where you are. Always." He laughed and ran away, leaping, like the electron he wanted to be.

I had brought Santiago's lung back to Mexico because I hadn't been able to muster the will to chuck it.

"You shouldn't feed it," Jackie said, finding my eyes, trying to scold me.

"I didn't think you believed the story."

"I don't. But just in case." Jackie stood up, fetching the last items of clothing from my suitcase. "I shouldn't have told you this story."

"Are you afraid?"

"I don't like hungry things." She snapped my suitcase closed. It was now empty.

At about three in the morning, I gave up on sleep and went downstairs to the kitchen carrying the lung with me. The cold tile on my bare feet perked me up. Outside, Almendra barked one lazy, reluctant bark. In the freezer I found a plastic container with chicken broth, and I put it in the microwave. The ice lump didn't melt all the way but enough that I could scoop some of it out. It was silly, spooning broth into the jar, bathing the lung while specks of chicken, carrot, and celery stuck to its skin.

But I couldn't sleep, so why not? At least for that night I had found a purpose: to feed the lung. The worst thing that could happen was it would rot, and I would finally have to get rid of it.

I put the remaining half-melted broth in the freezer, though my mother always told me I should not freeze food twice. Back in my room, I stared at the wet, dirty lung, waiting for a mouth to pop open and suck on the broth, though I had no idea how a lung would feed.

Nothing happened.

I lay on my bed, still unable to sleep. A crack ran along my bedroom's ceiling. It formed during a big earthquake, one of the few cracks that appeared in my mother's house. Unlike la Roma, where Joseph and I lived then, this house wasn't in a neighborhood where earthquakes hit the worst.

Santiago was a toddler when the earthquake happened. I ran out of the house holding him. He was very silent, so silent I thought he'd fainted except his large eyes were open, his thick eyebrows alert. I pulled Joseph out with us too. He had stayed under a doorframe, holding on to the edges, but outside was safest when we could run out easily. We saw a building fall half a block from our house, not completely collapse but sway, creak, and crack and finally lean on the building next to it. Joseph, like Santiago, stood silent, taking the disaster in, as if needing to acknowledge what would kill us. Dusty people fled, others stood in shock, others cried and screamed.

We didn't own a car then. We were content to figure out our movement by walking or metro—the city felt close, manageable still. There were no taxis I could hail to take us away. I needed to get us to my mother's house.

Joseph, shaken out of his shock, stayed in la Roma to help. People banded together carrying debris, offering water. Joseph found it easy to help strangers, a quality I admired but did not possess or have any particular interest in acquiring. I, instead, walked all the way to my mother's, a two-hour trek, carrying Santiago in my arms.

Santiago had an attack halfway there, near the Auditorio Nacional. His lung froze and he began choking, drowning. I laid him on the wide sidewalk, next to a group of dumbstruck people waiting for a bus that wasn't coming. His eyes bulged out in terror, his mouth gaping desperately, his arms flailing. People formed a circle around us, but I wouldn't let anyone come close. He was a trout

out of water, flopping, dying. I put a hand on his chest, making myself heavy. I searched his eyes and instructed him to not look away, to keep his eyes on mine. This calmed him enough that I could press into his chest and pump his lung in a steady rhythm. He grabbed my hand and brought it to his mouth. I made it into a fist, and he blew into it, as if trying to inflate me. Keep going, I told him. People knelt closer to us. I swatted at the air to keep them away. Santiago's lung was mine to conquer. Santiago's breath finally deepened, and as he exhaled, I felt his breath rush through my fist.

His eyes softened and the terror vanished, not oozing away but seeping inside him. Pulga, I called him. He was small and dark haired like a flea, and like a flea he bit life, sinking into it, refusing to let go. Some people clapped as I lifted him back into my arms, alive, as if I had performed some miracle. This was no miracle; there was no luck, no divinity. This was Santiago and me biting, jaws clenched, sucking life.

We didn't know there would be a second tremor later that day, a replica, and that the building we saw leaning earlier would fully collapse. I didn't know I would have to go back to la Roma, my mother driving me as close as she could to our street, to look for Joseph and save him from his own kindness.

I found Joseph stunned in a corner, caked in dust. At my mother's, I bathed him, and the three of us, Joseph, Santiago, and I, slept together in my old room, my room with a newly formed crack in the ceiling.

My mother took care to fix the few cracks in her house not long after the earthquake, but almost a decade later the crack showed again. I suspected this reappearance was a new event; otherwise my mother would have had it fixed. Little went unnoticed in her house. She kept it pristine: the indoor fountain running except at night; the plants well groomed, never dying, not even with a dog to destroy them; never dust; never a thing out of place. Jackie and my mother made a formidable team.

I hugged the jar with the lung in it and tried to sleep. I didn't, not deep sleep anyway.

The sun came out.

The jar was empty of broth. I had missed the lung eating, but it had eaten! None of the solid specks of food remained on the lung either. It had absorbed all of it. It also seemed a bit larger, firmer, as if inflated. I ran out of my room with it, ready to feed it more, but as I walked downstairs, I heard my mother's and Jackie's voices. I hurried back to my room and hid the lung in my empty suitcase. A sudden paranoia warned me that if my mother or Jackie knew of it, the lung would die. Jackie already knew of it, of course, but not that it had fed, not that I had gone against her fears. I would feed it again later.

"I WANT A MASS," my mother said. Jackie had made me entomatadas stuffed with panela cheese for breakfast. She knew my favorites, and her kindness felt warm. My mother had only fruit and coffee.

"A mass? For what?" I said, purposefully thick to annoy my mother.

"I will take care of it," she said. "I want to do this for my grandson. We can't have a wake, so at least I will give him a mass."

I hadn't been to many masses for the dead, none I could remember specifically except my father's. My mother had cried and so had I. We had worn black despite both our aversions to black clothes. I had been sufficiently sad. I loved my father, but his death seemed to fit my life; it did not shake any deep foundations, at least not mine—my mother's surely. Santiago's death didn't fit my life though I had known it was inevitable. It stopped my life as I'd built it. We had been a unit of three, Joseph, Santiago, and I, and without my son our unit ceased to exist. I was back by myself. Not back. I had never really been by myself.

"I don't want a mass," I said. My mother stood up from her seat at the kitchen's island to set her empty mug in the sink. Jackie took it from her and rinsed it. "Mami? Did you hear me? I don't want a mass."

"I heard you."

"You'll do it anyway."

"I will, and I hope you'll be part of it."

"What about Joseph?" I asked. Joseph, alone in Firgesan.

"He is welcome, of course. When is he coming back?"

"I don't know if he will come back." Would he? Would he go back to our house in la Roma?

"Did you fight?"

I shook my head.

"It's normal for couples to fight in such a situation."

"What situation?"

My mother sat next to me. The stools at our kitchen island table looked nice but were not in any way comfortable. She took my hand.

"I know you think you're alone. That your grief is only your own, that it is unfathomable to anyone but yourself. But you're wrong, Magos." I tried to find tears in my mother's eyes, but none formed. As much as my mother annoyed me, she was most formidable. "Mi niña, this grief is ours. Mine, Joseph's, even Jackie's.

Right, Jackie?" Jackie nodded, wiped her wet hands on her apron, and squeezed my other hand. "Let us carry this with you."

I felt the so-far-elusive lump in my throat but swallowed and slid my hands away from theirs. I would not give in to tears. They had refused themselves to me for so long I didn't want them anymore.

"How, Mami?" My mother tightened her lips, those thin lips I inherited. "I want to know how." I mimed taking a lump from my stomach and passing it to my mother. "Do I poop out my grief and hand it away?"

"Don't be vulgar, Magos."

"I really want to know, Mami. I'm not trying to be difficult. I promise. How do I do it?"

"Let's have a mass, for starters."

For a second there, I was afraid I would break or have some sort of epiphany. "What will a mass do? Will God help me?"

"This is not about God. It's the rite that's important. The occasion where you let yourself acknowledge this has happened in front of those who love you."

"I know this has happened, Mami." I stood up, pushed my back straight, lifted my chin. "My son is dead," I declared, and sat back down. "There you go. Acknowledged."

"You know what I mean."

I did. I knew the importance of an occasion, the importance of creating a space to honor. I used to be a big proponent of occasions: birthdays, anniversaries, throwing big unnecessary parties when Joseph opened his design studio, or Santiago finished third grade, or Lena got awarded a residency in a fancy hospital in New York, both when she went away and when she returned. I once loved to make a big deal.

"Do what you will, Mami. Just don't expect me to participate."

"Fine, but please call Joseph. He needs to be here."

My mother left me to finish my entomatadas.

"Delicious," I said to Jackie, pointing down at the last entomatada with my fork. Jackie nodded.

Santiago wasn't expected to live past his first day. We saw the X-rays, his chest empty except for a kumquat-looking ghost toward the middle. His lung, we were told. Like a second mini-heart. We were also told some people survived with one lung. In those cases, the one lung grows a bit more and carries the function of two. The problem was the one lung Santiago did have was underdeveloped. Doctors, pediatricians, and specialists had shaken their heads when he was born, a way to prepare us to say goodbye, to not get too attached. Except Lena. Lena told us Santiago would survive even though she was only a medical student then. She said that if he had survived the shock of birth, if his one tiny lung had worked out of the womb, somehow breathing those first few hours before we even knew what was happening—breathing with difficulty but breathing nonetheless—he would survive.

At three months old, Santiago's lung had not grown to the size it should have been, but it grew enough to keep him on this earth. On his first birthday, his lung still small but chugging along, we threw a birthday party as if it were a wedding. Joseph and I had moved into our house in la Roma, an old, narrow, two-story Art

Deco house with a patio and big planters decorated with broken mirrors. I filled that house with plants and turned the patio into a tiny jungle. But we held Santiago's first birthday party at my mother's house because our patio was too small, and my mother's garden easily fit a tent and several tables. Throughout the celebration Joseph didn't let go of Santiago, his eyes teary, afraid that if he let go, he'd wake up back at the hospital.

We had scares throughout, like in kindergarten when Santiago collapsed while playing. There was the time of the earthquake. Once, Santiago's lung short-circuited because he went into a rant about how some birds had been dinosaurs before, and you could tell they had been dinosaurs because the birds were red or had some red on them. Dinosaurs couldn't see red and so the smaller, weaker dinosaurs had evolved to be red in order to camouflage themselves and survive. He'd gotten so excited during this weird made-up tirade he passed out. After this, he became cautious with his rants, stopping himself before he became too excited. I hated the lung for teaching him such self-restraint.

Our lives had two seasons: one in which Santiago was active and cheerful, the other in which he wasn't able to do anything without wheezing, coughing, and giving up. These two seasons alternated throughout our life, though the latter eventually took over. Joseph transformed a room in our house into his design studio. He had been working in a firm in Coyoacán, but the commute was too long, and he couldn't bear being away from us, thinking every day he left would be the day he wouldn't return in time to see his son alive. I stayed in the house too, making sure our lives were as enjoyable as I could make them. I put on plays. Short comedies with bright endings. Santiago's stuffed toys were our audience and

Joseph, Santiago, and I the actors. On occasion, Lena would join, and either I would cast her as the narrator—the only role at which she excelled—or she would join the stuffed-toy audience. I cast myself as the protagonist; Joseph a villain or a lover, often both; and Santiago as the myriad other secondary characters, mostly monsters. Santiago didn't care that his roles didn't have names. He cherished changing into the different costumes he created for himself.

I should have been an actress, so much I enjoyed performing, but I was too occupied doing what I liked doing best: directing the way our three lives unfolded, tethered to one another, full.

I CALLED JOSEPH IN FIRGESAN.

"I slept in his room last night," he said. "Such a small bed. We should have bought him a bigger one."

"Santiago fit perfectly in his bed. That bed wasn't meant for you."

"He was so small, wasn't he?" He was eleven when he died, but he looked like a seven-year-old. We loved his smallness. "I tried not to smell his sheets too much because they lose smell every time I smell them, but I couldn't stop. I've lost his smell, Magos."

"Listen, Joseph. My mother's planning a mass for Santiago. She wants you here."

"Do you want me there?"

"I do." I was surprised this was true. Hearing his voice made me want to have him near.

"I don't think I can," he said.

"Why not?"

"It's too much, going back there. Mexico. It's all him."

"There's more to Mexico than Santiago. I'll be here."

I could see him, bedraggled and thin, slumping. I wished I could reach through the phone and straighten him. Maybe slap him. It was exhausting to bear his sadness.

"Jesus, Mary, and Joseph, Joseph!" I said. This usually made him laugh. He didn't this time.

"You left me," he said.

"I'm telling you to come and be with me."

"You did what you did. Why did you do that?"

"I wanted to take a bit of him."

"What bit?"

"A piece of his lung."

Joseph groaned into the phone, in pain or disbelief I could not decipher. "What is it like?"

"Like you would imagine a lung to be."

"He was horrible, open like that."

"He was dead. What does it matter?"

"He was our kid! A beautiful boy."

"Yes, he was beautiful."

Joseph sobbed hard into the phone, and I twirled the phone's cord.

"You have no heart," he said.

A fern near the French doors to the garden was dying. Brown and thin, its leaves drooped. It was odd to see a plant die in my mother's house. As a kid, I believed our house was enchanted, that nothing could die here.

"I'm telling you to come back. I want you here." We listened to each other breathe. "Please," I said.

"I'll think about it." He hung up.

My mother arranged the mass: she got the church and the flowers and contacted the people who needed to attend. Their names floated in my mind, familiar but not quite material; a name would conjure a voice, a unibrow, a pair of shockingly ugly shoes, but none a full human.

The smell of the church, flowery and ancient—rotting—paired with the drone of the priest's voice made me nod off in the sweet unavoidable way one has no control over. I would have truly slept, my first deep sleep since coming back to Mexico, if my mother hadn't kept elbowing me. I had agreed to attend the mass because saying no to my mother would've required more energy than I had.

Joseph was not religious, and I had found Catholicism boring ever since my mother took me to catechism when I was a young girl. We baptized Santiago because it was another occasion to celebrate his life, but other than that we had not stepped into church. Nevertheless, Santiago loved to talk about God, saying God liked to do this and that, as if God were a buddy of his—he desperately lacked friends. Once, while eating, Joseph was telling us some story and Santiago interrupted him to tell him not to worry. Joseph asked why. Santiago said God found it rude when people spoke with their mouths full, but he shouldn't worry because God wasn't looking over us. "God is supposed to look over all of us," Joseph explained. But Santiago said no, God chooses who he cares for, and he hadn't chosen us. But, Santiago added, we shouldn't be sad, God had too many rules anyway, and did we really want to follow so many rules?

People gathered in my mother's house after the mass. Those who came held my hands, their eyes downcast, their voices soft. As I squirmed away from their touch, my mother told them, "It's a difficult time for her, for all of us." I reveled in my brattiness, in my slouch, in my refusal to either cry or be the diligent woman who offered guests something to eat.

Soon, though, even my brattiness couldn't shield me from their pity and I wormed away from the gathering. I hid upstairs, behind a short ledge on the second floor that looked down on the house's main foyer, and spied on family and friends. Was I expected to find solace in these people? I felt alone, perfectly alone. So alone I felt divine. Divine like a lonely god unfathomable to anybody but herself. Perhaps I could believe in Santiago's God, a God who existed but had chosen not to look over me.

I heard an uncle ask my mother where I was. My mother's eyes shot up to mine directly, my eyes I thought hidden. I thought she would come and drag me back down, but instead she escorted the uncle away from the foyer.

"Let's find her," she said.

Lena appeared. She hated churches, God specifically, a deep scorn only possible if there was love to begin with, so she didn't go to the mass, not even for me, and I wouldn't have asked. She wore loose jeans, white sneakers, a white shirt, and a vermillion blazer—a shock of color against all the black. Scandalously inappropriate. Gorgeous.

My mother passed a hand over the lapel of Lena's blazer, a gesture to stipulate how ill-suited she was for such a grievous occasion, but she didn't say anything except to let her know I was not feeling well and had gone to bed. Then, my mother winked. Lena looked confused. My mother tilted her head upward until Lena understood. I often didn't understand my mother's schemes, but despite never having said so, I believed she thought of Lena as the one person who deserved me. The one person, perhaps, who I wouldn't ever swallow whole.

Lena handed my mother a bouquet of lilacs, also scandalously inappropriate: too lively and wild to be grievous. My mother thanked her with a kiss on her cheek, sneaking another glance up toward me. Lena waited in a corner behind a fanning palm until no one was looking at her anymore and slipped upstairs.

"Flaqui," I whispered as Lena passed me on her way to my room. Only I called Lena Flaqui, a pet name whose origins I couldn't remember given that Lena wasn't skinny. But it suited her, the sound of it, hard and tender at the same time.

"What are you doing?"

"Shh." I waved my arm downward so she would crouch next to me. "They'll see us."

She knelt next to me. "Who are all these people?" A lesser being would have asked how I was doing.

"Crows come to feed off my grief."

"Okay."

I enjoyed how she pretended to be put off by my dramatics knowing full well she secretly relished them.

"Let them starve," I said and rested my back on the ledge, bored of spying, while Lena, entranced by the theater of my family and friends, soaked up the gathering. I grew tired of hearing my name and Santiago's.

"Who's that?" Lena pointed to one of my cousins, hair bunned and highlighted. A woman with three children, all ugly and two stupendously dumb. For years, she tried to be my friend. Fruitlessly. She was crying in loud sobs while an aunt and her youngest son comforted her. She was performing the grieving mother, exactly the spectacle we were taught to expect.

"She's a cousin," I said.

"She's really putting on a show."

My mother rushed toward the sobs, but, finding the sobs did not come from me, she sighed, relieved. Then, because the cousin would not stop her sobbing, my mother's face changed from relief to disgust. She handed the cousin a tissue, and, once she blew her nose, my mother herded her into the bathroom. "Clean yourself," she said, then closed the door and walked away. How gauche, I imagined my mother whispering to me.

Lena and I made faces at each other like bored children at an adult party we were not allowed to attend. We took turns trying to slap each other's hands. We giggled.

"Do you think they think I killed him?" I asked Lena.

"Killed who?"

"Santiago. Maybe Joseph too."

"Why would they think that?"

"Because people love a good story. What a scandal, no?"

"You'd be notorious."

"A horror story."

I wiggled my fingers, pretending to perform a hex.

"Why didn't Joseph come?" Lena asked.

I shrugged. "Have you spoken to him?" Joseph was Lena's friend before he became my husband.

Lena nodded. "Our calls consist of him crying."

"Do you think he'll come back?"

"Do you want him back?"

"I don't know."

Lena put her hand on my thigh, and I put my hand on top of hers. In another life, she would have been my wife. In this life, I should have pushed her hand away, saved her from me. I let her touch linger.

"Shit, shit, shit!" Lena kicked her legs, threw her back into me, and squished me against the ledge's corner.

I pushed her off me. "What is wrong with you?"

She made herself small against my side. "Kill it!" she said and pointed to the linen closet. The shadow of a mouse, or a huge cockroach, squeezed under the closet's door.

I laughed. "Really? You're a surgeon."

"What does that have to do with anything? I'm not a rat surgeon."

I walked to the linen closet.

"Don't open it!"

I heard a scratching followed by two tiny squeals.

"Sounds like a mouse," I said. The scratching continued, now paired with high-pitched hissing.

"That doesn't sound like a mouse," Lena said. The sound made my hair stand on end, though it wasn't particularly threatening. Lena stood behind me before I had a chance to open the door. "Wait," she whispered.

"What?"

"Let me get a broom."

"You'd have to go downstairs to get it. No, wait." I ran to my mother's room and from the farthest corner of her walk-in closet I grabbed a tennis racket, wooden and heavy. Throughout all these years, it remained exactly where I knew it would be.

"Perfect." Lena snatched the racket from me and held it like a sword.

"One, two, three." I swung the door open. There was nothing.

"Maybe it went in there." Lena pointed to a dark nook on the bottommost shelf, next to a set of blankets wrapped in clear plastic. I took the racket from Lena and tried to push the blankets away with it. There was no space for the blankets to budge. "Do you see it?"

I shook my head. Then we heard a squeak. And another.

"It's in there," Lena said, peering from above my shoulder. "Do you have a flashlight?"

I didn't need a flashlight. "I'm going to pull these blankets out. You smash it if it runs out. Okay?" Lena nodded unconvincingly but took the racket back from me. "Ready?"

I pulled the blankets, but nothing ran out.

"What is it?" Lena asked from the very end of the hallway.

"Some help you are."

"What is it, Magos?"

"I don't know." I got down on the floor, flat on my stomach. The closet's bottom was dark and smelled like trapped moisture. In a corner, something moved. I realized what it was, unbelievable as it seemed. I reached for it, and it hissed. I snapped my arm back.

"What is it?" Lena remained at the end of the hall.

"A mouse," I lied.

"Don't touch it!"

"What will a mouse do?"

"It carries diseases," Lena said, and she walked a few steps closer. I felt a panic; she'd kill it if it ran out. I reached again and, ignoring the horrid hisses, grabbed it. A lump. A live, wriggling lump, like a pouch full of worms. I brought it close to my chest and ran to my room past Lena, who was too confused to stop me. The lung's jar lay smashed on the floor. I found an old shoebox while struggling to hold on to the wriggling creature. I put it inside.

It was the lung come alive.

"Magos?" Lena said outside my door.

"Coming!"

I tied one of my belts around the shoebox and shoved it in my closet. I opened my window. Lena came in.

"I threw it out," I lied, pointing to the garden below. "I didn't want to kill it."

"It's the second floor."

"A mouse can survive the fall."

"You're bleeding!" Lena rushed to me and held my hand. My blouse sleeve, long, teal, and silk, was wet. A bit of the bottom part of my left thumb seemed to be missing. Not a lot, a chunk the size of a pea, not even a pea, a lentil. Still, it bled substantially. Lena dragged me to my bathroom, scrunched up my sleeve, and ran cold water over my hand. She soaped and rinsed it. "Do you have alcohol?"

"In my mother's bathroom." She dragged me all the way there, holding my hand up, my arm folded at the elbow. She cleaned my wound with alcohol. The bite stung, but she didn't blow on it. She wrapped gauze around it.

"A mouse does not do this," Lena said.

"Maybe it wasn't a mouse. I didn't get a good look at it."

"You need a rabies shot. I'm taking you to the hospital."

"Now?" The idea wasn't terrible. The voices of the gathering drifted upstairs, and I wanted to be taken away from them. But I couldn't leave. The lung was here!

"What is going on?" My mother walked in the bathroom.

"A little accident," I said.

My mother stared at all the bloody cotton balls and then at my gauzed hand. "What happened?"

"We need to go to the hospital," Lena said.

"The hospital?"

"No, Mami. Lena exaggerates. I'll be fine."

"People are leaving," my mother said. "Your aunt Evangelina wants to say goodbye. She says she hasn't seen you."

"I'll be down."

"Are you sure she's all right?" my mother asked Lena.

Lena nodded reluctantly.

I came down and let family and friends hug me. After they left, Lena insisted I go to the hospital. "Rabies is not a joke," she said.

"I don't have rabies."

My mother and Jackie picked up glasses and china, cutlery loud against them.

"You can't know that."

But I did. The lung couldn't have rabies; it had just been born.

"Come," I said to Lena. "I'll show you."

The lung stood inside the shoebox.

"Ugh," Lena said.

It was roundish, the size of a baseball but a bit flatter, and with a protuberance—a tail or an arm, I couldn't decipher which—wagging slowly, like a periscope scanning the terrain, scanning us. It used this arm-tail to scuttle around inside the shoebox. The lung's skin had become grayer, smoother, and showed tufts of dark, downy hair growing in patches. It resembled a poorly drawn cartoon, like one of Santiago's monster drawings. Santiago had not inherited Joseph's talent.

"What is it?" Lena asked with a grimace.

"A lung."

"What's a lung?"

"You know, a lung to breathe." I inhaled to demonstrate.

"I know lungs, Magos. That is not a lung."

I told Lena the story of how I had opened Santiago and taken his lung and fed it. Lena wouldn't harm the lung, not if I didn't want her to.

"Impossible," Lena said, peering closer into the box. "A lung cannot be fed. It's an organ, not an independent being."

"Tissue can regrow, can't it?"

"Not all tissue and only under the right conditions. Not with chicken broth."

"It doesn't matter how. Point is it's here, alive."

Lena peered closer than I thought she would dare. As a doctor, I imagined, she had been trained to ignore her fear when necessary.

"My guess is it's a malformed rat," she said. "Severely deformed. It has the tail. No snout. Where are its eyes?" We couldn't find any eyes, only a mouth opening the tiniest amount with each breath. Its mouth was wide, fishlike, running halfway around its body. "Poor thing. We should put it down."

"Kill it?"

"It's suffering."

"You don't know that."

"This is not Santiago's lung, Magos. It's some unfortunate misshapen rodent. It can't live like this."

"It's growing."

"It bit you."

"I scared it."

"Magos, please. We cannot keep this thing."

"It's not ours. It's mine." I put the lid back on the shoebox and tightened it with the belt. I set the box in a corner of my closet and slid the heavy wooden door shut. I picked up the pieces of the broken jar. "It broke free," I said to Lena. "It wants to live."

"Can I take you to the hospital now?"

"The lung is not rabid. Did it seem rabid to you?"

Lena took me to the hospital. I got a rabies shot. She insisted I get rid of the lung, the rodent, as she called it. I said I would.

My days were split in two: time I spent with the lung and time I spent wondering what to do when bored of the lung. The lung grew. I fed it beef and pork—chicken it ate but with reluctance—and whatever leftovers I could scavenge without Jackie or my mother noticing. It liked beef the best, leaving the vegetables I tried to balance its diet with untouched. From the size of a baseball, the lung grew into the size of a small watermelon and just as round. It sprouted dark hair, fur, and with fur it looked much less repugnant. Its mouth remained a wide slit. When it ate or hissed—its hiss, I learned, was more a sound of pleasure than of threat—it showed two rows of tiny fangs, bottom and top, gray and sharp.

My hand healed and I forgave it for biting me.

Its eyes appeared black, wide-set, and beady, right above its mouth. It had no nose, or none I could find. To add to this awkward effect, its arm-tail grew not quite opposite its face but at an angle, with a paw at its end and three long black claws like talons. Regardless of the cumbersome placing, the lung handled it nimbly. With its arm-tail, the lung dragged itself around. It fed with it. It scratched. It dangled, hooking its arm-tail on the topmost part of the sofa, or my dresser, or—its favorite—the closet's rod where my clothes hung. Once it had a comfortable grip, it would let itself sway. This is how it slept.

When the lung rested—it slept a lot—I roamed the house making up games for myself. I found a bag of marbles tucked away in a drawer in my father's study next to some old, yellowed nudie magazines. I read the mystery novels I found in my mother's room. I played with Almendra, her favorite toy a dirtied stuffed squid—originally Santiago's—with one missing eye and a chewed-up tentacle. Some days I would just sit in a garden chair and watch the shadows move. Before, I hadn't been able to simply do nothing, but now I found it soothing to stare. I inspected my body and pinched my flesh. I was mostly skin. I did not leave the house. I had no reason to leave it. In addition, I feared if I did leave it, Jackie or my mother would find the lung and kill it.

Jackie, like me, was always at home and had an obsession with my room.

"You don't want to live like this," Jackie said in my doorway. "It's a mess." She had huge brown eyes, penetrating, offset by a small round nose that softened them.

"I do." My mess gave me peace. Jackie was intent on destroying the lung's and my ecosystem. "My mother won't mind if you don't clean it."

"I know that."

"Then why do you do it?"

Jackie's nose wrinkled, and I wondered if Jackie could smell the lung. It smelled of earth and rotting fruit. I hoped my own smell helped mask the lung's. I'd become smellier.

"I like to keep the house as best I can," Jackie said.

"Why?"

"It's my job. And it's my home too."

It would have been cruel to say this wasn't in fact her home, that she only worked here. It would also have been false. Jackie had lived with my mother for almost twenty years. It was her job to erase my mother's habits, smooth the dent on the side of the bed she preferred, pick up her night clothes wherever she left them, reorder her creams and lotions and makeup, learn what products she used most often. If Jackie wanted, she could probably deduce my mother's intimate life. I hadn't lived here in years, years in which Jackie had, years in which this was her home five days a week, then six, and now she didn't even go home on weekends anymore.

"Do you ever take days off, Jackie?"

"I don't need to." Her dad had died years ago, her main reason for traveling home on weekends.

"Are you not seeing anyone?"

She laughed. "I had a boyfriend once but he was an idiot."

"You could find another one."

"Too much trouble."

"And friends?"

"I go out sometimes. The girls around here are nice. They sometimes invite me to dances. But I think I'm getting too old for those."

"I don't think we're ever too old for dancing. Don't you get bored?"

"No." She looked at me, not unkindly. "Do you?"

I had no response.

"May I clean your room now?"

"I'll clean it."

"Fine," she said. "We're going to get mice if you don't." Jackie left with one last despondent look at the mess. I knew she would come back and try to clean it.

ON TUESDAYS AND SUNDAYS, Lena joined us for dinner. On those days I showered and wore nice clothes, remembering what it felt like to dress beautifully, combining bright colors and flattering silhouettes to produce chirpier versions of myself. Lena often brought gifts, cake or pan dulce, and sometimes a bracelet or necklace, all indicative of how well she knew my taste. Once she gave me a pair of silver earrings carved as tiny spiders.

"How awful," my mother said, turning them around in her manicured fingers. I wore them instantly.

Lena didn't ask me how I was doing, though I sensed she wondered. She avoided speaking of Santiago, though I wouldn't have cared if she had. I wasn't trying to forget him.

On one of these visits, she asked me if I had gotten rid of the rodent, and I assured her I had. I didn't fool myself into thinking she believed me, but she didn't bring up the subject again.

I asked her about the woman she was seeing. Lena, unlike with every other subject she expounded on, answered tersely.

"Do you not like her?" I asked, and when she told me she did, her plump cheeks flushed, I relished the knowledge that she was lying.

My mother and I sat in the kitchen helping Jackie snap string beans. The kitchen had large windows overlooking the part of the garden where most of my mother's flowers grew. A bright sun shone outside, yellow and thick.

"Do you need money?" I asked my mother.

My mother snapped a bean in half and held the pieces in her hands for a moment. "Why would you think that?"

I told my mother I had seen Jackie apologizing to the gardener, a gruff man who came once a week. He was owed two months' wages and threatened to stop coming. Jackie promised he would get paid. "Also, I've noticed the house needs repairs. It's not like you to let it become less than perfect."

"I forgot to leave Jackie the money. When he comes back, we'll pay him."

Jackie immersed herself deeper in the beans.

"Mami." I held her hand. "I can help. I have money."

My mother slid her hand away from mine and grabbed a handful of beans she then scattered in front of her. "I'm not taking Joseph's money."

"It's my money too."

"Did you earn it?"

"I did. As a matter of fact."

"I didn't know you had a job."

"I took care of my family. Everything Joseph and I had was for the three of us."

"I thought you lived mostly on Joseph's family's money."

"Who cares? I'm offering help here."

My mother took a handful of beans and snapped them all at once. "I have savings and the company's stipend. I can manage." The company my father built had been trying for years to reduce my mother's stipend or stop it completely.

"You could sell the house. It's too big for you. I'm sure it's awfully expensive to maintain."

"I will never sell this house. It's our home."

"You could get a good apartment with that money. Save the rest. Live comfortably."

"I'm comfortable here."

"Mami—"

"Stop it, Magos." My mother pushed the bowl of string beans away from us. "I'd rather struggle here, be a pauper, let the house crumble around me, and die with it."

Jackie slid the bowl of beans toward her and continued snapping. My mother's black hair was pulled back and glued closely to her head, tied in a styled bun. Her eyebrows were thick and expressive, passed down to me and Santiago, her cheekbones jutting, her lips thin and red, her wrinkles precise, falling in the exact spots to make her majestic.

"Don't be dramatic, Mami."

"There are things you don't give up on, Magos. Your father and I built this house, our dream house. Each room, each detail, ours. You grew up here. This house is our family."

"Our family is our family. Not the house."

"The house too. This place knows me, and I know myself in it." My mother snatched a string bean and bit into it. "Why isn't Joseph here?"

"Don't change the subject."

"I'm not. Joseph is your family. Figure out what you want to do with yours and let me have my own."

My throat was dry, but I couldn't manage the will to stand up and get myself water. "I have no family anymore," I said.

"Now who's being dramatic."

"My son died!"

My mother pinched my chin and swiveled my head left and right. She explored my face, my ears, my neck, my jaw, as if I were new to her.

"He did, my beautiful girl. But you didn't, did you?"

THAT NIGHT, I WAS LYING IN BED, drifting in and out of sleep, when I heard a yelp, then another one, then a howl and a door slam. I wasn't sure if I was dreaming or awake. Then Jackie screamed. I threw the blankets off me and ran down to the kitchen.

I stumbled through the dark. Another yelp. Then a growl.

"Almendra!" Jackie shouted.

I walked out to a narrow passageway, opening into the backyard and a patio flanked by the laundry room, an area for drying clothes, and Jackie's room. I found Jackie holding a broom high

above her. She was trying to untangle it from the clothesline.
Almendra snarled. Maybe she'd become feral. But then I saw—
with the help of the moonlight—the lung attached to Almendra's
hindquarters.

"No, Jackie!" She would swat the lung away from Almendra.
She only needed to get the broom unstuck. I held the broom. Jackie
tried to wrestle it away from me. I pulled. She pulled. The clothesline wouldn't hold much longer. "Please, Jackie, no."

Almendra yelped and scurried to a corner of the patio. The lung
held on, its arm-tail's claw fastened to one side of her hindquarters
while its ball-body bit the other.

"I'll get it." I yanked the broom from Jackie's hands.

"Get it off now!" Jackie said and grabbed the dog's collar, trying
to calm her. Almendra's legs shook, but she stopped yelping and
snarling.

I knelt by the dog, trying to figure out a way to remove the lung
without hurting it or Almendra. I held the lung's body with both
hands. Through its squishiness I felt something akin to a heartbeat. Stronger, like a gulping. The lung seemed to be drinking. I
pulled the lung. It wouldn't budge. I pulled harder. The lung
remained glued. I stopped pulling, afraid that if I used too much
force, I might tear a chunk out of Almendra.

I grabbed the lung's arm-tail instead, right below its claws. With
my thumb and index finger I squeezed what I thought would be its
wrist. With my other hand I tried to pry its claws out of Almendra.
The lung didn't let go. I squeezed its wrist harder, digging in my
nails. The lung squeaked. Its arm-tail loosened. I pulled it off and
held it away from Almendra's butt.

"Hold this." I handed Jackie the arm-tail.

"No."

"Take it!" The lung could fight back at any moment.

"It'll—"

"Jackie, please."

With disgust, Jackie held it.

"Don't let go!"

The lung's mouth still clung to the dog.

I squeezed the lung's body once more, hard, with both my hands. The lung squeaked but remained attached. I squeezed harder. Its body gave way, deflating. I squeezed more, in tiny increments, trying to gauge the point when I would have to stop before seriously hurting it. I kept squeezing. The lung became a fat, hairy Frisbee. Still biting. I dug in my nails, pinching folds of its skin. I dug deeper. Deeper. I didn't want to break its skin. But I might have to. Just so—

The lung squeaked, opened its mouth, and let go.

Hugging the lung, I scooted away from Almendra. Jackie dropped the arm-tail. It flopped limp at the lung's side. Almendra scampered to a nook under the boiler. I held fast to the lung in case it fought to return to Almendra, but it was immobile. If it hadn't been for the gurgling coming from its insides, I would have thought it dead.

Jackie sat next to Almendra and petted her. Almendra rested her head on Jackie's lap. The lung opened its mouth. I held it away from me in case it was trying to bite me. It burped. A droplet of blood slithered down the corner of its mouth. A reflex told me to apologize for the lung, to call it a monster out loud, to be disgusted. But such declarations would have been insincere. I felt sorry for Almendra, but the lung acted without malice. It was hungry. It didn't know not to attack her. The lung unfurled its arm-tail, stretched it, and wrapped it against its body, hugging itself. Jackie struggled with the words she wanted to say, a series of false starts and stammers.

"Don't tell my mother," I said. "She wouldn't understand."

"Is that the lung?"

I nodded.

"I told you not to feed it."

"I didn't think anything would happen." The lung burped again, shook once, and closed its beady eyes, ready to nap after a satisfying meal. I brought the lung closer to my chest and, like Jackie with Almendra, I stroked its fur.

"Is it really the lung?" Jackie asked.

I stepped closer to her so she could have a look, but she retreated. Almendra burrowed deeper into her lap. Jackie got on her feet and dragged Almendra from under the boiler. Almendra walked so close to Jackie they tripped over each other. I followed them.

In the kitchen, with full light, Jackie examined the dog.

"Is she okay?" I asked. There were two bloody areas on either side of Almendra's hindquarters.

"No," Jackie said. "But at least that thing didn't bite a chunk off. It would have, if—" I bent closer to Almendra to see the damage for myself, but Jackie pulled her away. Delicately, Jackie parted Almendra's fur to inspect her wounds. "You can't keep it."

I spread a protective arm over the lung's body. "I will."

"It's dangerous."

"We'll keep it contained."

"We?"

I squatted so I was eye to eye with Jackie. "Please, Jackie. I can't let it go. We'll teach it to behave."

"What if it doesn't want to behave?"

"It will."

"That thing is not your son."

"I know." I wasn't crazy. Jackie was right though; I had no idea if the lung could be taught or tamed in any way. I didn't even know how it had managed to escape my room.

"Right now, we need to help Almendra," Jackie said.

"I'll get some alcohol." I ran out of the kitchen carrying the lung. Back in my room, I hid it inside an empty suitcase, making sure I didn't leave any zipper unzipped. I snuck into my mother's bedroom. She snored lightly. From her bathroom I took a bottle of rubbing alcohol, Merthiolate, cotton, and gauze.

Back in the kitchen, Jackie was cleaning Almendra with a wet kitchen towel. She took a piece of cotton from me, doused it in alcohol, and swabbed Almendra's wounds with it. Almendra winced but remained subdued. Her wounds did not bleed anymore.

"It's not that bad," I said.

Jackie shot me an awful glance, then dabbed some Merthiolate with its little plastic paddle over the dog's worst gashes. Almendra kept her snout on her outstretched paws. I fetched a couple hot dogs from the fridge and offered them to Almendra. She smelled them, took one with her front teeth, and chewed on it unenthusiastically.

"She'll be okay. It's like donating blood," I said, though I had never donated blood. "Rest, eat, and you're fine."

"Almendra didn't donate anything."

"It's kind of the same principle, isn't it?"

"How are you explaining this to your mother?"

"We can say Almendra woke up bitten. That we don't know what happened."

"I won't lie to her." Jackie's face softened from fiery stare to concerned arching of her brows, almost tender. "I know where that thing came from, Magos, and what it must mean to you, but that is not really what you want. It's horrible."

"I can't just kill it."

"Let it starve."

"No!"

"I don't think it would feel much. It would just pass away. Maybe you could poison it. Quicker."

"This won't happen again, Jackie. If it does, I promise I'll get rid of the lung myself." I raised my hand, though this wasn't a promise I could keep.

"I'll keep your secret for a week. You can figure out what to do with it."

"A week is not enough."

"Then I'll have to tell your mother."

"She won't believe you."

"I'll show her the monster."

"I'm her daughter. She'll fire you before she disbelieves me. I'll make sure of that."

We both knew my mother would never fire Jackie, not on account of me, but I felt a burning urge to be mean.

"Come," Jackie told the dog. Almendra followed her out of the kitchen. As she left, Jackie said, "Do as you wish, miss."

WHEN I WAS ELEVEN, the age Santiago was when he died, I threw things out of my bedroom window to learn how they would break. Many of them did not—the plastic dolls and plush toys landed safely on the grassy yard below—but the wooden toys did break, or at least they came apart.

One day my father brought me a snow globe from a business trip to Québec. Inside it, a winter village stood, with snow-covered roofs and chimneys shooting up into the domed sky. In Mexico all the fireplaces I knew were purely decorative.

This snow globe was the last thing I threw out of my window, not because my mother punished me, which she did, but because this snow globe smashed so gloriously—an explosion of crystal, water, snow, and glitter, the village utterly destroyed—I thought I wouldn't be able to replicate such destruction again.

J ackie spoke to me only in requisite monosyllables. I let her be. I had my anger and she had hers. I didn't care if she told my mother about the lung anymore. Regardless of what happened, I was going to keep it. I only hoped for a little time to come up with a plan. Maybe Lena would let me stay with her. Maybe I would go back to Firgesan and live with Joseph and the lung, or we would go back to our house in la Roma and let the lung live on the patio I had transformed into a jungle. Joseph would understand. He was easy and loving.

"What did you do to her?" my mother asked, referring to Jackie's coldness.

My mother and I sat on the terrace overlooking the garden. Jackie shut herself up in her room claiming she had a headache. We had each brought one of my mother's noirs to read, but I couldn't concentrate. I'd kept the lung locked in a suitcase with a stack of books on top. I hated to keep it imprisoned, but what other choice did I have? I didn't want it to roam and be murdered. My mother had called the vet as soon as I pretended to discover

Almendra's wounds. The vet said her wounds were nothing to worry about. She gave her a rabies shot nevertheless.

"I think she's still worried about Almendra," I said.

"The dog looks fine to me now," my mother said. Despite the cone the vet had fitted her in, Almendra had indeed reverted to her old playful self. "Do you think Jackie wants to leave me?"

"I don't think so."

"I couldn't bear it."

"She loves you, Mami."

"I know, but she's getting older. I'm afraid I bore her."

"She doesn't seem bored. She runs this house like it's her own."

"It is her own." My mother pushed my hair back away from my face. It had gotten longer. For most of my life I had worn it in ponytails but lately I'd been letting it loose. "I can't stay here by myself," my mother said.

"I'm here now."

"But you won't be here long."

"Are you kicking me out?"

"Not now, but eventually."

Almendra jumped her front paws on me, dropping her stuffed squid on my lap. I threw it. Almendra ran. One of the terracotta tiles that made up the terrace's floor came loose, and my mother set it back in its place with her foot. It wasn't the only loose tile. The sun hid behind clouds and the afternoon cooled. I retook my book.

"What is it you want, Magos?"

"To read."

My mother smiled. She hated performance though she excelled at it. We both did.

"What about Joseph?"

"I don't know if he'll come back."

"What about his business?"

"He didn't have much business."

"Do you want him to come back?"

I set my book down. "I think I do. I miss him."

"And Lena?"

"What about Lena?"

"She's in love with you, you know."

"Mami!" Lena's love was a secret treasure I held dear, supposed to be only my own.

"Oh, Magos, it's quite evident."

"Do you think she would have me? It's been so long. And I'm still married. And I may still love Joseph."

"Do you love her?"

"I do, but I'm not attracted to her."

"Why not?"

"Are you?"

"I could see myself being attracted to her, if I were younger. One is free to explore."

"Jackie?" I asked.

My mother did not betray anything, not even a shrug. I laughed and interlaced my hand with hers. Her hand was more wrinkled than I remembered but still as regal, or perhaps even more. Her nails had been filed into neat, rounded points and had been painted perfectly in red. Her rings protruded shiny and elegant, as much part of her hands as her bones. My mother kissed my hand.

Back when Lena lived with us, during university, I thought about being with her. I was attracted to her intelligence, her ease. We kissed once. A delicious kiss full of saliva and desire. But I realized my desire was different from hers. She lusted carnally, her flesh hot, her hands horny on my body. I didn't lust, or at least my lust wasn't as physical, more of an admiration, a sense of pride in having someone like her want me. And besides, I was already enamored of Joseph by then.

A few drops of rain began to fall. I liked the rain in Mexico, somehow kinder.

"Lena can handle you."

"What if I like being alone?"

"You just said you missed Joseph."

"I should be alone, shouldn't I?"

"Fine, then be alone. But you still have to do something."

"What?"

"Find a job."

"Where? How?"

"Didn't you want to be an actress? Put on a play. Figure it out."

"I thought you hated my performances."

"I hate them less than this nothing."

It began to pour, and even though we were under the terrace's roof, the wind carried the rain to us. We gathered our books and stepped inside.

I HIRED A HANDYMAN to help with the repairs the house needed. When my mother caught him recementing the tiles on the terrace, she dismissed him immediately, job half-done. I paid the handyman in full.

"This is my house," my mother said. "Let me handle it."

The next day my mother and Jackie finished the handyman's work with the cement he'd left. My mother in sweatpants—I

couldn't remember seeing her in sweatpants, ever—Jackie with a
green bandana tied around her head. They spent the whole afternoon and the next day doing it. When finished, they toasted their
accomplishment with lemonade, happy with their newly refur-
bished floor, proud of their house.

I found a brand-new notebook in my room alongside a fancy
fountain pen. "Write yourself a new role," a note read in my mother's careful cursive. I hid the pen and notebook in a drawer and
called Joseph. We'd spoken sporadically, short conversations that
led nowhere.

"Come back," I said.

"Why?"

"Let's go back to our house." I hadn't been back to our house
in la Roma yet. Lena took care of it for us.

"Why do you want me back?"

"I don't want to stay in this house anymore."

"You could come back here."

"This is our home."

"It was."

"It's still mine. Come, Joseph. Stop being like this."

"I'm grieving my dead son, Magos. I'm allowed to be depressed."

Jackie walked by the bench where I sat. I smiled at her and she
ignored me.

"I have something to show you," I whispered into the phone.

"What?"

"Something I discovered of Santiago's."

"What?" I could sense him straightening up.

"Come and I'll tell you."

"Don't play games, Magos."

"You love games, though."

He breathed, his breath a roar on the phone. "I miss you," he said.

"Me too."

"Do you really?"

"I do. I promise. Will you come?"

"I could come for a couple of days."

"This week? I won't accept anything later than this week."

"I'll try to come this weekend."

"It's settled!" I said and hung up.

UNTIL JOSEPH CAME, I stayed in my room, leaving only to eat dinner with my mother and Jackie. My mother asked if I was writing. This seemed like the best excuse for my reclusiveness, so I said yes. I fed my lung and played with it. It liked me to toss it in the air, grabbing on to whatever it could before it fell all the way to the ground. It was incredibly limber, like a cat. It could hide inside the smallest nooks and make itself as thin as a pancake. It could slide under doors and escape. I kept a towel blocking the underside of my door. When it slept, I tried picking up the pen, but I couldn't get past a few mediocre ideas. I spent most of the time pacing, wondering what Joseph would think of the lung, if he would want to come back with us and retake our life back in la Roma. Three of us again.

When Joseph arrived, my mother greeted him with a huge smile, reaching up to hug him.

"My Joseph, how are you? Why did you abandon us for so long?"

Joseph looked as gaunt as when I'd left him; the only difference was he also looked clean, and his hair had recovered a bit of its blond sparkle. He bent down to hug me, and I held him tight. He didn't linger in my arms for long.

"You look well," my mother lied. "Have you eaten?"

Jackie took his duffel bag from him—a weekend bag. I was hoping for a bigger one.

"No, no," he said as he relinquished it. "I'm not staying here. I got a hotel in Coyoacán."

"Nonsense," my mother said. Jackie took this as an indication to go ahead and take his bag upstairs. To my room, I could only imagine. Joseph tried to protest but only stammered. "Come," my mother took him by the arm and led him to the living room. She sat him next to her on the longest couch. I sat across from them in a sofa chair. "Did you miss us?" my mother asked.

"I missed you, Lucía."

Joseph had won my mother's love, or at least tenderness, by being her most sincere admirer. He was too awkward for doling out compliments, but he stared like a kid watching magic, stooping more in her presence, as if he dared not be taller. My mother rubbed his back and he smiled so earnestly, I thought he might cry. Or I might. I missed him.

"You want a beer, maybe a Cuba?" It was strange playing host to my husband.

"I'm fine, thank you."

My mother did not leave us alone and I thanked her for it. We needed time to warm up to each other, and she was our buffer. I poured tequila for me and my mother.

"Okay, I'll have some too," Joseph said. We clinked glasses and, finding nothing else to toast to—Santiago could not be mentioned yet—we toasted to Mexico.

Jackie joined us. Feeling too shy to sit with my mother on the couch, she pulled up a chair from the dining room and sat there, sipping at the tequila I had diligently poured for her, her legs tight together, though she looked a bit more at ease than she had in the past few days. I brought out onion dip with crackers, pâté, and Japanese peanuts. My mother told the story of when she first met Joseph, how he had stepped into the fountain in the foyer.

"You were so embarrassed. You ruined your shoe, didn't you?"

"I was nervous." Joseph blushed, pleased.

The fountain was a mirror of water with a large round stone spewing water in the middle, delineated only by a pattern of river stones. As a kid I knew there were drains all around, but I wanted to believe the water vanished by magic, that a secret river beneath the stones carried it to another dimension. Joseph had barely wet his shoes then, but he enjoyed my mother's exaggeration, and I enjoyed that he enjoyed it.

I remembered what loving him felt like. I remembered how perfectly his long, skinny body felt against mine, how delicate he felt, how precious. I could find him again.

The doorbell rang. Jackie jumped up to answer it and Lena appeared.

"Flaqui!" I said. "I didn't know you were coming."

"Your mother told me Joseph was here."

"Mami?"

"I thought a little gathering was in order. One must celebrate these moments."

Lena spread her arms. "Joseph, Joseph!" she said, hugging him and pounding his back, as if he needed to pass gas.

Lena loved Joseph like a little brother, protective and charmed by most anything he did. During university they ran with a cool, rebel crowd—or at least I saw them that way. They saw me as the bratty sheltered girl from las Lomas. Lena and Joseph were more exciting than anyone I'd ever met. And though I didn't expect both Joseph and Lena to fall in love with me, it didn't feel outside the realm of possibility.

"Glad you came," Lena said. "Finally."

I poured more tequila, and we clinked our shot glasses.

The evening grew livelier with the tequila and Lena's loud stories. I forgot we had lost anything. I felt whole.

L ena had a bit too much to drink and accepted my mother's offer to stay in our guest room. Joseph insisted he sleep in the family room. Jackie and I helped him arrange the sofa bed.

"Are you sure you don't want to sleep with me?" I asked.

"I'm sure," he said.

"Are you angry with me?"

"I'm tired."

I COULDN'T SLEEP, so when the house had been still for a few hours, I snuck down to the family room and slipped into the sofa bed. Joseph mumbled something unintelligible but did not wake up.

I took his hand and placed it on my vagina.

"What are you doing?" Joseph said.

I pushed his hand aside and touched myself instead.

After a while of my breathing and his silence, I said, "Come on, help me."

He stretched his hand toward me and let me play with myself using his long fingers.

Minutes passed; my breath became heavier.

"Are you done?"

"Not yet."

But I was close. He let me keep using his fingers, his hand hot against my own. I came with such force my left leg cramped. My big toe curved as if in rictus.

"Ah. Ow." I reached for my foot. "I got a cramp."

His hand now free, Joseph took my leg and massaged my calf.

"I forgot you used to get these."

"Only when you were excellent."

"So you've missed me, huh?" The orgasm's pleasure lingered even as the pain of the cramp vanished.

"I did miss you, Joseph."

"I stopped missing you a while ago."

"That's not nice," I said with a smile. I understood anger. I couldn't stand politeness.

"I'm not trying to be mean."

"Be mean."

Joseph sat up and threw my leg away from him. I scooted up to him and rested my head on his lap.

"It got scary for a while," he said. "After you left and Uncle came to look after me, I suddenly couldn't feel anything anymore. When my mother died, Uncle absorbed all the grief and accumulated it inside his body so none of it reached me. That's why he's so gnarled and bent at odd angles. After Santiago, I expected to gnarl too. I wanted my grief, but instead I was left with a horrible nothingness, and I got really scared. But then I realized fear was a thing I could feel, and I clung to it. I was afraid of my loneliness. I was afraid I would never have anyone to love again. I blamed you for it. For leaving. I was angry. Furious. And then I had two emotions.

Fear and anger. The anger helped me wake up in the mornings and eat and clean the house and wash myself. The anger even distracted me long enough that I would forget my loneliness, and sometimes, in short bursts, I even felt cheerful."

"Are you angry at me now?"

"Yes."

"That's okay."

"I love you, Magos, but I don't know if I can live with you, or if I want to. So it really doesn't matter whether I love you or not. What do I do with it? What—this love doesn't make me feel better."

I pulled his hair, hoping that if I hurt his head, his heart might hurt a little bit less.

"Why did you bring me here?" he asked finally. I sat up.

"I want to wait until tomorrow when you're not so gloomy."

"Let's get it over with. Please, Magos."

I took his hand and led him upstairs. Asleep, the lung dangled upside down in my closet.

"Is it a possum?" Joseph asked.

"Remember the piece of lung I took?"

"Santiago's?"

"Yes. Well, I fed it, and it grew, and now it's this."

"Oh, Magos," he said, stepping away from me and onto a pile of clothes. "That's not possible."

"It is. Look at it!"

He sat on my bed, head in his hands. He shook, weeping.

"It's okay," I said, sitting next to him and rubbing his back. I was clumsy with his crying.

"Is this really what you wanted to show me?" He looked at me with worn, wet eyes.

"Don't you see? We can go back to our house in la Roma. Have the lung live on our patio. You'll go back to your studio. If you really wanted, we could go back to Firgesan. Firgesan would be good for the lung, actually, all that open space. We could—"

"Magos, stop!"

"I'm writing a one-woman show," I lied. "I'll perform it. We can make this work."

He turned to me with unbelievable pity.

"I'm trying," I said.

"By showing me some weird animal?"

"It's part of Santiago!"

"Look at this mess," Joseph burst out laughing. His face turned red, and he cried but this time with glee. Had I finally broken him? "This room! I can't even see the floor. It smells awful. And look at you, Magos. You look terrible!" He laughed more. "And I mean that in the best way possible. All of this is great. Really great."

"How is it great?"

Joseph wiped tears from his face. "You know what angered me most about you? I thought you didn't care Santiago died. Or not that you didn't care, but that you were somehow above suffering for him, that you were so strong you could move on. I hated to think you were rebuilding your life already. I hated I couldn't. But look at this! You're a mess. I don't think I've ever even seen a misplaced blouse of yours. Now they're all over." He picked up one of my wrinkled blouses. "Even the silk ones."

I snatched it from him, folded it, and jammed it in a drawer. "Happy?"

"Magos, it's fine. This is okay. You—"

"Don't patronize me, Joseph."

"I'm not. I swear. I'm a mess too."

"Can we just talk about the lung? Joseph, I really think we could—"

"Where even is it?" Joseph said, looking past me. The lung wasn't hanging in the closet anymore. Joseph hopped on one foot and then the other as if the floor burned him.

"Shit." I dug into a pile of clothes and flung garments.

"Is it dangerous?" Joseph asked, sifting through another pile of clothes.

"Of course not." I looked behind the curtains, where it sometimes liked to dangle. It wasn't there. "Look under the bed," I told Joseph.

He bent down, took a quick look, and shook his head. I threw myself on my belly and checked under the bed myself. The lung wasn't there.

"Maybe it ran away? Back to nature?"

"It didn't."

"Magos, it's just an animal."

"Help me look for it or leave, Joseph."

Joseph resumed sifting through the clothes. I opened the suitcase where I sometimes kept the lung but, apart from its poops, I found nothing.

My mother screamed.

"What was that?" Joseph asked.

My mother screamed again, "Jackie! Help me!"

"No, no, no," I muttered as I ran out. I burst into her room and flipped on the light. My mother thrashed her legs on her bed, her sheets and blankets a heap on the floor. "It's me, Mami," I said, louder than her screams.

She stopped screaming and threw her back to the bed's head-board, a barrier that wouldn't let her get away. The lung had attached itself to her thigh. My mother's face froze in panic. She looked awful, contorted, and pale. Her mouth opened and closed in short little gasps.

"Get it off!"

I jumped on the bed and scooched up to where she cowered. "It's okay, Mami. Stay still." I grabbed the lung with both my hands, squeezed, and pulled. I pinched its skin, but this time the lung wouldn't give up. "Do something," I said to Joseph, who stood by the bed.

"What do I do?"

"What's happening?" Lena asked, appearing by the side of the bed opposite Joseph. "What the fuck is that?"

"Get it off me!" My mother kicked.

"Stop kicking!"

"Move." Lena shoved me out of the way. I shoved her back, but she stood her ground.

"You'll hurt it," I said.

"Magos, hold your mother. Lucía, you need to calm down. Joseph, get me a hammer."

"Where?" he asked.

"Find one!"

"Don't hurt it! I can pry it off." I pushed Lena away.

My mother continued kicking. Lena gave up trying to get control of the lung and held my mother down instead. My mother stopped thrashing. I wedged my fingers in between the lung and my mother's thigh, wriggling them to find the opening of the lung's mouth. I managed to push one finger inside and, hooking it onto the side of its mouth, I pulled. Its fangs dug into my fingers. My mother cried out in pain. The lung was not letting go, and I was hurting my mother. I let go. My mother tried kicking the lung again, but she couldn't bend her leg far enough to kick it. She struck the side of my chest.

"Ow, Mami!" I winced, her kick much stronger than I could've imagined.

"You hold her," Lena said to me. "I'll get it off."

"Try to get inside the mouth. Don't hurt it, Flaqui. Please."

Lena maneuvered her fingers inside its mouth much more deftly than I had, her face serious and calm.

"Got the hammer!" Joseph announced, holding it high above him. Jackie came in behind him. She climbed on the bed opposite me and held my mother. My mother let herself fall on Jackie. The lung's arm-tail clung to the back of my mother's thigh. I tried to pry it off while Lena continued to struggle to free my mother from its mouth.

"Should I hit it?" Joseph asked.

"No!" I said. The lung loosened its arm-tail, and I was able to shove it off. "It's letting go."

But its mouth remained fastened to my mother. Blood pooled under her thigh, and she fainted on Jackie.

"Jackie, keep her awake," Lena said. "Lucía, stay with us."

"Mami?" I said.

Jackie patted her cheek with increasing force until my mother awoke back to her terror. She kicked her legs again, letting out howls, and in her desperation she kicked Lena in the face.

"Stop, Lucía," Jackie said, throwing her body on top of my mother. My mother settled down under Jackie's weight. Lena's nose bled but she didn't let go of the lung. She groaned and, pulling with two hands against the lung's jaws, she finally pried the lung's mouth open and snatched it away from my mother.

"Hit it," Lena ordered, holding the lung at arm's length, offering it like a sacrifice to Joseph.

"Joseph, don't you dare," I said. Joseph hesitated. "Joseph, please. This is Santiago's lung. Please."

The lung burped as if nothing was wrong.

"I'm sorry, Magos."

"Joseph, I'll take it away. You don't have to come with us. But please—"

Joseph brought the hammer down. The lung squeaked, a soft sound, and then nothing. Its arm-tail drooped, and its body slackened, melting on Lena's hands, its internal structures giving up. Lena let it drop, and it fell limp on the bed. My mother kicked it away.

"No, no, no." I picked it up and held it to my chest, trying to find its gurgling organs, but as much as I pressed it, I found nothing. Its beady eyes, once shiny and translucent like dark marbles, now looked opaque; a milky film covered them. No life remained in the lung anymore.

I wept, and the room went silent.

My tears were fat, and my snot ran. I wanted to scream but my voice could not find force. All the insults and curses I wanted to throw at them caught in my stomach. Only a wheeze came out. My stomach hardened and then my lungs. I lost my ability to draw breath in. I panted, gasping like Santiago had done so many times before.

"Magos?" Joseph stepped toward me.

I willed myself to calm down, to ease the rhythm of my lungs, to make them take in oxygen the way I had ordered Santiago's lung all those times it had failed him. I was drowning. My whole body tightened in panic. I tried gasping but I couldn't get any air in. I moved my mouth, but it was useless.

My vision darkened, leaving only a pinpoint of light.

I clenched my hand into a fist and blew into it. The blow eased my lungs enough that I could force a tiny breath in. I blew again and I drew in more air. I kept blowing until I inhaled deeply enough that my vision undarkened and the room appeared again. I was on the floor. The lung in front of me. Dead. My mother held her bleeding leg. Jackie held my mother, caressing her head. Joseph stood next to them, hammer still in hand. Lena knelt close by. They all stared at me.

I ran.

I snatched the lung, and I ran.

I ran out of my mother's bedroom, out of the house, and into the street.

LATE AT NIGHT, the streets of las Lomas are dead, dark, flanked by huge trees and huge houses. I walked, hiding when the odd car drove by. Carrying the lung, a monster, my monster, I felt like a fugitive, even if it was dead.

I wasn't sure where I was anymore. I found a park. The grass was wet. I was barefoot.

I thought of digging a grave. But as I began clawing at the grass, snapping its roots, I gave up. I wasn't going through one of these rites again. I sat the lung's dead body in the middle of a little garden fenced in by low shrubs. That was as much as I could do for it. I walked away.

LENA FOUND ME sitting on a curb.

"Hello, Flaqui," I said.

"Where were you going?"

"How's my mother?"

"We took her to the hospital. She'll live. Jackie is with her."

"Where's Joseph?"

"He's at the house waiting in case you came back."

"Where are we?"

"We're still in las Lomas. Where did you think we were?"

"I thought I'd gone far."

"You didn't." Lena sat next to me. "Where's the thing?"

"It's dead. Do you have your car?"

"Yes."

"Will you take me somewhere?"

"Where?"

I didn't answer. Lena stood up and offered me her hand. I took it. She lifted me up. We walked to her car, an old Vocho she adored.

"Where to, Magos de la Mora?"

"I don't want to go back."

"I won't take you back."

"Can you just drive?"

Lena stepped on the clutch, started the car, and shifted into first gear. We drove away.

MAGOS
LENA
JOSEPH
M

Magos stayed with me, pasted to my couch like a grub in a cocoon of blankets. It was Monday and the incident had happened over a week ago. I had to cancel my appointment with Maritoni that first Monday and I would have to cancel again.

Magos was unaware of these appointments, the women I hired to bathe me. Last Monday, Maritoni texted: *No problem. Next Monday (winky face and bar-of-soap emoji)*. It was next Monday. How many appointments had I missed in the last decade (without counting those months of my supposed enlightenment when I thought I could do without them)? Four. The previous Monday made it my fifth, and this one would be my sixth.

Carmina was the first woman I hired. I picked her up in front of a Catholic bookstore in Tlalpan. The storefront, newly painted in yellow with blue lettering and a white dove spreading its wings, was the most illuminated part of the street, which is why she and other women hung out there, pacing back and forth across the light's borders. Carmina asked if I was looking for a "holy good time" and laughed. "Divine sex!" a woman shouted from behind her. Carmina also laughed at my Vocho (my first car, bought for a pittance, though at the time I felt I was handing over a fortune). She laughed at the hacking sound it made each time I switched gears, laughed at my neon tracksuit, laughed because I had driven so far from home though I knew I couldn't have been the first client from a distant part of the city to pick her up. She laughed because I took her to my apartment and not a motel, laughed because I was an amateur. She laughed because I wasn't a man, and her laugh filled the car in carefree bursts, *jo jo jo* rather than *ja ja ja*. She was tall and her hair draped down past her breasts. When she sat on my couch, I stood in front of her because I was unsure how close I could get. Her miniskirt rode up her thighs to reveal the bottom edge of her pink underwear. She caught me staring and asked if I wanted to touch her. I shook my head. She grazed the edge of her underwear herself, her fingers teasing, and mmm'ed. I asked her to stop, and she reached to grab me. I stepped back.

"It's okay, baby," she said. I told her my name was Lena. "Come, Lena." She spread her legs wider, and her skirt rode higher.

"I'm not scared," I told her.

"I didn't say you were."

I unzipped my tracksuit jacket, shook it to unravel its rolled-up sleeves, and placed it folded on the couch next to Carmina.

"Yes. Strip for me, Lena."

She touched herself over her underwear. I took off my tank top next. I wasn't wearing a bra. Naked from the top up, I stood in front of her. I felt one of my breasts hang lower than the other, and the more she stared the more I felt this breast sag while the other remained stubbornly in place.

"You don't have to do that," I said after she let out a moan.

"You turn me on, baby."

"My name is Lena," I repeated.

"Lena," she said.

I asked her to bathe me. She followed me into the bathroom, where I stripped completely naked. She got naked too and placed her clothes on top of my pants, folded like mine. She tied her hair into a bun atop her head.

"Or do you want it down?"

I told her I had no preference. I let the water run until it became hot, the bathroom filling up with steam. I gave her a bar of soap, which she lathered in her hands before pressing it on my body. Not even that first time did I need to give her instructions. Carmina washed me starting from my neck all the way down to my toes. Her touch was firm and purposeful. She took shampoo and washed my hair, her fingers strong like a masseuse. She stayed silent throughout, no moans, no touching herself. Somehow, she realized that what I wanted wasn't explicitly sexual.

She came out of the shower first and told me to stay inside. She toweled herself off, wrapped the towel around her, then spread a dry towel and wrapped me in it. She rubbed my hair dry, my body too, like a mother would dry her child. She took my hand and found my bedroom. My nakedness felt more pronounced outside the bathroom as her hand led mine. She asked for pajamas, and I pointed to a drawer where I kept loose pajama bottoms and T-shirts. She handed me pants and a T-shirt and watched me dress.

"All set?" she asked.

I said, "Yes," satisfied in a way I'd never felt before and also rattled that this woman knew what I needed better than I did myself.

Carmina dressed in the bathroom, let her hair down, and reapplied her red lipstick. I paid her and offered to drive her back to Tlalpan.

"You're all set for bed," she said and asked for taxi money.

I gave it to her. She kissed my cheek and left. I slept through the whole night, my dreams so light, so inconsequential, I couldn't remember a single one.

For two years I hired Carmina every Monday, when her nights were less busy. Then she disappeared. The women in front of the Catholic bookstore told me she'd gone back north, where she was from. I pressed them for details, but they wouldn't tell me, protective of their own. I looked for Carmina, whose real name I didn't know, all over Mexico City. I couldn't convince myself that she'd really left. I thought she might be in danger, and I wanted to help her like she'd helped me. I found other Carminas but not her. I hired other women, but I drove to Tlalpan at least one Monday a month to see if Carmina was back. I was tempted to pray for her, but God is a scumbag; he wouldn't answer any prayers of mine. I wished instead, like one wishes on a birthday candle or a star. I wished Carmina was home and someone bathed her like she had bathed me, waiting for her with an open towel in which she nestled and went to sleep, safe and happy.

"Flaquiiiii," Magos moaned from the living room.

"What?" I answered from the kitchen.

"Come sit with me."

"I'm loading the dishwasher."

Maritoni's text appeared bright on my screen: *On my way.* I had accepted the fact that none of the other women would accomplish what Carmina did, her tenderness true and inimitable, but Maritoni did an acceptable job, even if after three years she retained a hint of fakeness.

"Flaquiiiii."

"Jesus. One second." Such a brat.

"Flaquiiiii."

"Fucking hell, Magos. I'm right here."

I wrote back to Maritoni: *I can't tonight. Sorry.*

My apartment shook with gunshots, moans, and sputterings, my sound system pushed to its very limits. Magos did nothing else but watch zombies gore and get gored on TV. The show was my favorite, but after a week of it playing nonstop, I realized none of it made sense; the characters made the stupidest decisions just so the show could keep them fighting zombies, never safe, never truly doomed. I tried to goad Magos into doing something else: play cards, put on a play, go out for a walk, even watch something besides zombies. She refused. I waited for a neighbor to complain about the noise, to give me an excuse to shut the zombies down, but none did. Maritoni texted: *Everything okay?*

Yes. I'll pay for tonight. Sorry.

Next Monday, she texted and then sent a lonely question mark: *?*

For sure, I typed, though I wasn't sure. What if Magos stayed longer? What was the plan? Could I go another week without an appointment? I would have to figure shit out day by day. Magos had upended my life. I finished loading the dishwasher and ran it.

On the couch, I carried Magos's feet onto my lap. Freezing.

"Do you have a fever?" I asked. Magos said nothing, so I reached to feel her forehead.

"I'm fine, Flaqui. Leave me." A swarm of zombies broke through doors. The main posse panicked. "They're in trouble now," Magos said, smiling.

Of course they were. Idiots. I would excel in a zombie apocalypse.

"Did you shower?" I asked.

One of the main characters was about to die. I had cried when I first witnessed his death, but now I couldn't wait for the dumbass to get it.

"Do I smell?"

"Yes."

Magos curled her feet away from my lap. For the past week, I'd managed to rearrange my work schedule to stay at home and keep an eye on Magos. I got us takeout, and though she ate very little I made sure she didn't starve. I brewed her tea that she left half-drunk on my coffee table. I tried to make her shower, telling her how good the warm water would feel on her body, but the one time she tried she didn't make it past slipping her sweatshirt halfway over her head. On-screen, the guy died.

"Oh no," Magos whispered, though it was her second run through the series.

"Do you want me to help?" I asked, scored by the show's mournful music.

"Help what?"

"I can bathe you, if you want."

"I'm not a child," she said.

There were moments when a gesture swept Magos—a pleased breath, a relaxing of her jaw, a silly hand movement—and she felt light, almost joyful, and I would think she was beginning to crawl out of the hole she was in. But then, the gesture disappeared, like a twitch, and I realized she was crawling out of nowhere. We hadn't talked about the incident. She didn't ask about her mother, or Joseph, who had disappeared. She didn't mention the monster.

I looked for creatures that resembled the monster on the internet or documented cases of people turning organs into independent organisms, but apart from fantasy and lore, there was nothing. I wished I could've examined the creature, determined what it was and where it had come from. What if it was Santiago's lung? Wouldn't that have been a groundbreaking discovery, someone bringing a creature to life solely with their own grief and a prodigious unwillingness to let go?

Magos pulled the blanket up to her nose. I reached for the most recent mug on the coffee table. Her tea was ice-cold.

"Do you want another?" I asked. She didn't answer. I gathered the rest of the half-finished mugs.

"No, Flaqui. Stay."

I sat back down.

I would be gone most of the next day, a surgery that I couldn't postpone. Alone, I worried what Magos would do. Magos sniffled, then cleared her throat. She hadn't cried. She sank deeper inside her blankets. She had lost twice, first Santiago and now her monster. People can endure quite a bit, more than we think we're able, but Magos was only now developing a callus for loss.

I couldn't ask Lucía to come and stay with her. Lucía wouldn't speak to us on account of the incident. Technically, she wouldn't speak to Magos, but because Magos was staying with me, I was included in her silence. I had tried hunting Joseph down by calling hotels in Coyoacán, where he said he was going to stay. I tried hotels in Polanco too, and in el Centro and the ones along Reforma. No Mr. Joseph Jansen anywhere. I even called his uncle, Luke, in New York. The man didn't speak, he only grunted, but Joseph called him every week regardless. Joseph swore he understood his grunts. They sounded mostly unintelligible to me, but by repeating myself to the edge of harassment, I managed to understand that Joseph hadn't gone back to the US. At least not to Luke's knowledge.

"Where are you going?" Magos asked.

"Pee," I said. She looked at me as if she would disintegrate without me in the room. "I'll be right back."

"You pee a lot."

"I keep hydrated."

In the bathroom, I called Jackie. I expected her to say no, she was Team Lucía through and through, but to my surprise she agreed to keep an eye on Magos for a few hours. I hung up. I would leave them a rotisserie chicken, half of it, the half we hadn't eaten that night. I didn't pee but I flushed to make my lie stick. I went back to the couch and zombies. Magos placed her feet on my lap. This time, I didn't mention how cold they were.

Through eight hours of surgery, I didn't think of Magos once. I was gifted at what I did. Colleagues trained themselves to achieve this kind of focus. It came easily to me, this compartmentalizing. So easy I sometimes worried that I was a type of psychopath as yet undiscovered, and then I remembered that if I were a true psychopath, I wouldn't fear being one.

Finished, as I peeled the gloves from my hands, the greenish light of the fluorescents glaring, Magos came crashing down on me like a stroke. I couldn't wash up fast enough. I called Magos but her phone was either off or out of battery. No surprise there. I called my house. No one picked up. Jackie must have left. I'd asked Magos to answer the damn phone.

Without traffic, I could drive back home in twenty minutes, but Mexico City traffic was cruel that night, as it enjoys being. I honked all the way, like a siren, stuck in the Periférico in a river of taillights, unable to take the second floor because I had no balance on my TAG. I kept meaning to link it to my credit card but hadn't. I honked. Cars blocked me on purpose to annoy me, the way I was annoying them. Fuckers! (Though I probably would've done the same thing.)

It took me more than an hour to get back home. I burst inside the apartment.

"What happened?" Magos asked, perfectly whole, standing at the kitchen's door. "Did someone die?"

"You're okay."

"I made supper."

All the lights in the apartment were on, the zombies gone and my windows open. I breathed in a freshness I hadn't encountered there in days.

"Why didn't you pick up the phone?"

"I hate talking to people I don't know."

"It was me! I called."

Magos walked up to me and placed a hand on my cheek. Crafty. She knew how I softened. "You look awful, Flaqui. Pale. Did something happen at the hospital?"

"Surgery went perfectly."

"You must be hungry." Magos walked back into the kitchen.

"You cooked? What did you make?" I collapsed in one of the dining room chairs, which was awfully rigid. Every time I sat on one of them, I thought of changing them, and yet I hadn't. I found it difficult to let things go.

"Baked chicken with potatoes." Magos handed me a steaming plate.

Usually I ate fruit for supper, maybe a quesadilla. Never anything as elaborate as this. Smelled delicious. She had showered and wore an old track suit of mine that fit her terribly but somehow enhanced how fresh she looked. Her hair was still moist and smelled fruity. She gobbled down her food.

"You seem chipper."

She nodded playfully but didn't offer why. The more I asked, the more she would delay satisfying my curiosity, so I didn't. She smiled from time to time, goading me to give in and ask again. The guy chanting "Tamales Oaxaqueños" passed by.

"Who made that recording?" Magos asked. "Do you think they paid him?"

"I like to think it's the voice of the original tamales vendor, passed on to all his descendants."

"I used to think it was one guy who made it all over the city," Magos said. "It was amazing. He worked so hard and drove his bicycle cart so fast! Have you ever bought tamales from one of them?"

I nodded. Magos looked at me like sunshine would shoot out of her eyes.

"Oh, come on. Tell me. Why the sudden rebirth?"

"Jackie came over."

"I told you she would. I asked her."

"She said something . . . ." Magos bit on a chicken bone and sucked its marrow. "Do all of you hate me? Was it that bad, what happened?"

"It was bad."

"Do you hate me for it?"

"It wasn't your fault. You didn't know how dangerous that thing was."

"I did know, Flaqui. It attacked Almendra before."

"You didn't tell me that."

"Why would I? Jackie wanted me to get rid of the lung and you would have too. I didn't care how dangerous it was."

I dropped my fleshless chicken bones on Magos's plate. "Doesn't matter now. Jackie says your mother is healing well. She'll forgive you. Joseph will reappear."

"Jackie said she saw the lung hanging from a tree three blocks from my mother's house."

The hanging dining room light flickered. Sometimes it flickered so much it made me nauseated. I didn't turn it on for this very reason. "She's mistaken."

"She said I need to come over there and hunt it." Magos laughed, bit, and sucked on a new bone. "'Hunt it,' she said."

A motorcycle roared outside. The light flickered more.

"Do you think this could be some plot?" I asked. "Some kind of revenge for what you put Jackie and Lucía through?"

Magos set the chicken bone down on her plate. "That'd be cruel. Jackie's not cruel." She pushed her plate away and leaned back on the chair. "Do you think she'd do that?"

I shook my head. She was right, Jackie wasn't cruel. "Jackie saw some other animal then. We're all still shook-up. Confused. Seeing monsters where there aren't any."

"Are you seeing monsters?"

I didn't see monsters. I had other problems. But my problems had nothing to do with monsters. "No," I said. "But I handle stress better than most people. It's my job."

"Jackie wouldn't mistake the lung for another animal. Not after all this. She wouldn't get my hopes up if she had any doubts."

"I don't think she's trying to get your hopes up. She wants you to take care of it."

"Kill it?"

I nodded. Magos took our plates and walked them to the kitchen. I turned off the flickering light. Magos brought two bowls filled with strawberries and a can of condensed milk. She drowned her strawberries in milk. I did a light swirl.

"You think I'll find it, Flaqui?"

"No."

"I'll find it."

"And?"

"We'll see." Magos took a strawberry and licked the dripping condensed milk from it. She caught me staring and smiled. I stuffed a strawberry in my mouth.

"Flaqui, it's been, what? Three weeks?"

"Ten days."

"Only ten?" Magos slumped on the chair, her spine quitting. "Wow. I . . . ." She stared past me, scanning the apartment as if she was just then realizing she was at my place.

I kept my apartment full of trinkets that encased moments I believed were worth remembering, a physical accumulation of my life in order to make sure it wasn't passing by unnoticed. Some of these things retained their memories: a brunch where I laughed until my belly ached; a trip to Argentina, farther than I ever thought I would travel; a day out in the rain; a complicated and successful surgery. But many others had given up their ghosts and stood soulless: a small Talavera vase, a framed poster of a film I couldn't remember watching, stained glass butterflies, a cat alebrije with a broken tail. I should've gotten rid of them, but I was waiting for their ghosts to come back. My apartment could only hold so many things. I could afford a larger one. I could afford a damn house. But I liked my tiny apartment. It had seen me grow from a person who could barely afford it to someone who could upgrade easily. It hadn't judged me; why would I judge it?

Magos straightened. "The lung must be looking for me. Wondering why I left it."

"If it's alive. Joseph hammered it. You told me yourself it was dead."

"I was distraught, Flaqui. All of you wanted it dead, so I thought it was too. It must have only passed out. My poor lung."

Magos pushed her bowl away though there were still a couple of strawberries left. I picked them out of her bowl. Magos cleared the rest of the table.

I didn't think we'd find the monster. Its cadaver had likely been taken by a tlacuache or stray dog or scavenger bird. But not finding it would be the worst outcome. What Magos needed was closure. If we found the monster dead, then we could pick up where we left off, with the zombies and her smell's prolonged stay in my apartment. Magos and her grief, lumbering along its course, twisted and potholed as that course was.

Of course, there was a chance we might find the monster alive. Jackie was indeed careful with what she said. And if we did find the monster alive, well, I had no clue what would happen.

We met Jackie outside Lucía's house. Almendra barked at us, wondering why we weren't going in. I brought a fishing net, Jackie a shovel, and Magos nothing. Magos made us promise we wouldn't attack the monster, only catch it. I wasn't sure if Jackie would keep her promise, and I didn't blame her.

Jackie led us west. I expected to go south to Chapultepec; a park seemed like where a monster would go. These streets were too residential, nothing but walls hiding huge houses. We tiptoed to the tree Jackie had seen the monster hanging from, Magos in the lead, Jackie and me behind with net and shovel raised and ready. The tree was empty. We walked up and down both sides of the street looking up the fat trees, trying to catch a glimpse of the black furry ball. Jackie walked tentatively, afraid the thing would jump on her and try to eat her. I wasn't afraid. I believed the thing was dead.

"Poop!" Magos screamed, and she lifted up a ball of excrement the size and shape of a golf ball. "It's the lung's poop!" Magos dropped it and wiped her hand on the tracksuit pants she was wearing. Mine. I offered her a tissue. She took it and stuffed it into the jacket pocket. Magos followed the monster's shit and we followed her. We spent an hour going up and down the streets of las Lomas, spiraling out from where Jackie first saw the monster, along the walled houses, past the manicured shrubs, under the jacarandas, ficuses, and other trees with names I didn't know, canopies spreading wide and pleasantly shading the sun. I had once been wonderstruck by these streets, so rich and alien, so not mine, back when Magos and Lucía first took me into their home. Magos hadn't known me well then. I hadn't cared. I'd latched on to the idea of becoming a doctor like a monomaniacal tick, and I would've had to quit school if she hadn't offered their help.

I was conceived unexpectedly when my parents were in their forties and my brother already sixteen. My mother believed I was a demon sent to ruin her family. She blamed me for her depression, for her quitting her job, and for my brother going to jail. Apart from church, she spent most days locked in her room watching TV. My father worked days at a pharmaceutical factory and nights as a watchman at an industrial park. She blamed me for his absence too.

My father said I had to be patient with my mother; she was sick. "Why can't she take medicine?" I asked, but my father said that her ailment was in her soul and only God could cure it. I prayed for her to get better. I was good. I kept the house spotless. I cooked my own meals and left my mother's on a tray outside her door. She seldom ate my food, afraid I would poison her. "Why can't you leave us alone?" she'd ask me, and I'd try harder. I wore old-fashioned dresses that made me look like a storybook good girl. Three starchy numbers with white scalloped necks that my father found at the tianguis: pastel blue, pastel pink, and pastel yellow. When I outgrew them, I wore my school uniform exclusively: skirt, knee-high socks, black shoes, and a forest-green cardigan.

Some days, if she was out of her room, she'd strip me naked, searching for marks on my body, something she could show her priest and my father to make them see I was in fact a demon. She'd scratch me as if my skin were peelable and my scaly demon flesh hid underneath. I brushed my long hair every night so it would shine. She'd mess it up when she tried to find horns on my head. I spoke softly and never cussed, but she would've been happier if I screeched and yelled obscenities.

In church, my mother was less afraid of me. She prayed for me with eyes tightly shut. There, she believed I could be saved, her family could be saved. I hated the kneeling, the Hail Marys, the Our Fathers, the bells and rituals, the priest's pious voice as if he weren't a regular man, the smell of incense and mothballs. Still, church was a respite, a place where my mother didn't attack me. Sometimes she'd buy me an oblea with cajeta outside.

It took me years to realize that my mother would never see me as her daughter. It didn't matter if I looked and acted the part of the sweet girl perfectly; to my mother I was a demon pretending to be good. Wily. Ready to destroy her whenever she let her guard down. At thirteen, when I finally understood that no matter what I did my mother would never love me, I acted even sweeter. Cloying. "Mamita," I called her, smiling grotesquely. I turned her crucifixes upside down, scratched the eyes out of her Virgins. She slapped me, pulled my hair. "Leave me be!" she'd scream, and she'd hit me harder. When she tired, I made my voice lower, smiled wider, and growled demon-like, "Mamita, I love you." I'd leave her weeping. I became her demon. I needed to break her before she broke me.

When I turned fourteen and my mother tried to poison me, my father sent me away to live with his aunt, my great-aunt Lety, a woman with a white buzz cut who spent her afternoons gossiping about family members I didn't know. She was the first one to call me smart. She despised church but not God. Becoming a doctor seemed the hardest thing to accomplish and the closest thing to being godly. Aunt Lety saw me get accepted into the UNAM but died shortly after. I couldn't quit school. So Magos took me in.

I lived with Magos, Lucía, and Jackie for over three years. Magos called us sisters but stopped once we both realized I was in love with her. Magos, the long-haired rich girl, friend of a friend, who had spoken to me at a party. Who had held on to my arm as if she'd known me for years. I left a month after she gave birth to Santiago. Joseph had moved in, and I was in the way. Besides, I could finally afford a place, the apartment in la del Valle I still lived in.

"Why can't we find any more?" Magos asked.

"The monster can't possibly shit all over las Lomas," I said. "It's shit is finite."

"It must be around."

"I hope so," Jackie said. "Lucía won't be able to sleep with that thing around."

"You told Mami?"

"I'll have to if we don't catch it."

Ten minutes later, Magos found a new trail of shit that led us to the entrance of the park that overlooks Barranca de Barrilaco.

"Should we go inside?" Magos asked.

"You're the poop tracker," I said.

In parts, the park was a forest, wild and chaotic, but in others it showed the manicuring hand of humans, cobbled paths, bougain-villeas in tended shrubs, handrails. We walked a series of woody trails crisscrossing the barranca over bridges. It had rained the past few days, making the park lush, green, and muddy.

"Over there." Jackie pointed to a group of people peering down into the barranca.

A teenage couple held hands while a man poked a pair of eviscerated cats with a stick. The cats lay just centimeters away from where the barranca dropped. A woman held a hand over her mouth but didn't look away. Trees shadowed the area. The smell of blood and insides betrayed no rot. These cats had been freshly killed.

"What happened?" I asked.

The man with the stick pointed to a tree that rose from deep in the barranca. On one of the branches hung the monster like a black, round, furry fruit. "That thing killed them."

"My lung!" Magos tried to run to it, but the drop was steep. She tried sliding down, but I pulled her away before she tumbled below. "Lung!" she shouted. The monster curled up to face us. "Lung!"

"Don't call it," the woman who covered her mouth said.

"Lung!" The monster swung to a branch closer to us, nimble with its arm-tail. "Lung!" It swung closer.

The woman scrambled away. The monster landed on a shrub that stuck out from the barranca's wall, just a few meters down from us. The girl in the couple threw a rock at it. Missed. The man hit the ground with his stick, but the monster didn't flinch. The girl picked up another rock.

"Don't," Magos said. "We're professionals. Lena, tell them we're professionals."

"What?"

"We've come to take this animal away. Lena, tell them."

"We've come to take this animal away."

"Professional what?" the girl asked. The man with the stick stepped closer.

"Step back," I said, surgeon mode activated. I waved my net high in the air. "We're professionals." I elbowed Jackie, and she raised her shovel too. "Step back now," I said.

The teenage couple and the man with the stick joined the woman down the trail. The monster opened its mouth and growled. Its fangs glistened bloody. Magos slid toward it, but I pulled her back up.

"I'll get it," I said. "Jackie, hold me." Jackie took my hand. "Magos, hold Jackie and anchor yourself to that tree, okay?" We made a chain. I slid down the barranca. The monster recoiled. "Magos, call it."

"Let me get it."

"Call it!"

"Lung! Lung, come here." The monster's black marble eyes bulged out at Magos's voice. It growled inquisitively. I would get one shot with the net. If I failed to catch it, I was pretty sure it wouldn't stay put. "Lung. Little lung," Magos called.

The monster let go of the shrub. It didn't fall. It was wedged in. Its arm-tail curled up, like a periscope. Its eyes froze on mine. I swung the net. The monster jumped toward me. I slipped from Jackie's grip.

Fuck.

I scratched but couldn't get a grip on anything. I hit something as I tumbled down. Leaves fluttered above me.

I saw sky.

The barranca's wall loomed above me. I inhaled to confirm I was alive. I smelled mud. I hurt. I was wet. I shifted to get up, but there was no ground to hold me. I was on a ledge. I held on. Pain shot through my left wrist, but I didn't let go. There was still a steep drop into the barranca below. I managed to sit up, my legs dangling. I touched my head, trying to find out if I'd hit it. I could've broken my neck.

"Help!" I screamed. "Help!" I couldn't see Jackie or Magos, or anyone, but I heard commotion above me.

"Lena." Jackie peered from above.

"Help!"

She disappeared. I heard voices. Arguments.

"Help!"

I couldn't climb out of the barranca on my own. And I didn't know how much longer the ledge would support me. I didn't know if I could survive another fall.

"Help!"

"Hold on!" Jackie said.

She slid down slowly, holding on to the man with the stick. The man with the stick slid too. I reached toward Jackie, but we were too far apart. Jackie told the man to go down farther. He tried but the mud was too slippery. He almost let Jackie fall. She held his hand with both of hers. He pulled Jackie back up. I got on my knees. Something cracked. I hugged the wall and dug my fingers in.

Jackie slid down again. Slower. The man held her hand. The boy in the couple held the man's hand. Someone held him. I placed a foot on the rock to test its strength. To make sure it wouldn't crumble. I pushed myself up. My foot slipped on the mud. Jackie grabbed my hand. I held on to a crevice in the wall with the other. I didn't care how much it hurt. How much my hand wanted to slip away. The man pulled. Jackie pulled.

I crawled out.

I was muddy and scratched up, but no one was paying any attention to me. Magos was holding the monster like a baby. The girl wanted to touch it but was too scared to dare. The boy and the man didn't come near the thing.

"What is it?" the girl asked.

"A rare species," Magos said.

"Where are you taking it?" the man asked humbly, impressed by our heroics, fumbling as they were.

"A reserve."

"In Chapultepec?"

"North. To Sonora. It's a desert species."

The group looked at each other, awed. My jeans were torn at the knee. My arm bled. I had more than one thorn stuck in my hand.

"Time to go," I said.

"Flaqui. My goodness." Magos picked a twig from my hair. The monster stared at me and growled. Magos held it closer and kissed its head.

My mother thought I was a monster and didn't love me because of it. This thing, an actual fucking monster, was loved.

I pushed Magos on her way. Jackie hesitated to follow us. She could've told the group that we were impostors, that that thing wasn't some desert animal, that it was dangerous and that the group should help her destroy it. Magos looked at her with pleading eyes. Jackie picked up her shovel, thanked the group, and walked away with us.

"How did you catch it?" I asked when we were close to Lucía's house. The sky had darkened, and raindrops began to fall.

"Jackie tackled it," Magos said, combing the monster's fur with her fingers. "Has it grown? I think it's grown. It's heavier for sure."

"Gotten fat on a diet of neighborhood cats," I said.

Jackie stepped in front, halting us. "What are you going to do with it?"

"Take it home. With Lena."

"I don't want a monster in my house."

"Please, Flaqui. We'll keep it in your spare bedroom until we figure out something permanent."

"Permanent?" Jackie asked. A car drove by, and we instinctively huddled toward a wall as if we were doing something criminal. "You mean to keep it?" Jackie whispered. "Mi niña, please. You just said that thing grew. How big is it going to get? It's dangerous now. Imagine it larger."

"Jackie's got a point," I said.

"Did it attack you? Any of you? It could have, but it didn't. It's learned its lesson."

"Didn't seem that way for the cats."

"It just needs time. The lung will become a boy. You told me so, Jackie. Like your great-grandmother's cousin."

Magos held the monster out to Jackie. Jackie took a step back.

"What if it doesn't grow into a boy? What if it remains like this? A wild thing? How will you keep it? Caged?"

"What's the alternative?"

"Kill it," I said.

"Flaqui!"

"Well, that is the alternative."

Thunder rumbled. The rain got fatter.

"Enough!" Magos screamed, and she squeezed the monster. The monster squeaked. "Sorry." It snaked its arm-tail around Magos's bicep. "Jackie, thank you so much for leading me back to my lung. Thank you. Really. But it's not your problem anymore. I'm sorry I kept it at the house. I'm sorry it attacked my mother. But from now on I swear you will never have to see it again if you don't want to. We're keeping it safe with us."

"Us?" I asked.

"For now, Flaqui. Please. I don't have anywhere else to go."

She had her house in la Roma, but I didn't say this. I wanted her to stay with me even if the price of her company was keeping the monster too. Jackie lifted her hands up in surrender.

"Fine," she said and walked away.

"Please don't tell my mother," Magos screamed after her. "Please. Not yet."

Jackie kept walking.

W e kept the monster inside my spare bedroom with the door shut except when Magos went in to feed or play with it. The gap under the door was too narrow for the monster to squeeze through, Magos assured me, but at night we stuffed a towel in it. I was unable to sleep. I'd lost my Monday bathing routine, plus now Magos slept in my bed and I was housing a monster in the room across the hall. At night, I heard it scratch, hiss, and growl.

After a week of catching sleep only through brief naps in my office, I was exhausted. Magos didn't snore but her breaths were loud. I tried to be lured into sleep by her breathing but after each exhale, her breath paused, and at every moment of stillness, I grew unsure if she would ever breathe again. I got out of bed.

Outside the monster's door, I heard a growl, almost like a purr, like it was happy. I peered inside. The monster dangled from the ceiling's light fixture. The streetlight's glow illuminated its furry balloon body, swaying as if a breeze were blowing. I stepped in and closed the door behind me. A car's headlights ran through the room. The monster curled up to face me and bared its fangs. It could attack me like it had attacked Lucía, but I didn't run away. I stared back. The room stank despite Magos's constant cleaning.

It opened its mouth wide, revealing the fullness of its fangs. Two rows extending halfway across its body. I was jealous of the monster, how it didn't care what it was or did. No shame. It held itself up with a certain pride. But mostly I was jealous of the way Magos cared for it despite it being a monster.

"I'm not scared," I said.

It hissed.

I hissed back.

It closed its mouth but kept looking at me, deciphering who I was.

"I can't sleep," I said.

The monster growled, swung, and leapt to the curtain rod. I grabbed the doorknob, ready to flee in case it jumped on me next, but it swung back to the light fixture. It continued leaping from fixture to rod, rod to fixture. It flipped and cartwheeled in the air, putting on a show. I sat on the carpeted floor and watched. After a while, it tired, dangling from the light to let its momentum ebb. I clapped, my jealousy mutating into something like kinship. I watched it sway.

I woke up to Magos's voice, "Flaqui. Flaqui." She knelt by me, holding the monster in her arms. The monster peered and unfurled its arm-tail toward me. "Monstrilio likes you."

"Monstrilio?"

"I can't keep calling it Lung."

She was right; we don't go around calling people Ovum. We fed Monstrilio raw meat, mostly leftovers from the butcher, beef, or pork, sometimes lamb. It wasn't discerning as to what it ate as long as the meat was raw. I bought it a four-tiered cat tower so it would have something else to entertain itself with besides the hanging light and curtain rod. Monstrilio plopped on top of it and stared out the window. I often found it lying there, particularly when the sun was bright.

Magos said it was developing, that it wasn't as round anymore and would soon stand upright. I wasn't sure it would stand upright, but it was getting bigger and was growing four stumps that resembled paws, or possibly hands and feet. At times, Monstrilio stretched wormlike and stared at its new extremities. It bit at them, wondering what they were, or perhaps trying to get rid of them. Magos began referring to Monstrilio as *he*. Monstrilio wasn't Santiago, but he was becoming his own being, the ties that bound him to Magos's pain thinning, his original darkness giving way to something new and independent.

I got used to Magos sleeping next to me. We didn't cuddle or hold hands or kiss or touch. To her, we were friends sleeping in the same bed. For me, it was an ancient hope reviving, that she would love me like I loved her. Maritoni texted asking when we would return to our sessions. I wrote, *Soon*, and though my routine of baths was the one remedy I'd found for my insomnia, I didn't want "Soon" to happen.

The bell rang one morning. Joseph stood at the door. He was tan and his hair had grown down past his shoulders.

"Where the fuck were you?" I asked.

"I took off." Joseph pushed his hair behind his ears.

"No shit. Come in."

"Magos," he said, freezing just past the entrance. "I thought you were at your mother's."

"I'm not allowed after what happened," Magos said.

Joseph turned to me, his face pale. I wrapped my arm around his, just in case he tried escaping again. I held him tight.

"Lucía is coming around," I said. "She's talking to me at least."

"How is she?"

"She uses a cane now."

"Her leg's fine," Magos butted in. "My mother just loves the air of grandeur the cane gives her."

"Coffee?" I asked and led Joseph to the table.

"Where were you?" Magos asked after we had seated ourselves.

"Oaxaca," he said.

"I like Oaxaca," she said.

Joseph sat up straighter and shifted his body toward me.

"I found a tiny beach town. An inn with only three rooms. I ate and slept and swam belly up in the ocean until water plugged my ears and the only thing I could see was the sky." Joseph took a sip of coffee and stared at the mug cradled in his hands. "Killing that thing and the chaos of that night made me forget myself. Holy moly, it was bliss."

"Why are you back then?" Magos asked.

He stared at Magos, his face red. I imagined he wanted to scream at her after what she had done. His jaw tensed with boldness that dissipated just as quickly as he had raised it. He drank more coffee instead. Magos tried to take his hand. He snapped it away.

"Will you stay in Mexico City?" I asked.

"I don't know."

Magos looked at me.

"They're staying here," I said. "With me."

"They?"

Magos reached out to him again, but he scooted away so forcefully he almost tipped his chair backward.

"Joseph," she said. "That thing, as you called him, is not dead."

Magos rose and asked Joseph to follow her. He stayed seated. I took his hand and, because it was me, he relented.

Monstrilio lay on top of the cat tower. He folded up his body to look at us, showed his fangs in what I liked to think was a smile (but possibly wasn't), and produced a series of growls.

"What the—" Joseph whispered in English.

Monstrilio let out another string of sounds unlike any I'd heard him make before. Joseph choked, the start of a sob. I waited for him to lose it. My heart pounded. Maybe he would try to kill Monstrilio. I wouldn't let that happen.

Joseph didn't breathe back in, and his stasis made it hard for me to breathe too. Magos poked Joseph. He didn't react. Magos poked him again until he turned to her with bulging blue eyes. He bent his head down to his knees. Was he about to puke? Did I have time to steer him away from the carpet?

I rubbed his back, but he straightened back up so abruptly he made me jump. He was laughing. A weird jerky laugh.

"Oh, man," he said, again in English, red in the face, tears in his eyes.

Magos took his hand and this time he let her. He probably didn't even notice.

"Don't cry, Joseph. Please."

Joseph wept long unabashed sobs. His tears free and drenching. Magos looked at me as if I knew some way to stop his crying. I closed the door to Monstrilio's room. Magos held Joseph by the waist and, like a puppeteer, walked him to the living room and plopped him on the couch. She sat next to him.

"What is happening?" he said among blubbers. "Magos, did we kill ourselves in Firgesan?"

"We're not dead," Magos answered in Spanish.

"I can confirm that," I said.

"Did that thing just call me Papi?"

"What? No," Magos said.

"He did make a weird sound," I said.

"Monstrilio doesn't speak," Magos said.

"You call it Monstrilio?"

"He's got to have a name."

Joseph inhaled what was left of his tears and snot, wiped his nose with the back of his hand, got up, and walked back to the room. We followed. Monstrilio turned to us, and then, maybe because we were waiting for it, maybe because we were holding our breaths (it seemed as if the whole of Mexico City had held its breath too), we heard it.

"Papi!" Monstrilio said in a raspy voice, his eyes carrying a light within. He bared his fangs, said "Papi!" again, and draped back down to dangle.

Joseph closed the door.

"You heard it this time," he said.

"Yes," I said.

Magos stared at the closed door, as if there were something else to it besides wood.

My phone rang. An emergency. My patient, Mrs. Rodriguez, wasn't recovering nearly as well as I'd hoped. I left Magos and Joseph outside Monstrilio's door.

I spent the rest of the morning in the hospital reviewing Mrs. Rodriguez's tests, ordering a couple more, and assuring her family she would make a full recovery, in time.

Traffic that afternoon was light. I drove directly to Magos and Joseph's house in la Roma, past my favorite tacos de canasta place, a bright orange tarp selling tortas ahogadas, a green one selling fruit, restaurant terraces with planters determining their territories, a stationery store with backpacks hanging on a rope, and sidewalks raised by tree roots. The smell of fresh tortillas made it into my car. I turned right at the tortillería and onto a narrow street where the city quieted and their house stood, thin and tall, painted sky blue, its windows framed into dark squares.

The main gate, wrought iron in an Art Deco pattern, led into the living room, which opened into the dining room and then the kitchen. The house had been unoccupied for a while, but it was tidy. I called out for Mrs. Rosa, the woman who cleaned my apartment on Tuesdays and Thursdays and whom I'd hired to clean and water the plants at Magos and Joseph's house once a week. I didn't want to give her a heart attack in case she was around—I didn't know what days she came. The house was empty. The furniture was covered in sheets, the floors and counters held minimum dust, and the plants in the house and on the patio spilled from their pots, fat and conceited. Mrs. Rosa was thorough. Magos and Joseph could move back in the next day if they wanted. They might. Now that Joseph was back and Monstrilio was calling out to him.

I went up to Santiago's room. Sat on his bed. Sunlight seeped at the edges of his closed curtains. The room smelled of fabric softener. I sniffed his cartoon-dinosaur bedspread. Maybe Magos would hate me for having erased Santiago's smell from his room. Time would have erased it anyway. On his desk there were mugs and mason jars filled with rainbows of colored pencils, markers, and pens.

I noticed a notebook with "Santiago Jansen de la Mora" on the cover. On the first page, he had written, "Hello, today is Tuesday," and drawn a sort of fox with a tail three times the size of its body. The next page read, "Hello, today is Wednesday," and showed a drawing of a pink creature. Its shape most resembled a giraffe's, but with two large fangs protruding from its mouth. On one of the last filled pages ("Hello, today is Saturday"), he drew a creature that looked just like Monstrilio, same ball-body, same arm-tail sticking out awkwardly from its side, same row of fangs across half

of its body. A few pages later, he wrote, "Hello, today is Monday."
Then, instead of a creature, he wrote, "The End." There were a
bunch of blank pages remaining in the notebook.

I closed the book and set it down the way he'd left it. I opened
his curtains and the window. I sat back on his bed hoping for a
breeze to waft in and cool my face and for the sunlight to lift the
shadows that clung to me.

I t didn't take long for Monstrilio to win Joseph over.

"Papi! Papi! Papi!" he called out as he leapt from light to cat tower to curtain rod, thrilled simply because Joseph had entered the room. The sound of his voice was raspy and low, but there was a childlike quality to its intonation: fresh, awed, and loving. Joseph pretended aloofness at first, as if it weren't evident Monstrilio was melting his heart. It was possible Monstrilio had said "Papi" as a reflex, a sound which only meant something to us. But then he started saying "Mami" and "Lena" too.

Magos and Joseph decided to move back into their house in la Roma, as I suspected they would. Joseph flew back to New York to pick up the things he and Magos had left behind. While he was gone, Magos asked me to empty Santiago's room. I told Magos to wait for Joseph, but she told me neither she nor Joseph could do it. I didn't want to either, but Magos pleaded, and I was unable to say no. I packed Santiago's clothes, books, and toys into boxes and stowed them in a small storage room on their rooftop. His furniture, I gave away to an orphanage. I kept his monster notebook for myself.

The room empty, I took a magazine from Joseph's studio, a thick designer-looking thing, brought it to the stove, and set fire to it. Flames curled its pages and I dropped it onto the floor. I watched the fire turn the magazine to ash. The tiles wouldn't catch fire, but smoke filled the kitchen.

I wanted to delay their move, make Magos see that her place, and Monstrilio's, was with me. I would give up my apartment and Magos and I would buy a house. I would convince Joseph to stay in New York, tell him Magos didn't want him. She had abandoned him, twice. She hadn't even looked for him, had come to me instead. I would tell him Monstrilio was a monster that couldn't love him.

I put out what was left of the fire with stomps, picked up the remnants of the magazine, dropped them in the sink, and drenched them with water. I opened the door that led to their patio to air out the smoke. The tiles stayed blackened and uglied the kitchen. I didn't regret it.

A day later, I helped Magos move back into their house. There wasn't much to move in except the few clothes she had been wearing since she came back to Mexico and Monstrilio's cat tower. We pulled blankets off furniture, swept, and dusted. Magos walked around the house staring at the furniture and Joseph's and Santiago's framed artwork. As if in a museum, she touched nothing, her hands held behind her back. I waited for something to pierce the coolness with which she was holding herself, but nothing did.

We put Monstrilio in Santiago's old room, empty except for the cat tower. In the kitchen, Magos rubbed the darkened tiles with her foot. I pretended I didn't notice. On the patio, Magos caressed her plants, held some leaves as if determining their weight. She mumbled to them, then stood frozen in the middle of her tiny jungle.

"Okay?" I asked.

"Why wouldn't I be?"

I offered to stay with her, but she said she'd be fine, that I'd done enough.

"At least buy me pizza."

Magos was mopping the kitchen when the bell rang. I went to answer, but there was no pizza. Lucía and Jackie stood at the door.

"We've come to help," Lucía said.

"Help?"

"With the move." Using her cane, wooden with a silver handle, Lucía pushed the door open and stepped in. Jackie followed. Magos stood in the living room. "Nice to be back here," Lucía said.

"I thought you were the pizza," Magos said.

Jackie sat on the couch and Lucía sat next to her.

"So, may I see it?" Lucía asked.

"See what?" Magos asked.

"The monster."

"What monster?" I said, high-pitched.

Magos smiled. "He's in his room."

"Santiago's room?" Lucía asked. "Isn't that a bit disrespectful?" Magos's lips thinned, the way Lucía's did when she was upset. Lucía put her hands up. "I haven't come to fight."

Magos led the way upstairs. I walked behind the three of them, trying to figure out if Lucía or Jackie were hiding any weapons to murder the monster. I saw no obvious weapons, though Lucía's cane could be used as one. I stayed close to her. Monstrilio lay on the topmost tier of his tower staring out the window. There wasn't much to see except the walls of the house next door, but he enjoyed the light.

"Is that it?" Lucía said from the doorway. "Wasn't it larger?"

"It was smaller before," Magos said.

Monstrilio turned toward us and bared his fangs. Lucía stepped back. Jackie walked forward protectively.

"It's okay," Magos said. Monstrilio let himself fall, grabbed a rod from the tower with his arm-tail, and swung toward us, building momentum. He did this when we fed him, a pantomime of hunting. "No," Magos said. "It's not time to eat." Monstrilio kept swinging, building more momentum. "Monstrilio. No." Monstrilio gave up and dangled.

"Mami," he said in a croak.

"Did it say 'Mami'?" Jackie asked.

Magos waved Lucía and Jackie nearer. "This is Lucía, my mom, and this is Jackie."

"Hungry," Monstrilio said.

"You just ate."

"Meat."

"It speaks," Lucía said. "Jackie, you didn't tell me it speaks!"

"I didn't know."

"He started speaking only recently," Magos said. "Simple words: *mami, papi, meat, hungry, play, light, thank you.*"

"It says 'thank you'?" Lucía asked.

"Sometimes. Mostly to Joseph."

"He says 'Lena' too," I said.

Monstrilio swung and, with a somersault, threw himself on top of the tower to face the window again. Lucía took Jackie's hand and they stepped closer. "What did you call it?"

"Monstrilio."

"Monstrilio," Lucía said. Monstrilio turned to her, fangs bared. She flinched.

"It's how he smiles," I said, though I wasn't sure if this was true.

"You're ugly." Lucía tapped Monstrilio with her cane.

"Mami, don't!"

"It is. Don't think I've forgiven it." She tapped his head again. Monstrilio scratched the spot Lucía tapped. "Can you say 'Lucía'?"

"It doesn't work like that, Mami."

"Lu-cí-a." Lucía's mouth moved in slow, wide gestures. Monstrilio eyed her. "Stupid thing," she said.

"Lucía," Monstrilio said. Lucía stared at him. "Lucía," Monstrilio repeated.

"Don't you try to eat me again, you hear me?"

Monstrilio growled, not menacing, more like a question. Lucía shook her cane and tapped him for a third time. One more and I was confiscating that cane. Monstrilio bared his fangs. They stared each other down until Monstrilio swiveled away from her.

"Okay, I'm done," Lucía said. Magos followed her out of the room.

Jackie asked if she might touch him. I nodded. She poked him as if making sure he was real. "When I told Lucía it was alive, she wanted to kill it."

Monstrilio growled.

Jackie stepped back. "Does it understand me?"

"I'm not sure."

Monstrilio yawned and his fur bristled.

"Goodness," Jackie said.

"I know." Monstrilio's mouth, when outstretched, split half of his body wide open. "Does Lucía still want to kill him?" I asked.

"I don't think so. Do you think it's Santiago's lung?"

"Maybe, but he's not Santiago."

"You don't think it'll become a man?"

"Do you?"

Jackie looked at me with sad eyes. "I told Magos a story in which a heart became a man. That story didn't end well."

Monstrilio slumped on the platform. Jackie poked him again. Monstrilio scratched. He enjoyed rubbing himself against rough textures, but there were no rugs or carpet in this room. In my spare bedroom, the carpet was bald on Monstrilio's favorite spot to rub. He also scratched many of my towels and sheets into ribbons. Magos got him industrial rugs so he wouldn't totally wreck my apartment, but we forgot to bring them. I'd bring them later. Or was Monstrilio not my business anymore? This room overlooked the patio, and none of the city sounds wafted in. It was too silent, hermetic, like a tomb. I panicked. I was about to lose something I wouldn't get back. I concentrated on Jackie's hair as I tried to swallow my panic. She permed it into curls that framed her head like a halo, pushed back by headbands. The one she wore that day was orange.

"Flaqui! Jackie!" Magos called from downstairs. "Pizza's here."

Jackie walked out of the room. I petted Monstrilio. He hissed and I hissed back.

I got a carton of beer from the corner store. We sat at the dining table. Magos and I ate pizza. Jackie and Lucía joined us with beers. From time to time, Lucía patted Jackie's hand. I wondered if they fucked. Night came, and I said I had to go. Lucía asked why I wasn't staying with Magos, especially with "that thing" in the house. I made up a lie about having surgery early the next morning. Magos kissed my cheek and I left.

La del Valle, the neighborhood I lived in, wasn't far, and I drove there too quickly. I stayed inside my car. Other cars rushed by. *Are you free tonight?* I texted Maritoni though it wasn't a Monday. I waited for fifteen minutes, but she didn't answer. I drove to one of my favorite bars, an old cantina with large wooden tables covered in plastic, gruff service, and amazing tuna tostadas. The waitress knew me and led me to a table for four, the smallest they had. I drank mezcal chased by beer. A group of office people walked in, already half-drunk, laughing. A woman held two men by the waist as if they were about to fall over or she was. They all spoke over one another. The woman sat first, and the party arranged itself around her. When their drinks came, they cheered. She had accomplished some work victory. After the cheers died down, she noticed me staring. I would've normally shifted my eyes away, but I held her gaze. She lifted her Cuba to me, I lifted my mezcal to her, and we drank together though we sat at different tables. Maybe she was thinking, I want to be like her. Brave. Independent. Drinking by herself, getting a tuna tostada, who cares if she's alone. In fact, better alone! I gulped down the rest of my mezcal. My third. Fourth? I ordered another.

The woman immersed herself in her party and I lost interest. Joseph also loved this cantina. We hadn't been here together since before they left for Firgesan. Magos claimed she liked it too, but by the way she held herself here, barely touching anything at all, I could tell she found it grimy. Joseph and Magos would be a family again, with Monstrilio instead of Santiago. Even Lucía had come around, begrudgingly perhaps. Everything seemed to be falling into place, returning back to a life in which I had no place.

"Hello."

The office woman appeared in front of me. She wore her hair in a stylish bob, her blouse loose enough to drape fashionably, her bra's edges noticeable, her pants high waisted.

"Sit," I said. She looked back at her group, but they weren't paying attention to her. She sat. "Want anything to drink?" I asked.

"Are you a doctor?"

I looked down at myself, trying to deduce if my clothes gave it away, but I wasn't wearing anything doctor-y. "How did you know?"

"Dr. Álvarez?"

"Yes. Lena Álvarez."

"My grandfather is—" She said a name that sounded familiar but did not conjure up a specific man, rather a type, rich and old, with a big family of smiling pretties that call you *Doctor* with such reverence (because you've successfully saved their beloved elder) that you come to believe you're someone important.

"Ah, yes, of course," I said.

"You look good," she said, her words slightly slurred. "Younger."

"Youngest surgeon in Mexico."

"Is that true?"

"Yes," I said, though I wasn't sure it was. I was the youngest surgeon at my hospital. "I'm a genius," I whispered.

She laughed. I wanted to say something else, something witty and flirty, but words betrayed me. She got up.

"It was great to see you. I'll tell Grandpa I ran into you."

She offered me her hand. I held it. She squirmed, unable to decide whether to sit back down or run away from me. I didn't let go of her hand.

"What's your name?" She told me her name, but I didn't know what to do with it. She tugged away. I held on tighter, now with both hands. The woman was so uncomfortable, I felt like crying.

"Nice to meet you," I said, and I finally let go of her hand.

She stumbled back to her group. What the fuck was that? her friend's bulging eyes said. I ordered another mezcal.

Magos wasn't home when I arrived. "Out on errands," Joseph said. She'd asked me to come over but said to text her before I left and I hadn't. Joseph was sweaty and wore workman gloves.

"What are you working on now?" I asked.

Joseph had built Monstrilio a jungle gym on the patio with wooden platforms and logs sticking out of walls, platforms on high posts, a little house structure with a roof, and rope ladders connecting it all. Inside the little house, Joseph had put in a dog bed. Monstrilio collected old towels and crumpled sheets and had lined the bed with them, apparently preferring this now to sleeping upside down. Joseph called it a nest. He painted Monstrilio's house yellow and the platforms and logs in reds, blues, and greens. He integrated Magos's plants into this playground and added in some of his own, palms, ferns, a hydrangea. He brought the big, leafy monstera from the nook next to the stairs right next to Monstrilio's house. Joseph had also fastened a net from the roof of their house to their neighbor's wall after an incident in which Monstrilio escaped the patio, only to be found hours later by a terrified Joseph and Magos, waiting for them atop a tree in front of their house as if nothing were amiss. The net ensured Monstrilio had an open sky but prevented him from escaping again.

"See that corner over there?" Joseph pointed to a patch of dirt at the far end of the patio. "That's where Monstrilio goes to the bathroom. I thought I'd make it nicer." We walked to the end where Joseph had a table set up with tools and several pieces of wood. "I have to remove some of the cement, but there's a guy that can do that for me. I'll build an enclosure around it, fill it with better dirt, and grow grass. Monstrilio will love that. It'll be easier to clean too."

"Nice."

Joseph nodded, pleased. "So, what's up? I haven't seen you in a while."

"Did you miss me?"

"I did, actually." Joseph measured the wood.

I'd been busy lately, taking on more surgeries than I could reasonably manage. The only way I could find sleep anymore was if I went to bed at maximum exhaustion. Maritoni had quit. She'd found an exclusive gig. I didn't know exactly what that meant, but I knew not to ask for details. I spent weeks searching for the right woman to replace her. I tried finding someone online. One woman seemed bored and washed me like a robot, harsh and mechanic. Another cooed and patted my head as if I were some sort of mangy animal she was rescuing. Another washed me pretty acceptably but then ran off with my bag and my blender. I had finally settled on Estrella. Excellent. Comparable to Carmina. But I still couldn't sleep. I supposed that my body needed time to adjust to Estrella. She was good. No. She was excellent and would soon make me sleep.

"Hand me that saw," Joseph said. I did. He stared at me and with his free hand pulled my right cheek down as if he knew what to look for in the whites of my eyes. "Are you okay?"

I pushed his hand away. "Peachy." Monstrilio landed on my shoulders. "Shit." I jumped. "You scared me."

"Lena," Monstrilio said, and he leapt onto Joseph's table.

"Go play," Joseph said. "We're working." Monstrilio swatted Joseph with his arm-tail. Joseph laughed. "Go!"

Monstrilio swatted him again and bared his long row of fangs. I was sure it was a smile this time; his eyes glittered, silly and eager. Joseph swatted him back, and they began to play-wrestle, Monstrilio on top of Joseph, growling, while Joseph, grunting, pretended to pin him down. Monstrilio had developed four defined legs complete with furry hand-and-feet-looking appendages, which Joseph tried to hold. Monstrilio wiggled them but didn't use them for anything else. His arm-tail was all that he needed. They rolled on the ground until Monstrilio escaped by grabbing a rope and swinging to a sky-blue platform.

"Papi. Bye-bye."

"Cheater!" Joseph wiped his brow.

"You didn't win?"

"He wins every time. He knows I can't follow him up there."

"Has he ever hurt you?"

"A few scratches. Sometimes he forgets how sharp his claws and teeth are. But I like that about him. Like he's indestructible." Joseph grabbed a pencil and measured again. He began sawing. "No work today?" he asked.

"Not until later. You?"

"The yogurt people said they might commission illustrations for a new kid's line they're launching, but they haven't made a decision yet."

"Sounds fun."

"It's work. Not all of us have a surgeon salary."

"Not all of us come from money."

"Barely any money left these days. I'd rather not dip into it if I can help it."

"Will Luke be okay?"

"He's good. There's still enough for him." He blew on the edge of the cut piece, took a piece of sandpaper, and filed the edge in swift strokes.

"And Magos?" I asked.

Joseph set down the wood and stared at it like a puzzle piece he didn't quite know where to fit. "She's always out."

For the next couple of hours, I helped him as if I were his nurse, handing him instruments, holding things down, clasping others. I was reminded how warm his friendship was and how much I missed it. I couldn't blame him for ending my fantasy with Magos.

She finally showed up.

"Flaqui! Just the person I wanted. Like I summoned you."

"You did summon me."

She asked me to help her carry stuff in from her car. We unloaded four cans of white paint, a tripod, a video camera, lights, and rolls of colored paper and brought them up to Santiago's old room. "What's all this?"

"Now that Joseph has built Monstrilio his own wonderland, I thought I'd make this room my studio." She opened the curtains. Light shone, bouncing warm off of the room's yellow walls.

"Like a movie studio?"

"Performance art," she said. "Remember that show that we went to last month? I want to do that."

"That weird video thing?" The show had been almost two months ago, the last time I'd seen her.

"I kept thinking about it and I have so many ideas. I'm an artist, Flaqui. Isn't that wonderful? I always wanted to be one but never thought I could. I can't draw or paint like Joseph can. I can't sculpt. I'm not good with my hands. But I can perform."

"Can you live off of that?"

She carried the paint cans to a corner of the room. "If you mean money, probably not, but that's not the point, Flaqui."

"Then what's the point?"

"Creating. Expressing. Sharing my voice."

"You sound possessed."

"Possessed by creativity. Are you free this afternoon?"

"I have to be at the hospital by six."

She looked at her watch. "Good. We have enough time."

Magos took me to the MUAC. I'd never been inside the museum, only seen its windows shooting outward, like an inverted slide. Inside, the museum was bright, everything glass or concrete. Three young people wearing boots and totes stood in front of a set of hanging acrylic panels I wasn't sure were art or decoration. Magos walked right past them and into one of the inner rooms. She wanted to show me an exhibition by a Chilean performance artist she'd seen three times already. The artist, a woman with long black hair, not unlike Magos's, ripped books apart in videos projected on the walls. Benches had been set up in front of each projection, though only one woman sat.

"Come," Magos pulled me to watch the artist destroy a children's book, the kind with large, glossy pages.

"This is what you want to do? Destroy books?"

"Isn't it fantastic?"

"I don't get it," I said, though I was spellbound.

The woman fought to rip the book apart, and I wanted her to succeed. When she did, the book a pile of ripped pages and spine, I felt a great sense of accomplishment. So absurd, I chuckled. We moved on to the next video. In this one the woman held the Yellow Pages in her hands. A tough one! She grabbed the book and tried to split it down its spine. She failed. She tore some pages, crumpled them, and threw them. This didn't satisfy her. I thought, "You can do it!" but she didn't need my encouragement, only someone to watch her. Me, her audience.

"All we say these days is 'Good morning.' 'Good night.' 'Have you eaten?'" Magos's voice brought me back to the museum. "I think he hates me. Or not hate. Like I taste bitter."

"Who?"

"Joseph." The artist bit into the Yellow Pages. "He tastes bitter to me."

"It'll pass," I said. I wasn't entirely sure what she was talking about. The artist spit shreds of yellow paper.

"I don't know if I want it to pass, Flaqui. Maybe it's okay that we taste bitter to each other."

I turned to Magos. The same height as me. Her ponytail swung as she turned to me; the dark in her eyes sparkled. She had drawn a slight cat eye. I pushed a stray strand of her hair behind her ear.

"I don't want to talk about him, Magos."

She gestured a zipping of her mouth, turned an invisible key, flicked it away, whipped around, and took my arm with a hop of her step. She led me to the next projection. In this one the artist was trying to destroy an ancient-looking leather-bound book.

"She's beautiful, don't you think?" Magos said.

"Very."

The pages inside the book ripped out easily, but the woman wanted to destroy the leather cover too and she had only her body to help her. I watched as she tried different ways to obliterate it. When she finally found a way, by chewing on it nibble by nibble, I realized Magos was gone. I found her in a room with an alien-looking orb sculpture (onyx?) watching rain pour down outside. Two other people watched the rain from the museum's large windows, impatient, as if it couldn't go away fast enough. Magos watched as if the rain were part of the art.

"Did you bring an umbrella?" Magos asked me. I hadn't. "Do you mind getting wet?" I didn't.

She grabbed my hand and we walked out into the rain. We stood at the center of the museum's esplanade and blew on the streams that fell over our mouths. Rebel strands that escaped her ponytail stuck to her face.

"Flaqui! We're soaked." She laughed.

I was too knotted in emotions to laugh, or cry, or kiss her. She was gorgeous.

A wall fell in Lucía's house, one of the outside walls that kept the house from the street. No one was hurt, but it knocked into the garden, the kitchen, and the area where Jackie's room was. I drove to Lucía's house. Magos, Joseph, Lucía, and Jackie, with Almendra on a leash, stood in a row on the street staring at the debris. Dusk made them seem like a painting.

"What happened?" I asked.

"We don't know," Lucía said, and she prodded one of the stones with her cane.

"The wind, I think," Jackie said.

"It must have already been weak," Joseph said.

I patted Lucía on the shoulder. I thought her house was invincible.

"Mami, let's get you some clothes," Magos said. "You and Jackie can come stay with us until we fix it."

"We're staying here. Aren't we, Jackie?"

"Lucía doesn't want to leave the house unattended," Jackie said. "Now that anyone can come in."

"Can't someone come and fix it?" Joseph asked.

"I called someone," Lucía said. "But he can't come until tomorrow."

"So you'll stay here alone?" Magos asked.

"We'll be fine."

"I'll stay with you."

"I'll stay too," Joseph said. "Maybe we can clear this rubble a bit. Patch up the kitchen. It seems like the wall only knocked down some of the windows. Nothing structural." Joseph picked up a rock, formerly part of the wall, and heaved it into the street.

"Thank you," Lucía said. She stared at the collapse with both hands resting on her cane. Magos put an arm around her. Lucía turned away from the debris. "Let's make us some tea."

"I can't stay," I said. The crumbling of the house was making my nose itch and my bones feel like rubber. "I have to be at the hospital. I just came to check if you were all okay."

Magos hugged me and kissed my cheek. Lucía squeezed my hand.

"Bye, Joseph," I said as he heaved another rock into the street.

"Lena, hey, wait. Monstrilio will be hungry soon. I can go and feed him if it's too much trouble, but if you don't mind—"

"Just tell me what to do."

Joseph said there was a bag of meat in the fridge that I should separate into five portions and distribute among the bowls spread out on Monstrilio's patio. "He likes to feel like he's hunting," Joseph said.

After finishing a few things at the hospital and with the house's collapse nagging in my stomach, I was ready to call it a day. Then one of my closest colleagues, a friend even, called for a consultation. I met him at his office a floor down from mine and spent a good part of the night discussing a patient he wanted to refer to me. A difficult case, vertebral osteomyelitis. By the time I got home, I was so exhausted I went straight to bed. I woke up a good four hours later—longer than I had slept in a while—made myself coffee, glanced at the paper, and it wasn't until I was in the shower singing "Qué monstruos son" that I remembered I hadn't fed Monstrilio. Half wet and dressed in a mismatched tracksuit, I drove to Joseph and Magos's.

I tiptoed through their house. I couldn't be sure a hungry Monstrilio wouldn't forget who I was and attack me.

"Monstrilio. It's your friend, Lena. Please don't eat me."

I heard a creak. I spun around and tripped over a sofa chair. Monstrilio was on top of me. "Get off me!" I kicked and knocked over a stool with a plant on it. Monstrilio wasn't on top of me. Only the chair I tripped on. I took a moment on the floor to catch my breath.

"Monstrilio," I called out to the patio. "Monstrilio?" I stepped outside. I heard rustling. Monstrilio plopped down at my feet. He smiled. Fangs bloody. "Fuck. What did you do?"

Cats and small dogs (some not so small), also a few rats, lay dead all over the patio, in pieces, eviscerated. It stank of innards and blood. Monstrilio leapt, grabbed a post with his arm-tail, and swung to another. He growled from up in his perch, chomped on something, then threw it at my feet. Bloody and furry. I stepped back in the kitchen and closed the door behind me.

I took three long breaths to push myself into surgeon mode and went back out. Monstrilio's yellow house had a gate so they could lock him inside when they had strangers over. I ordered Monstrilio to get in, but he didn't obey.

"Monstrilio, please."

He leapt away. "Lena," he said, playful.

I took a piece of who knows what animal and threw it in Monstrilio's house. Monstrilio leapt inside. I locked the gate.

There was a rip on the net above. Joseph's job to fix. I grabbed a shovel and a trash bag from a tool shed at the back of the patio and shoveled up a mostly whole hairy dog. Threw it in the bag. Monstrilio burped. I tried to pick up part of a cat, but it kept slipping off the shovel. The bell on its collar jingled. I went back inside the kitchen to find some gloves. It would be easier to pick up the dead animals with my hands.

"What are you doing here?"

I jumped.

Joseph laughed. "I didn't mean to scare you."

"Don't go out there."

"Why?" Joseph's face turned eggshell white. "Did something happen to Monstrilio?"

"I'm sorry, Joseph. I really am. I forgot to feed him yesterday. I guess he must've been hungry because he got out."

"He's lost?"

"He's here. But his leftovers are too." Joseph stormed past me, opened the door to the patio, stepped out, and then stepped back in. He was paler. I told him to sit. Asked him if he needed to hurl. He told me he didn't, but I slid a bucket next to him, just in case. I rubbed his back. "I should have fed him. I'm sorry."

"How many did he kill?"

"A lot."

"Why so many?"

"I don't know, Joseph. Instinct?"

"And he brought them here?"

"Kind of makes sense. This is where he usually feeds."

"Magos can't see this."

"She needs to know what happened. Don't you think?" I found a pair of dishwashing gloves, slipped them on, and headed outside.

"I'll be with you in a minute," Joseph said, so pale that the veins on his temple showed.

"You don't need to."

"I'll be there."

Joseph and I spent the next hour picking up as much of the animals as we could find. He threw bucket after bucket of soapy water on the floor. He mopped, and even when there was no blood left, he kept mopping. His face became red and sweaty. The day was too sunny for such a scene. Joseph didn't acknowledge Monstrilio, who called out "Papi!" from behind the gate. I scrubbed the walls and flowerpots where blood had splattered. Some stains wouldn't fully come out, but at least I made them less incandescently red—more brownish, like dirt.

"I think it's clean now," I said, and I picked off a bit of pet from one of the plants.

Joseph gave the floor a final mop. Monstrilio scratched the metal-bar gate with his arm-tail claws and asked, "Papi?" Joseph's face muscles quit; his eyebrows and cheeks drooped.

"I can't let you out," Joseph said. Monstrilio scratched again. Joseph pushed his fingers through the gate, and Monstrilio placed his arm-tail on top of them. He stared at Joseph with big, beady eyes and showed his fangs, still bloody. "I'm sorry." Joseph walked inside the house.

ESTRELLA CAME THAT NIGHT. It was a Monday. She bathed me, the frosted tips of her bunned-up hair soggy on her forehead. I pushed them away, and my hand lingered on her cheek.

"Is this okay?" I asked.

She nodded, her hands busy soaping my breasts. I didn't normally touch the women I hired, but sleep was coming so rarely I wondered if I needed to do more to earn it. My hand traveled down from Estrella's cheek to one of her naked breasts. I lingered on her large, beautiful nipple before going down past the curve of her belly to her vagina. I fingered her. It seemed she wasn't sure if she should stop washing me or if she should just relax. She opted for the latter. I asked her to finger me too. After we came (I wasn't sure if she came or if she pretended to come for my sake, though if it was fake, it was amazingly convincing), she toweled me off like in our regular sessions. She watched me dress in my nightclothes. I paid her more to account for the sex, and she left. I went to bed with the same ease I had each Monday before the incident, before Magos and Monstrilio jumbled up my life. I was confident I would sleep through the night.

I woke up an hour later and had no trace of sleep left in my body. I called Joseph and asked him to meet me at our favorite cantina.

"It's midnight," he said. I didn't answer. "Okay. I'll meet you there."

Joseph showed up in sweatpants. I wore a tracksuit. We ordered beers, and it was only after we drank most of our pints that we found the spirit to speak.

"Thank you," Joseph said. "I needed this."

"You and me both." We clinked glasses and downed the remainder of our beers. We asked for more.

"It was horrible, wasn't it?" Joseph said. "I told Magos what happened. She's still at Lucía's. Apparently there are more things to be fixed apart from the wall. She said it was natural if Monstrilio was hungry. But she didn't see what Monstrilio did, Lena. You saw it. This wasn't hunger. It was like he was showing off."

"A horror show."

"Right? I mean, it was excessive."

"Is Monstrilio still locked up?"

"I spent the day installing metal fencing instead of the net so I could let Monstrilio out. He seemed so sad in there, and it broke my heart to leave him, but I couldn't let him out again."

"It's not Monstrilio's fault. He's wild."

"I thought he was getting tamer, you know? I play with him. And he speaks for chrissakes. What the hell is he?"

"A monster."

A table next to us cheered and clinked glasses. Joseph drank. I drank too.

"Should we even keep him? I mean, he had no qualms about mauling every pet in the neighborhood and bringing them home."

"He doesn't know any better."

"I don't believe he's a monster, Lena. At least not a full one. He can learn."

"Learn what?"

"To behave." Joseph burped. "Magos wants to cut his arm-tail off. She says now that Monstrilio is growing into a more human body, he doesn't need it anymore. She has a theory that the arm-tail is what makes him wild."

"Where did she get that from?"

"I don't know, but she seemed pretty sure."

"Do you think it's true?"

The table next to us erupted in laughter and I smiled, unsuccessfully trying to absorb their merriment.

"His body is changing," Joseph said. "He didn't have limbs before and now he has four. He's getting less round. He's not looking more human but at least more like a normal animal. His arm-tail is the only thing that's off, coming out of the side like that."

"So you're going to chop it off." I was angry for Monstrilio. I thought they loved him just as he was. "That's bullshit, Joseph."

I chugged the rest of my beer down and Joseph did too. The waitress, her hair so unnaturally red it was purple, took our empties away. We asked for one more round.

"I'm teaching him new words, and I want to keep teaching him. He learns quicker now. The other day he said, 'Papi, water more.' He's constructing sentences. I saw notches scratched on one of the wooden posts, and when I asked him what it was, he said, 'Sleep.' He's counting the times he sleeps! Like a calendar."

"What for?"

"No clue. But you see how smart he is. And he says 'Monstrilio' now, did you know? He says 'Monstrilio' and points to himself. He knows who he is!" Joseph smiled. Then he became sad. "I don't know what to do, Lena. I don't know if I can keep this up."

"Keep what up?"

"This life, here, with Monstrilio. With Magos. It's like she's acting. She does all the things Magos would do. She says all the things she would say, but there's nothing inside her. Like she's on automatic."

"Faking it until it becomes real."

"I've been doing it too, you know? I'm working. I'm smiling. I'm out here caring for Monstrilio. And sometimes, it does seem like it's real, like I can actually be this person." He pushed strands of hair behind his ears. "It just feels like I should be doing something else."

"Like what?"

"Crying."

"Then cry."

"I've cried myself out."

"I'd say."

"Shouldn't I be holed up in a dark room somewhere with a scraggly beard, dirty and insane?"

"Why aren't you?"

"I guess I already did that. Back in New York. Uncle watched me cry. I could go back there or live somewhere else. End things, finally. That's why I came back here. Why I showed up at your door that day. I still could. Start over for real, I mean." He stared at me. I scratched at a bump on the table's plastic covering until a small hole appeared. "Well. What do you think? Aren't you going to tell me to stay?"

"Why would I?"

"Because it's what's best for me? For Magos and me. And Monstrilio too, I think."

"Is it?"

"I don't know. Help me."

"Sometimes I think I should disappear to a cabin in Greenland, become a lumberjack."

"Why Greenland?"

"Why the fuck not?"

Joseph lifted his glass and looked at me through his beer, his face the color of sunshine. He smiled, his teeth in full view, even the crooked one to the side. I stuck my tongue out. He did the same, put his beer down, and excused himself to go pee.

arrived at their house at seven sharp. Most people wouldn't dare arrive exactly on time, but I hated calculating how much cushion I should give (when is too late or just right), so I came at the time asked. Joseph received me. I pulled him down to hug him and he winced. His forearm was bandaged.

"It's nothing," he said.

"Doesn't look like nothing. Let me see."

"Flaqui!" Magos walked into the living room and kissed my cheeks. "You look great. A bit pale. You're working too much, no?" I nodded. Also, Estrella had left me, and I hadn't had the energy to look for a new woman. I'd begun to wonder if my routine of baths had run its course. "I got some of that Tempranillo you like. Come. Come."

Magos had set the dining room table with candles, linen napkins, glittering silver, and beautiful earthenware dishes.

"Is this all for me?"

"I wanted tonight to be special."

Joseph had combed his hair back and was wearing a shirt with a mauve blazer over it. Magos wore a flowy black-and-white-patterned dress with a chunky red necklace and heavy silver bracelets. I was wearing jeans and a shirt. I tucked my shirt in. Magos told me not to worry.

"Always beautiful," she said, and she disappeared into the kitchen.

"Was it Monstrilio?" I asked, pointing at Joseph's arm.

"It was an accident."

"Give it here." Joseph handed me his arm, and I undid his badly wrapped bandage. A gash ran from his elbow to his wrist, luckily sparing his radial artery. "Did you have this looked at? You need stitches."

"I didn't want to go to the hospital and have to answer questions."

"You should've told me."

"I'm fine."

I left to get a suturing kit, alcohol, and gauze from a pharmacy three blocks away. When I came back, Magos and Joseph sat in the living room with wine glasses. Mine sat ready on the coffee table.

Magos lifted her glass. "Salud."

"Wait. I need to take care of Joseph first."

"Can't you do that later?"

"Nope. I plan to drink tonight."

I opened the bottle of rubbing alcohol and wiped the instruments with it. Magos left us. Joseph moaned when I cleaned his wound.

"Lucky it's not infected."

I gave him eleven stitches.

"He didn't mean it," Joseph said. "I was trying to get him down from the mesh ceiling, but I must have surprised him because when he realized it was me he had hurt, he became, I don't know if *sad* is the word, but he wouldn't stop whimpering and climbing on me. He's been doing whatever I tell him to since then."

"You're back to being friends with him?"

"I never stopped. I was just shaken. I didn't know how to handle the pet thing."

I bandaged his arm with fresh gauze.

"Now can we say salud?" Magos asked, appearing back in the living room.

Magos had cooked budín Azteca, my favorite, and had made a spinach-and-nut salad with jamaica dressing, and, for dessert, Joseph had baked a tres leches. He poured wine.

"How are your videos coming along?" I asked Magos.

"I'm fiddling with some ideas. I wrote a lot while staying with my mother, but I haven't really done much video-wise."

"Really?" Joseph said. "You're in your studio a whole lot."

"Practicing. Testing. But nothing concrete yet. I haven't found my project."

"What does that mean?" I asked.

"What I want to say, explore. Something that will make my work cohere. I think I might try a live performance."

"Sounds intense."

"It is," Magos said. Joseph took a big gulp of his wine.

After dessert, and one more round of wine, they became silent and stared at me ominously.

"What?" I asked. "You're not planning on feeding me to Monstrilio, are you?"

Magos laughed. "You're an idiot."

"What is it?"

"We need to ask you a favor."

"Oh, man."

"We want you to remove Monstrilio's arm-tail."

"Fuck no."

Magos looked at Joseph as if it was his turn to say something, but he stared down at his wine glass.

"You're fine with this?" I asked him.

"Magos says it'll help Monstrilio be less wild, but maybe he's not supposed to be."

"Monstrilio almost tore your arm off, Joseph," Magos said.

"He scratched it. Barely."

"Lena just gave you stitches!" Magos placed her elbows on the table. "We have to do something, Flaqui. He can't stay savage forever."

"You had no problem with him being savage before," I said.

"Yes, but Monstrilio must evolve. We have to help him evolve."

"I don't want to mutilate him," Joseph said.

"It's not mutilation. It's removing something that will ultimately hurt him. Like removing a tumor, right, Flaqui?"

"Not like that at all," I said.

Magos leaned back on her chair, took a sip of wine, and stared at the lamp, half a metal sphere painted in an acrylic orange. I was with Magos when she bought it at La Lagunilla, years ago, with Santiago in tow. He had observed each item with his hands held at his back like a tiny collector. I bought him a tin robot. He kept it on his lap when we drove back home. I told him he was allowed to play with it, but he told me the substances on his fingers might damage it. I remembered laughing. I loved his weirdness. I couldn't remember seeing the robot when I packed away his things.

Joseph picked at the crumbs of his tres leches with his fork.

"There's nothing wrong with Monstrilio being wild," I said. "He's a monster. And anyway, why do you think removing his arm-tail will make him less wild?"

"Instinct," Magos said. "Like I had with the lung. This feels right, Flaqui. You both have to trust me."

"Let's say you're right, Magos," Joseph said. "Chopping off his arm-tail still feels cruel to me. Monstrilio does everything with it."

"Why is he growing other limbs then? We have to help him learn to use them, but he won't if he can keep relying on his arm-tail."

"Besides the cruelty of it," I said, "removing his arm-tail is not just whacking it off. We don't know anything about Monstrilio's anatomy. What if his arm-tail holds his brain, or his heart, or another essential organ? We need to know what muscles can be severed, if any. Bones. Tendons. Monstrilio could be one interconnected membrane. We don't know. And healing? Do we know if he heals?"

Joseph said, "After the—the pet situation—Monstrilio was scratched up pretty bad, but he healed fast."

"What would you need to do this?" Magos asked.

"I'm not going to do it. But you'd need X-rays, at the very least. Ideally an MRI. You need to know if Monstrilio responds to anesthetic and if he can handle it. We don't even know if he has veins."

"He bleeds," Joseph said. "Red blood, like us."

"You'd need a hospital."

"You work in one," Magos said.

"I'm not going to do this, Magos. Monstrilio is wild. If you loved him, you wouldn't want to change him."

Magos's lips became thin.

"I don't want to remove his arm-tail either," Joseph said. Magos glared at him. "But I think we should do the tests. If anything, we might discover something. Some other way to help him, perhaps?"

The tests sounded reasonable and, regardless of what they showed, I could still refuse to remove the arm-tail. Besides, I was curious. I scheduled an MRI under a made-up patient's name. The tricky part would be keeping Monstrilio still. I'd need to sedate him, but I didn't know how he would react to sedatives. I would've taken some blood samples if I had somewhere to send them without raising alarms.

MONSTRILIO SWUNG FROM post to platform to rope, saying, "Meat. Meat. Meat," after I had given him a small-dose sedative to test for any adverse reaction. Joseph pulled Monstrilio down. I inspected him. He growled, pleased, as if he were getting a rub-down. His skin was gray, and his fur made it difficult to spot a rash, but I became sufficiently convinced that Monstrilio wasn't allergic. Next, I had to test whether the sedative would actually sedate him, for which I needed a full dose.

Joseph got on his knees and struggled to contain Monstrilio on his bed. I injected him. After a few seconds, he stopped struggling, whimpered, growled from deep inside, and went limp.

"Is he okay?" Joseph asked. "Shouldn't he be breathing? When he sleeps you can still feel him breathing and a whole lot of gurgling inside. I feel nothing."

"It's okay, Joseph," Magos said.

"No, something's wrong!" Joseph rubbed Monstrilio's head. "Lena, do something."

I took one of his limbs and pressed the area below a small hand. I wasn't sure this was the spot to feel for his pulse or if there was a pulse to be felt even in regular circumstances. I felt nothing.

"What is it?" Joseph asked.

I tried another limb. Nothing. I tried the area where his neck would be. Nothing.

"He's dead, isn't he?" Joseph sprang to his feet, paced, and wiped tears from his face. "You killed him!" His chin scrunched up. "He's dead. Again!" He slapped one of the plants. A leaf flew twirling in the air.

"Jesus Christ, Joseph. Keep it together," I said, and I placed my outstretched palm on Monstrilio's body.

"He's dead," Joseph blubbered.

"Shh. I feel something."

Joseph knelt back down, put his palm where I had mine, and closed his eyes. He opened them in terror and picked Monstrilio up. He hugged him tight.

"Joseph, don't," Magos said. She was also terrified. "Let Lena—" Joseph collapsed on the floor with Monstrilio on his lap and wept over him. Magos tried to grab Monstrilio. "Joseph! Let Lena—"

I tried to grab Monstrilio too.

"No!" Joseph swatted my hand.

"Joseph. Joseph! Look at me. I need to check Monstrilio. If anyone can do something about it, it's me. So, please, let me. Now!" Joseph handed Monstrilio to me. "Out of here. Both of you."

I laid Monstrilio on his bed and put my ear to his body. Any sound coming from him, particularly if repetitive, would mean life. I heard a faint gurgle. I pressed on his body harder. I heard a thump. I waited for another.

Thump. Thump.

His pulse was low. Low to which standard? Maybe this was what it was supposed to be. The important thing was that Monstrilio had a heartbeat, if this thumping could be called that. We didn't know if Monstrilio had a heart. To be sure, I waited a few more minutes and listened to Monstrilio again. His thumps were louder. His body rose and fell, like breathing. He was alive. And the sedative had worked. I called Magos and Joseph back onto the patio. Joseph sat cross-legged next to Monstrilio and stroked his fur, waiting for him to awaken even though I told him it could take hours.

Magos and I walked back inside the house.

"Monstrilio is not Santiago," I said. "You want to make him something he's not."

"I know what Monstrilio is," she said. "I made him."

The hospital wing that held the MRI scanner was deserted except for a nurse that kept watch, given that the wing also held a supply room. I distracted him with inane questions while Magos and Joseph slipped in with Monstrilio. The nurse could have caught us if he decided to patrol the floor, but he wasn't a watchman, and the MRI room was far enough away that I was confident we'd go unnoticed. I sedated Monstrilio. Once he was asleep, Joseph and I placed him on the MRI table. Magos, Joseph, and I went into the observation room while the machine scanned. Monstrilio's anatomy began to appear on the screen. Fuck me, I thought, but I waited for his whole body to be scanned before I said anything.

"Look," I said, pointing to an empty area covering half of Monstrilio's body, on his back and pooling where his arm-tail protruded from. "There's nothing here, no discernible organs, bones, or cartilage. It may be liquid or simply one continuous membrane. There's no structure."

"Monstrilio was super squishy before," Magos said.

"Right. But look here." I pointed to the other half of Monstrilio. "There are bones here, you see?" They nodded. "And this here is a heart. And these are his digestive organs. And this right here at the bottom of his head is a cranium with a brain inside. Do you see it?" They squinted at the images. "Look!"

"We're looking, Flaqui. What?"

"This is the anatomy of a young child."

"What?" Joseph said.

"Half of Monstrilio has a young boy's anatomy. Like a person gestating inside."

"Like Monstrilio evolving," Magos said.

"He's a boy," Joseph said.

"He's not a boy," I said. "Not fully."

"What then?" Joseph asked. I didn't have an answer. I hadn't expected this. Magos was right. There was a person inside Monstrilio, at least anatomically. Joseph leaned forward, his nose almost touching the monitor. "That's his heart, right?"

"No." I pointed to where his heart was.

"Then what's this?"

"A lung. He has only one."

After the MRI, Magos and Joseph decided to remove Monstrilio's arm-tail. His arm-tail, like Magos intuited, was not part of his new anatomy and perhaps was hindering Monstrilio's transformation into his final form. Nevertheless, I remained uncomfortable performing the operation. I conveyed my reservations to Joseph and Magos, mainly that it felt wrong to interfere with a living body. And also that I loved Monstrilio as a monster.

In the end, I agreed. Of course I did.

I performed the operation at their house with instruments surreptitiously borrowed from the hospital. The scalpel sliced right through the base of his arm-tail, with no bones or muscles or tendons to hinder it, only bloodlike goo. Contrary to what Joseph had said, Monstrilio oozed something similar to blood but not quite blood, thicker and browner, like molasses. The only trace of his arm-tail became a sewn-shut stump that among all his fur was barely noticeable.

Soon, Monstrilio's stump showed every sign of being healed. Without his arm-tail, though, Monstrilio became clumsy. He fell. He tripped. He couldn't climb. He couldn't swing. He stayed in his nest inside his yellow house. He barely spoke anymore. Before, when he slept, nothing but the loudest noise could rouse him. But now he curled into a ball, his breaths shallow, and at any noise, any whisper or sigh, he jumped up, alert and fully awake. I checked on him every few days. Physically, Monstrilio was in perfect shape. However, as the days passed, he moved less and less.

Magos became irritated that instead of making him move to where his food was, Joseph hand-fed him. Joseph told me Monstrilio would starve if he didn't. Monstrilio grew thinner and longer, with patches of gray skin showing through where his fur had fallen off. Joseph said he was dying and Magos said he was shedding his old body. The one thing he retained was his same dumb-looking face, though his eyes were duller, and he didn't bare his fangs anymore. I managed to avoid the three of them for a few weeks, waiting (hoping?) for the day Joseph or Magos would call to tell me Monstrilio was dead.

Finally, late one night, Joseph called.

"I'm going to put Monstrilio down."

"It's three a.m.," I said, pretending he had woken me up. He hadn't. I hadn't been able to sleep and was watching TV.

"I can't let him suffer, Lena," Joseph said. "It's been almost two months! I'm going to do it tonight. You can't stop me."

"Then why are you calling me?"

"Listen to him." I heard a faint whimper. "He whimpers like this all night. I can't sleep. Breaks my heart."

"Can you wait for me to get there?"

"Tonight? Why? No. I'm going to do it myself."

"I'll help you do it painlessly. We'll put him to sleep."

"Tonight?"

"Yes."

"You'll tell Magos."

"I won't."

"You promise you'll help me?"

"I promise."

Thirty minutes later, Joseph received me in boxers and a T-shirt. He looked awful, red eyes, crunchy sallow skin, sunken cheeks. He took me to the kitchen. Monstrilio curled on his bed by the door to the patio. The sheets and towels that had lined his nest were gone. Monstrilio poked his head up.

"Papi?" Monstrilio said, his voice pitchier.

"Hey there. It's okay," Joseph said in English. He sat down next to Monstrilio. "Lena's come to visit."

Monstrilio lowered his head and hid it between his front legs. The kitchen seemed dimmer than normal. I realized it was Monstrilio's sadness that radiated thick around us and blocked out the light. We had fucked up. I'd fucked up. But I was going to set things right. I showed Joseph a vial with a sedative that could stop a rhino's heart.

"Are you sure?" I asked.

"No," he said. "But what else can I do? We've destroyed him. He's suffering." Joseph stroked Monstrilio's head. "I can't go through this suffering again, Lena. Waiting for death. Convincing myself he'll get better."

"Monstrilio is not Santiago," I said.

And yet. I filled a syringe with the sedative and showed it to Monstrilio. I wanted Monstrilio to know what was happening. I needed at least a hint of volition.

"This will help you die," I said. Monstrilio stretched his head toward it. Sniffed. Joseph shook next to me. He was crying.

The lights came on in the kitchen, blinding me.

"Flaqui?" Magos said. "Why are you here?"

I clenched the syringe in my fist.

"Joseph thought Monstrilio was ill," I said, shielding my eyes. "I came to check."

"Joseph thinks Monstrilio's ill every day."

Joseph rose. "She came to help me put Monstrilio down."

"Kill him?"

"He can't live like this, Magos," Joseph said. "Look at him. Scared out of his mind."

"He's adjusting!"

"He's lost all joy."

"He's growing. Transforming. Of course he's going to be disoriented."

"This isn't confusion, Magos. This is despair."

Magos turned to me. Here I was again, trapped in this family.

"And you? You were going to help him do this?" Magos stepped forward. Her nightgown fluttered. "Were you going to poison him? Or hit him with a hammer again?"

"I shouldn't have come," I said. "This is not my business."

"Damn right it's not your business," Magos said.

My stomach tightened and an ooze of panic filled me, but I didn't try to fight it. I let it overtake me.

"Actually, it is my business, Magos. You made it my business. You asked me to perform the surgery. You've made your whole fucking life my business. And I was happy to oblige. More than happy. But I won't anymore. I just won't fucking do it."

"Great," Magos said. "Get out of my house."

"I thought you loved Monstrilio. But you only wanted Santiago back. Monstrilio was amazing. Look what we did to him."

"Get out."

"Lena stays," Joseph said. "This is my house too."

"You get out too!"

"You can't kick me out."

"The hell I can't." She pointed toward the door and snapped her fingers. "Out! Both of you."

Monstrilio growled, a low growl, almost a whimper, his black marble eyes wet. I hoped Monstrilio would fight, defend us, but he curled back in on himself, hiding inside his body. Joseph knelt to him, kissed his head, wiped tears, walked past Magos and out of the kitchen. I trailed behind him until he stormed upstairs.

I let myself out.

t was a week before Joseph called. He'd gone back to Brooklyn with Luke. I didn't hear from Magos. My ability to summon focus, my surgeon mode, had become erratic. I decided to take time off, rescheduled whatever patients I could, and referred the others. I wasn't sure what to do with myself. I visited the cantina. I hired women to bathe me, not just on Mondays but any day I needed them. Almost every day. More often than not I had sex with them. My insomnia continued.

I wrote to an old mentor from my residency in New York. He told me there wasn't a vacancy for a neurosurgeon but that he could bring me in as a consultant. He was confident that once I was there, the director of the hospital would be so impressed she'd beg me to stay.

"Let's do it," I wrote back.

I didn't expect much, but it excited me in a way I thought I'd lost the ability for. A few weeks later I was hired.

The day before my departure, I visited Jackie and Lucía to say goodbye.

"You're leaving us," Lucía said, kissing both my cheeks.

"Do you want a beer?" Jackie asked.

"What are you drinking?"

"Tequila."

"I'll join you with a tequila, if that's all right."

We sat in the living room and sipped our tequilas. The sun shone through the French doors in the house in las Lomas. I used to study by these windows. Magos would sit next to me and pretend to read a novel or a magazine before she started talking, though she wasn't supposed to interrupt me. She'd ask me about what I was learning. I'd tell her, hoping I would bore her enough that she'd leave me alone, but she would listen to every word I said. She said my voice soothed her.

"To New York!" Lucía raised her shot glass.

I downed my tequila and poured myself another. I was tired. My insomnia would find me in New York. But it would have to travel all the way from Mexico and perhaps get distorted along the way, like a shitty signal on an old TV, speckled and blurry, weak.

"It's good you're leaving. You're bigger than all of this, dear Lena. Bigger than us."

I smiled. Lucía's compliments, like Magos's, had always resounded loudly in me. Outside, Almendra ran by barking at some birds. Lucía watched the dog, and I noticed her face had lost its plumpness. Her bones jutted out markedly, and she had bags under her eyes.

"Have you been well, Lucía?" I asked.

"I'm perfect."

"That's not true," Jackie said. "She's been tired."

"It's just a spell. It'll pass."

"I can recommend a good—"

"Have you seen Monstrilio lately?" Lucía asked. "Jackie and I saw him last week. He speaks more and he's attempting to walk upright. Can you believe it? He can't walk yet, of course. He's still very crooked. His bones haven't quite settled where they should be."

"He doesn't know how to use them yet," Jackie said. "His body, in general."

"Magos calls him a boy, but he's not a boy yet. Not with that fur. And those fangs! But I believe he will be." Lucía sipped her tequila. "To think that the thing that tried to eat me, that grief creature Magos created, is becoming a boy."

"Is Monstrilio still sad?" I asked.

"He's confused, I think," Jackie said.

"Confused. Yes," Lucía said. "And a bit meek, for my taste."

"Hard to picture Monstrilio as meek," I said.

Lucía stood up, the first time I'd seen her use her cane earnestly for support. She handed me a small gift-wrapped box. I opened it and found a silver necklace with two tiny calaveritas as pendants.

"I think they're quite horrid," Lucía said. "But Jackie tells me calaveritas help ward off fear."

"Why two?" I asked. "Do I have that much fear to ward off?"

"For my two girls, of course. This one is Magos. This one is Lena."

Something beeped in the kitchen and Jackie got up to check. Lucía made me get up and fastened the necklace around my neck. They asked me to stay for dinner, but I lied and said I had things left to pack. They hugged and kissed me goodbye. I wetted my fingers in the fountain by the entrance, waved goodbye once more, and walked out.

A taxi honked, startling me. New Yorkers next to me screamed at the taxi driver, riled under their umbrellas. The city's noise, its rain, splashes, honks, and insults, though similar to Mexico City's, felt foreign, and I froze. The taxi honked more angrily but, before I moved on, I relished its noise. Though it rained, a crowd of people had gathered at the Columbus Circle entrance to Central Park.

I would buy lots of plants for my new apartment. I would need to move things here from Mexico, too, my trinkets, even the ghostless ones. Or maybe I would get rid of all my shit. But that would happen another day. I stood in the middle of Manhattan, a speck among such tall buildings and large crowds that stared at me, annoyed because I didn't move.

"I'm not a fucking speck," I said. "I'm Lena."

MAGOS

LENA

JOSEPH

M

To get a table at the restaurant one either had to know the chef, be a celebrity, or wait months. We had been waiting only about one month when Peter got a call telling him they had a sudden cancellation—a table for two had opened up at nine that night. Peter took it immediately. He didn't care that it was already eight and I was done cooking pork stir-fry for dinner.

"Get ready," Peter said, and he ran to our bedroom.

I ran too, hoping that if I imitated his zest, a zest for most anything, I would one day catch it. I found him in his underwear trying to choose between black jeans and slim gray trousers. I stripped down to my underwear too, relishing the moment as if we were boys at camp. I pinched his ass. Peter told me to dress. I wore a sweater without a T-shirt underneath, which made me feel sexy. Our room, the shared air, the warm light coming from our bedside lamps, and Peter's giddiness invited a kind of euphoria.

We arrived at an abandoned garage in Red Hook.

"Are you sure this is it?" I asked.

Peter took my hand and led me to a door with a single light bulb shining above it. After confirming Peter's name on an iPad, a woman let us inside and led us through a long dark corridor whose ceiling stood just a couple inches above my head. Peter grazed the silver-and-black wallpaper with his fingers and whispered, "How special!"

The light dimmed as we walked in farther, dim enough that I could barely see the woman who led us. We continued walking. The corridor seemed to have no end.

"Is this right?" I whispered.

Peter squeezed my shoulder. We walked some more, and I got the sense we were being swallowed. Before I could run back toward the light, toward the Brooklyn night outside, toward our home and enjoyably boring life, we stopped in absolute darkness. Peter laughed. "How exciting!"

With a flick, the woman drew open a set of curtains and stood aside. We entered a roofed patio lit by chaotic clusters of light bulbs spread throughout. Peter gasped. I squinted at the sudden brightness, the coziness of it all, an enchantment too perfect to completely ease my nerves. She pointed to a table set for two. Our table was one of only six, nestled next to a tree and a couple of planters growing bamboo.

"Isn't this marvelous?" Peter said, gaping all around. One of the things I loved most about him was how he used words like *marvelous* earnestly, so committed to their meaning that any hint of affect dissipated and the words lingered full and sweet.

A waiter appeared and recited our menu for the evening. Seven courses, all paired. We would begin with cheeseballs covered in ash on top of a sauce mirror whose ingredients I didn't catch though I was paying attention.

Peter raised his sparkling white wine and said, "To us."

"To us." I clinked his glass.

Peter mmm'ed his approval throughout the whole meal, looking at me to check if I was enjoying it too. I echoed him happily—it was all delicious—and by dessert, paired with a limoncello cocktail, I was at the drunker end of tipsy and finally fully relaxed. Peter, though, kept wiping his mouth with his napkin and pushing the remaining crumbs of his dessert around his plate. He snuck glances at me, as if shy.

"What?" I asked.

"I've been trying to come here for so long."

"It was worth it."

"This is the moment, isn't it?"

"What moment?" My face tingled. Was he going to break up with me? Go out in style? Leave me on this fairy patio to go back through that awful corridor by myself? Peter wiped his mouth once more and set his napkin on his plate. I sipped the last of my limoncello cocktail.

"So," he said. It was awful seeing him this jittery. "I have something for you."

Was he about to tell me these two years together had been a prank? Perhaps an experiment? He had liked me too much from the very first day. Peter couldn't be real, as I was about to find out.

Peter fished a small black box from his blazer's inside pocket and set it open in front of me. A silver ring poked out from a pillow of black velvet.

"For me?"

Peter laughed and I sensed his body relaxing. "Will you marry me?"

The ring had been polished smooth and showed no stones. Classy and exactly to my taste. I imagined there was an inscription inside it, but I was too afraid to pick it up and see. The restaurant became silent. Not quiet, mute. There was no clinking of cutlery on china, no low voices or whispers, no sips or gulps or scratches, no birds, no cars, no airplanes, no crickets, not even the beating of my own heart. I heard nothing, like an interrupted movie.

"Joe?" he asked.

Peter's stare, his anticipation, his body coiling up in tension froze me. I needed to give an answer, but my mouth was dry, my tongue like a stone, and I'd forgotten how to breathe.

"Joe?"

My head snapped up in a reflex. I looked at his face. He retained a smile, but it seemed to be held by toothpicks. My body took over my indecisiveness.

"Yes," I said in a spasm.

Of course, yes. One doesn't say no to a marriage proposal! Especially when asked by someone like Peter. I loved Peter. I'd loved our two years together.

"Yes? Yes? Yes!" Peter clapped once and jumped from his seat. "Yes!"

The closest table turned to us and stared unapologetically because moments like these, proposals, are meant to have an audience. They're meant to be enjoyed and celebrated. Peter picked up the ring and motioned for me to give him my hand. He slipped the ring on my finger. His touch was cold, as was mine. He magicked another box from his blazer and gave it to me.

"Another?" I asked, looking at a replica of my ring.

"For me," Peter whispered, extending his hand.

"Shouldn't I have bought it?"

"It's fine." Peter wiggled his fingers. I slipped the ring on. "We're engaged!"

He shot his two fists into the sky. A cork popped. The table next to us was clapping. The waiter was aiming champagne glasses under a bottle's torrent. Peter was next to me. He was kissing my mouth. Tables were whooping. I was drinking champagne, a ring glimmered on my hand, and a cluster of bulbs above shone bright, so bright I thought they might explode.

The long dark corridor felt much shorter going out than going in, the restaurant spitting us out, excited for Peter and me to step into a new life. The woman at the entrance congratulated us and it took a second for me to realize why.

I thought of Magos, the way this woman held the end of her ponytail and whipped it back, asserting her space. We too had gotten engaged once, but this night felt nothing like Magos. I didn't feel the weightlessness or the certainty that this was it, that from here on out this was what life would be.

"Where are you going?" Peter shouted.

I stopped at a corner. The streets were empty, and the wind was spring chilly, but I couldn't really feel it. A construction site stood next to me, protected by a wire fence, which I held, my fingers tight in the mesh.

Peter's face glowed above his phone's light. "Uber's coming."

Inside the Uber, Peter asked if I was happy.

"Yes," I said. He mmm'ed as if he had just tasted something delicious.

THERE WERE TWO HUGE SETS OF windows in our Williamsburg apartment—Peter's technically—one set in our bedroom and the other in the dining room, which led to a narrow balcony where I kept a dying hydrangea, a gift from Lena, the one failing element in our home and yet the one I loved the most.

Peter went to sleep, but not before calling me his fiancé a dozen more times. I stepped onto the balcony and sat in the folding chair we kept there. Looking at Manhattan from Brooklyn had cheered me up ever since I was a kid in Cobble Hill and my uncle took me to the piers. New York City in general, but particularly Manhattan, made me feel small, and I enjoyed the particular sense of joy one gets when feeling small, because when small, someone will protect you, or at least, someone should.

I had expected Peter and me to end. Maybe that's why it was so good between us. I had no other motive to be with him than to enjoy him. Whatever irked me about him, whatever his faults, were easily overlooked since I knew they weren't really mine to deal with. I was temporary. Soon, he'd leave. Why fight when he used my nail clippers and lost them, or woke me up on weekends just because he was already up, or hinted that my hair would look better trimmed and shaped?

My ring caught a twinkle. There was a time I fantasized about someone proposing to me, their eyes deep in love, someone who wanted to announce to the world that we were each other's. I stroked my ring's smoothness, and a happy flutter rocked my belly. A romantic Joseph still existed somewhere.

After my divorce from Magos, I'd found singledom easy. I'd loved Magos in blind awe, an all-consuming crush on her confidence, her ability to wield the world to her liking. I loved how curious she was of me and the hidden frailty she allowed me to see in her while nestled against my body, trusting that I could function as her cocoon. I had never been a cocoon before. With her, I became powerful, more exciting, grander. Beautiful. Then Santiago came,

and every time he looked up at me like I was a superhero, each time
he called me "Papi" to tell me something half-invented-half-true—
"Papi, did you know there's water on the moon where tiny dinosaurs live?"—each time he clung to me breathless and my touch
soothed him enough to make him breathe again, pulled me deeper
into a love I had no idea could exist. One I had no idea what to do
with. When it all went away, I was content not to love again.

Then Peter messaged me on a dating app I used solely for sex.
He was hot and I was horny. But after sex, he didn't disappear like
the others. He wanted a date. I only agreed because I wanted more
of his body. He wanted to know me and listened as if my life were
astonishing, though I told him little. He asked for a second date
and a third. I waited for the moment he would become disen-
chanted. I had a messy and unfinished previous life I would eventually have to go back to. I was simply enjoying a respite, this break
from all that had happened, but it couldn't be my future.

I sat on our balcony until the sky began to lighten. I considered
going to bed, to Peter and his snores, which comforted me, but
sleep overtook me, and I woke up to Peter shaking me.

"You slept out here?"

"I needed some air."

"Too much excitement?" He knelt so that our faces were on the
same level. "You're not . . . ."

"No. No."

Whatever he was going to say, I didn't want to hear. I didn't
want him doubting me. I wanted to marry him. I was stepping
closer to a life where my past had no place. I was shedding them,
Magos, Santiago, and M.

n Saturday morning, Peter dashed around in his pajamas. A week had passed, and I hadn't yet told anyone. Meanwhile we were being swamped by congratulatory bouquets from Peter's family and friends. Peter placed an orchid on a table in the corner where sunlight wouldn't hit it directly. My intention to cook pancakes was halted by so many mean, accusatory flowers.

"Marvelous," he said.

I sat at our dining table, weighted down into a chair. I hadn't known where to start. Lena was the obvious choice, but she'd been busy at the hospital, and I wanted to tell her in person. An excuse, really, because she'd meet me for a beer anytime if I told her it was important. She wouldn't send flowers. But she'd ask me why as soon as she saw the ring on my hand. She'd ask if I was sure. And I wouldn't know how to answer.

Peter had made me promise we'd go to my uncle's later that day and announce our engagement. Peter's family lived in Michigan, so my uncle was the one blood relative we—we, we, we, now it was always *we*—had in New York.

"I should go by myself," I said.

Peter froze holding a spritzing bottle in his hand. "To Uncle Luke's?" I nodded. His face twitched, all his arguments stuck in a grimace. Pipes gargled, something creaked, and a dog barked. He inhaled and with the same breath whispered, "Okay."

He was so put together, so easy, so respectful. I was happy he didn't fight. If he did, I'd have to flee or tell him all about my past. Our engagement would certainly be called off. Or worse! He'd want to be involved and I wouldn't be able to stand it.

"I'm sorry," I said.

"Why are you sorry?"

When I didn't answer, Peter spritzed more flowers. He moved on to tend the plants. Soon he would make himself a coffee and ask if I wanted some. Sometimes I felt as if all the care he bestowed upon me was simply to keep himself from discovering what I hid.

I ARRIVED AT MY uncle's house in Cobble Hill. The house was old and handsome, and Uncle kept it furnished as if it were a museum. My family had been rich once, but our wealth dwindled. We rented out the top floor and the basement and my uncle kept the first and second floors—more room than he needed, but he enjoyed the space. As did M when he visited. The living room was filled with newspapers, books, old notepads with his scribblings, and the robes my uncle shed when he felt too warm. The fireplace didn't work anymore but made the room homey, alongside a long couch, two leather chairs, a couple of ottomans, rugs, damask wallpaper, a few paintings, some of my framed illustrations, and a huge bay window that showcased the tree-lined street in front.

"Hello, Uncle."

I called him Uncle, instead of Uncle Luke or Luke. Uncle had seemed formal and funny when I was a kid, like how an old-timey orphan would address his caretaker. He used to laugh every time.

He grunted from his favorite armchair, his spine a semicircle against the cushioned back. I sat down on the couch in front of him, keeping my ringed hand on my chest, hoping he would notice it and ask. But he was too busy reading a French leather-bound book, his gnarled fingers keeping a tight grip on the edges. He grunted again without taking his eyes off the book.

"M?" I asked.

Uncle nodded.

"He's in Berlin. You know that."

Uncle grunted three times in increasing exasperation.

"I'm aware it's his birthday next week." I leaned back. "Santiago's, technically."

Uncle put the book down on the table next to him and took one of his yellow pads.

He should be here, he wrote.

"Berlin will be good for him. A fresh start. No one there knows . . . you know."

He is what he is.

"What is he?"

Uncle smiled, flipped to a new page, and wrote, INCREDIBLE.

"He has a chance to be a boy now. A man. Magos agrees. She's trying to get him a job."

Uncle pondered this. He deferred to Magos's opinion much more readily than mine.

Magos had been right; removing Monstrilio's arm-tail propelled his transformation. I didn't go back to live in Mexico City, but I visited Monstrilio often. Each time I visited, and he looked more human, I dared not hope for more. But he became a teenager, and most traces of his earlier form vanished. A patch of fur on his forehead and his fangs, long and sharp, never replaced by human teeth, were the only clues of what he'd once been. Magos called him Santiago now, but I couldn't. He wasn't Monstrilio anymore, but he wasn't Santiago either. Santiago was dead. There was solace in keeping his memory unchanged. He was a place to visit, like a book reread.

M stayed with us in Cobble Hill during the summers, away from Magos, Lucía, Jackie, and his tutors. Magos thought school would be too much for him and I agreed. M looked like a boy, but he was shy, as unsure of his new body as he'd been sure of his arm-tail. Uncle relished his summers with M, an understanding between the pair that surpassed words. Bonded, I suspected, by the unique bodies each had acquired, so different from their original ones. Uncle celebrated the part of M that was most monstrous, a belief in a pure freedom.

One summer, I caught M eating a couple of crows in his backyard. Uncle watched him, bent over, as if waiting for a cue to join in. I rushed to stop them. Magos and I had agreed to weed out whichever Monstrilian instincts remained in M. Uncle protested in grunts, but M froze, his jaw unhinged, feathers in his hair, fangs bloody. I grabbed the dead bird from his hands, scooped up the remains of the other, and said, "We don't do this, M! Not anymore." M looked scared but I kept firm. A fight brewed in my chest between a sense that it was unnatural to stop him and another that yearned for M to be like us, completely. "And you." I turned to Uncle. "You know better than to encourage this." Uncle grabbed M and cannoned past me, angry that I couldn't understand M so fully or accept him so easily.

Uncle grunted and pointed to his yellow pad: *Stuck in apartment*. He raised three crooked fingers.

Lucía had died almost a year ago. She was watching telenovelas with Jackie, dozed off, and never woke up. Jackie stayed in the house in las Lomas, but the house, as if sensing the loss of one of its two pillars, decayed. A window fell from the second story all the way to the yard, a chunk of ceiling in Magos's old room collapsed, and a family of skunks took over part of the garden and sprayed Almendra incessantly. Jackie put the house up for sale, and when it sold, she took an old and sluggish Almendra back to her hometown in la Sierra Gorda. Without Lucía and Jackie, M retreated more into himself and refused to leave the house in la Roma.

Then, Magos was offered an opportunity to do a performance in Berlin with one of the best European art galleries. She told me that if she and M were going to be lonely, better to be lonely in a brand-new place. I agreed. We hoped Berlin would shake M's malaise and he would start living like the young man he was. Magos and M had been living in Berlin for three months, but M still refused to leave their apartment.

"He'll adapt," I said, and I straightened up on the couch. "But I didn't come here to talk about M."

Uncle grunted inquisitively. What other topic could I possibly have to discuss? I wiggled my fingers to show my ring finger like I'd seen people do in movies. Uncle made no sound, no movement, no hint of acknowledgment.

"The ring." I pointed. Uncle let his head drop on his shoulder, as if he were confused. He was going to make me say it. "I'm getting married."

Uncle turned his face toward the ceiling.

"So?" I asked. Uncle didn't move. "It's happening," I said. "We haven't set a date, but I think he wants to do it in the fall. And why not? He's good, isn't he? Nice, caring, smart? I don't see why I shouldn't."

Uncle furled forward, grabbed his pad, and wrote, *Peter?*

"Of course, Peter! Who else?"

Uncle shrugged.

"You're supposed to give me your blessing."

Uncle opened his eyes wide, blue like mine, amused. He turned to a new yellow page. *It's Peter I have to give blessing.* He turned to another page. *No need to ask.* He reached his hand toward me, and I took it. Though impossibly thin, he pulled me to him with enormous strength. He kissed my forehead, pricking me with his day-old beard, and let go with a grunt. He wrote, *Happy?*

His hairline had receded from the top sides, and the rest of his hair was longish, gray, and unkempt. The lines next to his eyes denoted not cheeriness but a hidden softness.

"I don't know," I said.

Will you tell Peter?

"About M? Should I?"

The year I moved out of Cobble Hill and in with Peter, he suggested M stay with us for the summer. I told him Uncle would be too lonely without M, which was true, but really, I was afraid Peter would discover what M was. Peter had met him only a few times and knew little of his past, except that he was my son and had been in a coma for a couple of years. I hadn't known how else to explain his tutors, the way he stared as if everything was new, his raspy voice, his awkward movements, too sharp at times, too fluid at others, the dentures he wore to hide his fangs, too large and forwardly protruding. I couldn't explain that I had lost one son and gained another. Is that what had happened? I still wasn't sure myself.

Uncle grunted "No," pushed his way out of his chair, patted me on the shoulder, and walked out of the living room.

waited for Peter to leave for work. As an analyst for financial markets, he woke up at four each morning and by five he was out the door. It would be close to noon in Berlin. I sat up in bed, refusing to turn on the light, and called Magos's cell phone. M didn't own one. He picked up.

"Hey, M! Happy birthday!"

"Are you okay?"

"Yes."

"Uncle Luke?"

"He's fine. We're all fine. Happy birthday! Are you having fun?"

"Mami got me a tart."

"And?"

"I was knitting."

During his self-imposed lockup, M had taught himself how to knit. Magos told me he was knitting an endless scarf that was currently ten meters long. I strived to separate M from Santiago, and these new, non-Santiago abilities helped. But sometimes M saw something and a memory from Santiago popped up, like when we were in the supermarket and he stood in front of a box of Froot

Loops and pointed, calling them "Fruti Lupis" the way Santiago would have. "I like those." M ate bowl after bowl.

"I finished reading *Bestiario* this morning," M said.

"Uncle will want you to tell him all about it. You know he made me read Cortázar growing up too. Are you going to do anything else?"

"No."

"You need to get out, M. Maybe you could go visit the Tiergarten. I hear it's beautiful."

"Mami got me a job. A birthday gift, she said."

"Awesome! Where?"

"You think it's a good idea?"

"I think it's an excellent idea. You'll do amazing. Where will you work?"

"At the gallery."

"Doing what?"

"Mami said Assistant."

"Cool! Look at you! Gallery jobs are the best." My voice bounced inside my dark, empty room.

"You worked in a gallery?"

"No. But everyone I knew back in art school wanted to."

"I'll have to practice going outside."

"You can do that."

"I'll be okay?"

"Absolutely."

"You promise?"

"I promise."

This was the moment to tell him I was engaged, but my tongue tied. I tried to spit it out, but by the time I rallied enough gumption, Magos came on the phone.

"Bueno," she said.

"Hola," I said, switching to Spanish. "He sounds better."

"You think?" Magos asked. "At least he didn't refuse the job flat out."

"Maybe he's finally coming out of it."

"You'd think it was his mother that died."

"I don't think that's all M is struggling with. He loved Lucía, but he's also confused. You know . . . about not being Monstrilio anymore."

Magos aha'ed absentmindedly, shutting down.

"How's work?" I asked.

Magos's career as a performance artist had blown up in the past couple of years. She was MAGOS DE LA MORA, bold and marquee'd. The year before, she had performed a piece here in Brooklyn in which she asked visitors to write down their dreams on pieces of paper, which she ate. She ate them all. So many in fact that an annoyed Lena had to take her to the hospital to have her stomach pumped. "How is getting sick art?" Lena had asked. "How is it not?" Magos answered. Peter had been so impressed by her, if a little overwhelmed. It only added to my mystery. Who was I, really, who could have once been married to this woman?

"Awful," Magos said on the phone. "I'm scrapping it all."

"Why?"

Magos stayed silent. I pictured her on a sofa, picking at the polish on her toenails, forgetting I was on the other end of the line. I turned on my bedside lamp. The light hurt my eyes. I shut it off. In the darkness, I saw M, his eyebrows, beautifully full and arched like Magos's. Santiago also had those eyebrows.

"Hey, do you think Santiago would have looked like him? M, I mean?"

Magos never openly acknowledged M as separate from Santiago, and I wasn't sure what I expected, or wanted, as a response. The question lingered like a wet blanket.

"Does Peter touch you?" she said finally. She laughed. "Of course he does. But does he grab or caress? I suppose he does both, yes? But if you had to say what his preference is, what would you say?"

"How is this . . . ."

"Tell me, Joseph."

"Grab."

"Really?"

Peter rarely touched anything he didn't eventually squeeze. He loved to lick, too, his tongue more efficient than his fingers. Magos used to graze my clavicle bones with two fingers, pause at the intersection just below my throat, fondle the shape of it, and continue across my chest until she reached one of my shoulders. Then, she would follow my arm down to the crook of my elbow, trace its wrinkles, caress my forearm hairs, and gingerly pinch my fingers, learning each of their shapes. She did this while I slept, while she thought I slept. If I gave any indication that I was awake, she would stop and pretend she was also sleeping. Nights I lay on my side, or on my belly, she'd explore my spinal column, walking her fingers down each vertebrae, sometimes jumping, like leaping from stone to stone to cross a river. She'd reach my ass, slide her hand under my shorts, place her full palm on each of my cheeks, trying to gauge, it seemed, if they were identical. Sometimes she would pull the covers off me and tour my legs. This required her to kneel on the bed or shift her body, so her head was by my feet. She had to realize all this movement would wake me. But what mattered wasn't that I was asleep, but that I pretended. She'd kiss my thighs.

Her kisses tickled, especially when she kissed close to my knee. Sometimes I wouldn't be able to contain a giggle and she would jump back into a sleeping position, her eyes shut tight with a big mischievous smile on her face. I'd kiss her forehead or her shoulder, whichever part was closest to me, and she would hum cozily, lovingly, as if I were the one who had decided to be tender all of a sudden.

"Joseph?" Magos asked on the phone, startling me.

"I'm here."

"I've got to go. Santiago is waving goodbye."

"Tell him happy birthday."

Magos hung up. I stayed faceup in bed staring at the darkness. I tried to forget M and Magos, pushing myself to think of nothing else but the day ahead, the illustrations I had to finish, the invoices I still hadn't sent, the payments I had to chase. It soothed me to focus on tasks I could accomplish within a day, nothing complicated, making myself believe there were no decisions or uncertain futures looming beyond today.

Peter flirted with the owner of our local wine shop, a man with thick glasses, fitted sweaters, and an Australian accent. I enjoyed the way Peter played awed student to this man's lecture on the different grape blends of Californian wines. There was no pretense in Peter. He paid attention and asked basic questions that the man answered patiently, if not without a hint of arrogance, an arrogance Peter seemed unbothered by. I stepped away from them and browsed the wine selection stocked sparingly on wooden shelves, as if I recognized anything about the bottles other than the attractiveness of their labels.

Peter appeared next to me. "What do you think?" He showed me a bottle of red wine with a sketch of a golden cat on a cerulean background.

"Nice label."

"It's a gift."

"From who?"

Peter nudged his chin toward the store owner.

"What for?"

"Our engagement!"

Along with Peter's family, friends, coworkers, the owner of our favorite bodega, her son, the family who ran the Puerto Rican restaurant on Grand, and two cashiers at Trader Joe's, now the wine-store owner also knew of our engagement. We were a month into it, and I still hadn't told anyone but Uncle, not even Lena. I wasn't even sure why I was terrified of telling people anymore. M and Magos were in Berlin, and M was adapting to his job much better than either Magos or I had imagined. There was no need for things to change, for monstrosities to be revealed, for my two lives to merge.

I grabbed Peter's face and kissed him. He laughed.

"Congrats, you guys," the owner said as we left the store. Though it was Tuesday, the streets were packed with people enjoying the first warm spring night of the year. The largest lumps of snow had been reduced to tiny, dirty, pockmarked mounds, leaving the streets shiny with water.

"I think he's jealous," I said, looking back toward the wine shop.

"Absolutely seething!" Peter said, and he took my hand. We played at splashing each other as we made our way back home.

I texted Lena: *I have news. Meet me for a beer? Tomorrow night?*

LENA MET ME IN WILLIAMSBURG, and we walked up to Greenpoint. She knew an old bar that was hanging on for dear life. Except for a quartet of young intellectuals sitting in a booth, the place was empty. We sat at the bar and ordered IPAs. I didn't know

how she found these places. She lived in the Upper West Side, still
in the same apartment as when she first moved here.

To me, Lena's life consisted mainly of work, occasionally
interrupted by one of us, Magos, Uncle, M, or me. Everything
else that she did—the places she knew, neighborhoods she walked
through as if she'd been born there, texts that made her smile or
get nervous in ways that couldn't be work-related—surprised me
every time. Her depths were a mystery, but I felt most comfortable with her.

"Married!" she said.

"Why is it so shocking?"

"Again?"

"It's different this time."

"How? Never mind."

She grabbed her pint and drank. The bartender, a fifty-something
woman with a tattoo of vines crawling up her neck, set two glasses
of bourbon in front of us and winked at Lena.

"You know her?"

"I used to frequent this bar." She lifted her bourbon.

"I'm impressed," I said. The bourbon felt good. "She seems
cool."

"Does Magos know?"

"No."

"You're scared." The young group of intellectuals burst into a
baaing that took a minute to decipher as laughter. "You shouldn't
be. Magos seems different these days. Calmer? More centered?"
Lena seemed unperturbed by the roar. "I don't know what the
right word is. Magos should have her own vocabulary."

"What are you talking about?"

"She's been calling me every other night, sometimes every night. We haven't talked this much since I was living with her in las Lomas. I'm not sure what's going on."

"What does she say?"

"She'll tell me about going out and trying to speak her bad German. About how bulky some of Berlin's buildings are. How sometimes it seems like a city about to, what's the word she used, *bleed* open, so much is going on underneath. Mostly she talks about her day. It should be boring, but—"

"You've loved her your whole life."

Lena licked her upper lip. "Even I am capable of getting over things, Joseph."

"What else does she say?"

"She's excited about her upcoming performance but won't tell me any of the details. You know she changed it all? Classic Magos. And then the cat. Goddamn cat. She's crazy about this cat—not hers, the next-door neighbor's. It comes through their window and hangs out with them most of the day. She thinks the neighbor, Elias, is smitten with M. She has plans to invite him for dinner, play matchmaker. She says M loves that cat too. She repeats that a lot. Like proof he won't eat it."

"M wouldn't eat it. Not now."

Lena downed her whisky. "Oh, Joseph."

"I'm serious. He's doing good."

"Magos had to find M a job where she herself works."

"She doesn't work at the gallery. She does her thing somewhere else."

"Right. The warehouse. 'Splendid space,' she called it the other day. When did she learn to talk like a fucking artist?"

The whole first year after moving to New York, Lena refused to talk to, or about, Magos. This renewed, loving familiarity was pleasant.

"Is she with someone?" I asked.

"There was a Polish guy for a bit. She talks about an Argentinian sometimes, some sort of corporate honcho. He bores her but keeps popping up from time to time. She doesn't tell me that much, actually. Mostly I talk and she listens, like back in the day. She says my voice soothes her." Lena got lost in her own voice. Then she turned to me and inhaled as if surprised I was still there. "So, how's M?" she asked. "Really."

"Good. He's . . . yes. Really good."

I tried to find hints, subtext during our calls these past few weeks that would indicate that I shouldn't be so hopeful, but there weren't any. He really was doing well. He loved his menial job, perfect because thinking tired him out and as an assistant at the gallery he didn't have to think much. Lugging artwork, sending packages, sweeping, hanging. Only three other people worked there with him: Samara the gallery owner, Thomas, his boss and operations manager, and Silvia, Samara's direct assistant. M found out he enjoyed art. Art had no answer, he said, and no right way to be.

"He has a crush on Thomas, his boss. Not on the neighbor," I said. "Apparently, they spend most of their time together. M wants to kiss him."

"M said that?"

"Yes. What's more human than wanting to kiss someone?"

A woman in a chunky sweater and a fanny pack came in. "Cas-san-dra!" someone shouted. The fanny-pack woman waved and joined the intellectuals. I imagined M in a group like theirs. Now, it felt possible.

"So you're in Magos's camp now."

"There are no camps, Lena. Just because I don't think he's Santiago doesn't mean I don't think he has a right to be human. I like hearing he's happy."

"Have you told Peter?"

"Told Peter what?"

"About M."

"What about M?"

Lena rolled her eyes so wildly I thought they might leave their sockets.

"No. How can I?"

"Isn't that what couples do? Tell each other things, secrets? Especially couples that are about to be married?"

Surely Peter had his own secrets. I just couldn't imagine what they could be.

"Peter calls M Santiago," I said, and I tried to drink but my glass was empty. A Leonard Cohen song came on. "He heard Magos call him Santiago once and got all flustered because I hadn't shared his 'real' name. He actually scolded me for calling him M instead of using such a glorious name like Santiago. What could I say? That Santiago is a glorious name, but you shouldn't use it because the real Santiago is dead? I shut up and let him."

The bartender refilled our whiskeys. Leonard Cohen's voice made it to my stomach, where it boomed, making me ticklish. I was getting drunk. Keeping M's secret felt safer than letting it out where its threads could come loose and knot, making a mess impossible for me to untangle.

Lena and I clinked and drank some more.

was coloring in the last of a chubby dinosaur that was going to be used to launch a new yogurt flavor called Yellow-Dino-Bang— it had pineapple in it, maybe banana—when Magos's name flashed on my phone's screen. It was past midnight in Berlin.

"Magos?"

"Papi?"

"M? What is it? Are you okay?"

"How are you?"

"Good. You?"

"I had sex with Thomas."

It was hard to decipher M's tone. At times it was starkly flat and at others it was curious, his statements uplifted by the rising emphasis of a question, but it hardly ever revealed any strong emotion. His eyes were what carried the weight of his feelings.

"Wait." I tapped my phone to request a video call. Darkness answered, the phone trying to make the best of the little light there was to display M's grainy silhouette. "I can't see you."

The screen lit up, blurred by the phone's attempts to find focus. Finally, M's face appeared. The sharp tips of his fangs peeked through his lips. He wasn't wearing his dentures. There was anxiety in his eyes.

"Did he do something to you?"

"Thomas?"

"Yes."

M took a moment, as if evaluating what he and Thomas had done.

"Nothing bad. He was nervous. I was too. He said he liked my body. Even my stump. Ugly, no?" On the left side of his hip, M retained a furry mound of flesh where his arm-tail used to be. It hurt to realize he thought it was ugly. "Do you know the smell, Papi? The smell before sex? I hadn't smelled it before. Maybe a little when Thomas and I kissed. The smell made me dizzy. Happy dizzy. Also hungry. But he was hungry too I think because he kept pushing into me. Grabbing me. Like he didn't know what part of me he wanted. I asked him to get naked. He wanted to. But wouldn't at first. Why is it sometimes people don't do what they want to do? He wanted me naked too. I could tell. It was the smell. We were going to have sex."

As he spoke, the fear I had seen in his eyes faded into a soft joy, so pure I wasn't sure if I had seen it before. But then he swallowed, stared into the phone, and the fear returned.

"I bit him, Papi. I know I'm not supposed to. I couldn't help it. I bit his belly. He bled a little. But I helped cure him."

His head left the phone's frame for a moment. Behind him there was a poster of an old Italian film.

"Is he okay?"

His face reappeared. "Thomas?"

"Yes! Thomas. Is he okay?"

"Yes."

"Are you sure? He's alive, right?"

"Yes. He was angry at first, but it didn't last long. I asked him if he was scared. He said no. But didn't understand why I bit him. Hungry, I said. And I said he was very tasty. He laughed, but I wasn't joking."

"Is Thomas really okay? You can tell me. I won't be mad."

"Thomas is fine. He even asked me to stay the night. But I wanted to call you."

"You can't go around biting people, M." I told him that I was sure other people did, in sex and maybe in other circumstances too. But he wasn't just any person, he was M, and he had to be extra careful.

"Don't worry, Papi. Thomas didn't like the bite. I promised I wouldn't bite him again." There was heartbreak in his voice.

Sometimes I hoped M's hunger would disappear. Other times I feared that if his Monstrilioness totally disappeared, M would be left an empty husk.

"People don't understand what you are, M."

As my words traveled to Berlin, I hated myself. I smiled to keep myself from telling him to forget everything I had just said and to go ahead and bite if he wanted to bite. For a second, I believed myself strong enough to take on whatever consequences came from setting him free. Instead, I told him he should go to bed and rest. The screen went dark.

I WENT DOWN TO THE PIERS in Cobble Hill. I thought I might go and talk to Uncle, get his take on M biting his boyfriend. But I imagined he would just write *M is M* and stare smugly at me as if those three words contained the whole truth. I didn't have the energy to be annoyed.

I sat on a bench and looked at Governors Island. The sky was overcast, a crisp drizzle fell, and soon it would be dark. I zipped up my jacket. A tourist boat made its way back to Manhattan, though it was a bit late for tourists. Perhaps it wasn't a tourist boat, but one full of children on a school trip. I could be their attraction. "Look! A sad Brooklyn man," their teacher would say. "Let's cheer him up!" The children would wave and clap. Maybe the boat would sink, tipped by some inexplicable whirlwind. The parents of those dead kids would think it a bad prank when they received the news because it is other children who die, never your own. They would sue the boat company. They would sue the school. They'd hire divers to make sure their kid wasn't one of the ones lying at the bottom of the sea; their kid had somehow been spared, somehow drifted onto a safe shore. They'd form a support group but soon grow to hate one another because what they needed wasn't acknowledgment or empathy or closure; it was escape.

The boat honked. It had reached Manhattan. A dog jumped on the bench next to me. I reached to pet it, but the owner pulled it down as if it had committed a crime. Our eyes met; she mouthed *sorry* and walked away. My phone vibrated. A picture of Peter that I took just as he was turning to look at me appeared on my screen, his face at his most handsome.

"Hey!" I said.

The chill of dusk that had stuck to me like frozen film lifted just knowing Peter was at the other end of the line.

"Where are you?" he asked.

"Out for a walk."

"In Williamsburg? We have a situation, Joe. Can you come? Now? Right away?"

sweated all the way home. Peter must've found out. I couldn't imagine what else the situation could be. M had called him, told him he'd bitten Thomas. Of course, M had no reason to do so, unless, possibly, because I had let him down. I'd scolded him when I should have celebrated his steps into humanhood. Wobbly steps, but we're all wobbly at first. I was still wobbly.

I couldn't picture M scheming. He didn't even have Peter's phone number. Unless Magos finagled it. Maybe she wanted Peter to know the person he was marrying, not as sabotage but to stand up for herself and M, and Santiago, for those I was leaving behind. These thoughts, absurd and paranoid at first, became more plausible as the taxi neared Williamsburg. I wiped my sweaty palms on my pants.

I found Peter crouching on top of the coffee table in our living room, shrouded in one of our blankets, forest-green cashmere, leaving only his eyes uncovered.

"Careful!" he shouted. I swiveled, expecting to find someone behind the door ready to club me. "No. Over there!"

Peter gave no indication as to where *there* was. I crouched, an instinct to leave less of my body unprotected, and crab walked over to Peter.

"What's—"

"Up there!" Peter turned his gaze up. I folded my arms up over my head in case something was about to fall on me.

"Where?"

"There!"

I finally saw it, clinging to the edge of a high shelf next to a philodendron—a tarantula. My body slackened. I wanted to laugh.

"Do something, Joe."

I walked closer to the tarantula. I couldn't believe it was real, not in New York! Fat, brown, leggy, hairy, the size of my palm. It could've been a prank, but that wasn't Peter's sense of humor. Also, it was moving, two of its legs undulating as if testing what its next step would be.

"It's a tarantula, I think."

"I don't care what it is, Joe! Kill it!"

Before Monstrilio, I probably would have slapped it dumb with a broom, swept it off of the balcony, and let it splat downstairs. It was hideous, but its careful, tentative movements proved it was as bewildered as we were. I stepped closer, and it contracted.

"It's going to jump!"

"Get me a box."

"Kill it!"

"A shoebox."

"We don't have shoeboxes."

"You have tons."

"With shoes in them!"

"Tupperware. Something!"

Peter remained immobile inside his green cashmere cocoon. I waved him to go, but he stayed in place.

"You're not going to trap it," he said.

"I am."

"What if it jumps and hides?"

"It won't."

"How do you know?"

"Peter, get me something."

Peter hesitated. Inside the blanket his movements were constricted, but he wouldn't let it drop. Wormish, he climbed down the table and in short quick steps made it to the kitchen. He yelped.

"What?"

"Nothing. I'm okay."

After rummaging, and probably deciding there were no Tupperware containers he could fathom using to house a tarantula, he picked a used yogurt container from the recycling. He threw it at me. I asked for a lid. Peter tiny-stepped his way back, rummaged again, and came back with a blue lid that he also tossed at me. Perched back atop the coffee table, he crouched deeper into the blanket. I dragged a chair to stand on because, though I was tall enough to reach the tarantula without it if I stretched, I wanted to be as steady as possible. On the chair, my head grazed the ceiling, and my eyes came directly in front of the tarantula. It turned around, butt facing me, which meant I would have to nudge it.

"Don't touch it!"

Peter's shout startled me, and I almost fell. I recentered myself, shushed him, and stretched my arm to lower my fingers in front of the tarantula. The plan was to pull them back like a shovel. But as I lowered them, the tarantula swiped one of my fingers with one of its legs, an exploratory caress. I didn't pull back. Instead, I let my hand flatten on the ledge. The tarantula stepped onto it and, huge but lighter than I expected, it settled right in the middle of my palm. As slowly as I could, I swiveled around to show Peter. He yelped and told me to kill it immediately.

The tarantula shifted and, unbalanced, slid off my hand.

"Grab it!"

But I couldn't grab it because I would squish it and hurt it. Maybe it would bite me. It had to drop. But then, as the tarantula fell, in a miracle of reflexes, I grabbed the yogurt container and caught it midair. Thunk.

"You got it?"

I nodded.

"Trap it!"

I stepped down from the chair. I couldn't find the lid.

"Get away!" Peter balled himself inside his shroud.

I found the lid on a shelf below.

"Do you have it?" Peter asked without showing his face.

"I have it."

Peter peered. "Is it really in there? Don't lie to me, Joe."

"It's in there."

"Should we let it suffocate?"

"I'll take it outside."

"Where, Joe? Not here. Joe, not near the building. We should call animal control. It'll lay eggs."

"I'll take it to the river."

"What river?"

"That river." I pointed in the general direction of the East River. The tarantula scuttled inside. I went to grab my jacket but realized I was still wearing it.

Walking on the street, carrying the yogurt container with both hands, pressing down with my thumbs so the lid wouldn't open, I felt the strange exhilaration of a criminal. I walked to a park close to the Williamsburg Bridge. There was a sandy stretch past the lawns, where the river lapped and chunks of concrete and rocks rested on sand as if both had originated there. It was still drizzling, the weather unable to commit to rain. Tarantulas liked damp, dark places, I had read somewhere. Or maybe that was bats. Regardless, I couldn't think of a better place for the tarantula to live in New York than in a crevice near the river. Surely there'd be enough bugs to eat.

I knelt on a slab of concrete sticking out from under other slabs. The slabs and rocks created a series of tiny caves, one of which I was sure the tarantula would make its home. I peeled the container's lid open. The tarantula stood in a ball, legs crammed into its body. I petted it, hoping to soothe it, but I only made it cringe more. I tipped the container to let the tarantula out, tapping the bottom to make it slide. It froze, balled up on the concrete slab. My hair dripped with all the drizzle it had accumulated, but I couldn't leave, not without knowing that the tarantula would live. Slowly, it unfurled one of its legs. Once this leg felt safe enough, it began unspooling the rest, a slow stretching out onto the slab until it stood fully at ease. Then, with a speed I couldn't have guessed, it scuttled away into a tiny cave, so fast it gave me goose bumps.

PETER STARED AT ME all through dinner, Thai takeout because neither of us had felt like cooking.

"Why didn't you kill it?" he asked.

I slurped the last of my noodles. I tried to find accusation in his face but could only see curiosity.

"I didn't think it deserved to die."

Peter nodded and took his plate and empty food carton to the kitchen. I followed him.

"Let me," I told him as he began scooping the food remains from our dishes. He gave me the plate, pressed himself against my back, and slid his arms across my belly. I froze with a dirty plate in my hand. He wriggled his hand inside my pants. "Let me finish the dishes first," I said.

"You were so hot taking care of that thing," he whispered in what was supposed to be his sexy voice.

He kissed my neck, nudging my hair away with his nose. My hair was my tiny rebellion, something that assured me I was still me. Also, Santiago had loved it, calling out the different shades of yellows and browns he found in it. Peter tugged at my penis, as much as the tightness of my pants allowed. I got hard. Peter removed his hand. He enjoyed this teasing. I set the dish in the dishwasher, turned to him, and kissed him. He tried to return the intensity of my kiss but fumbled. I pushed him on the counter. I unbuttoned the top button of his shirt, grabbed each side, and tore his shirt open. Buttons flew.

"Hey," he said, looking down at his mangled shirt.

I swiveled his head up by pulling his hair and kissed him again. He had no idea what the hell was going on. Neither did I. I found his nipples and pinched them.

"Ow!" I twisted. He pushed me away. "What's going on?" he asked, covering his chest with his hands.

The skin around his mouth was red. I kissed him again, softly so he would come back to me, and he did. He was sweet, almost rotten, a sexy rotten that I suspected was the smell M had talked about, the horny sweetness right before sex. I licked the nape of his neck, squeezed his ass, and moved down his chest with my tongue as he undid his pants and shoved them down. I took his hard penis in my mouth. He moaned a moan that seemed to have traveled from far within his depths. He'd never moaned like this before. I moved up, twirled the inside of his belly button with my tongue. I pressed my face into his belly. I sucked one fold of his skin into my mouth, where it was most tender, and played with it. I tested my teeth against it, barely grazing it at first. Peter tousled my hair, pulling it gently.

I bit.

"Ow," he said.

I sank my teeth deeper.

"No!"

But I wouldn't let go. There was an exhilarating power in hurting him. Pleasure in doing something I shouldn't do.

"Stop!" He shoved me hard. "What's wrong with you?"

My teeth showed as purplish rows on his stomach. He bent down to gauge the damage. The shape of my bite tattooed on his skin.

"Why would you do this?"

There was no blood. M had drawn blood. I tried to caress the spot I had bitten, but he slapped my hand away.

"Not okay, Joe."

"I thought I might try something new."

"Biting?"

"People do it. It's not so bad, is it?"

"I'm not into it." Peter stopped rubbing his belly, and his face relaxed almost to a smile. "I suppose nibbles are okay." He turned back to inspect the bite. "You were too darn enthusiastic."

I didn't want to be the first to laugh, though a big hearty laugh was brewing between us. I scooched up against the oven. My pants were halfway down, but pulling them up would've meant we were done having sex. The floor tile pressed cold against my ass.

He sat next to me. I leaned my head on his shoulder, looking past his mangled shirt at his naked groin.

"You fool," he said, and he began kissing me.

An invitation came in the mail, a postcard, minimalist in design, with white block letters on a teal background: *Magos de la Mora.* Her name bled out of the card's edges. Peter showed it to me as we rode the G back home from a movie at BAM. Thick, premium cardstock. On the back it read, "You are cordially invited to Magos de la Mora's new groundbreaking performance: SON," then listed an address in Berlin and a date two weeks away.

"Did you know this was happening?" Peter snatched the card from me, flipping it back and forth as if it would suddenly reveal more information. "Son," he read. "Is this about Santiago? Maybe an homage? A leaving-the-nest-type thing now that he's eighteen?" The train stopped; seats freed up but neither Peter nor I made a move to sit. "What's her work's theme, her oeuvre, do you think?" The train sped up again. "Her performance here was stupendous, remember? Funny, in a way, but vicious, really. Do you think this piece will be about motherhood? We're going, right, Joe? It'd be amazing to . . . ."

Peter kept talking, but I couldn't make sense of his words. The train rattled and swerved. I gripped the pole tighter. Magos had already called telling me she wanted all of us there, but I didn't know how to handle Peter with all of us together. Especially if Magos had planned a performance like this. Lena was going. I'd hoped to ignore the whole thing.

The train stopped at Metropolitan, and I followed Peter out.

"We're going, yes?" Peter said.

"I have work."

"Nothing that you can't advance or postpone. I'll take time off. Come on, Joe. I'm dying to spend time with your family. I barely know them." Peter leapt up in front of me and grabbed my shoulders, his face inches away from mine. People transferring trains avoided us. "Are you embarrassed of me?"

"No."

"You haven't told them, have you?"

I shook my head.

Peter breathed in. "I won't even get upset about it. We'll tell them in person, together. It'll be perfect. They're our family now."

Peter walked on toward the L. I followed a few steps behind.

PETER, LENA, AND I ARRIVED in Berlin three days before Magos's premiere and met Magos and M at a traditional German restaurant. Magos got up to hug us as soon as we came in, but M remained seated until we got to the table. Under my hug, he felt sturdier. He wore his hair a bit longer, in dark curls that swirled all over his head. He touched my hair.

"You cut it."

"Only a trim." I pushed it behind my ears. "I missed you."

"Me too."

"I thought I had convinced Uncle Luke to come too," Magos said, stretching her head as if he would suddenly materialize behind us.

"No chance," Lena said. "That man hasn't gotten on a plane in fifteen years."

"Twenty," I said.

"Hello, Santiago," Peter said, and he offered him his hand. M shook it.

"Sit," Magos said, and she took Lena by the elbow to lead her to a seat beside her.

"Beer, M?" I asked as he sipped from a pint. "I didn't know you liked it."

"I learned."

"Thomas likes it?" I winked.

"Yes," he said. M ordered in German: Schnitzel, Sauerkraut, and Kartoffelsalat. I said I would have the same. Peter too. Magos and Lena ordered pig's feet to share.

"Joe, I can't wait any longer," Peter said, pushing his hands out. "We have news." Magos eyed him as Lena leaned back in her chair and rearranged the napkin on her lap. "We're getting married!"

Peter grabbed my hand and lifted it. I smiled as the restaurant became darker, as if half the lights had gone out. M began to cough and turned red. I placed one hand on his chest and the other on his back. Magos rose. Lena sat up straighter. M continued coughing. Magos offered him her fist. She would do this when Santiago's lung gave out and he couldn't breathe. It usually reignited his lung, but M pushed her fist away gently, cleared his throat, and recovered his breath by himself.

"I'm okay," he said. Lena relaxed back into her seat. "Really. I'm fine."

Unlike Santiago's, M's lung worked fine. We just forgot sometimes.

"I was shocked, too, when this one said yes," Peter said, his glass
lifted, waiting for us to cheer. He had no context with which to
worry for M. "I thought Joe had sworn off marriage forever!"

Magos turned to Peter. "Why would he have sworn off marriage?"

Peter's eyes ballooned to the size of a cartoon fox's. "I didn't
mean . . . I just meant, he, you know, he didn't give any—"

"It's fine, Peter." Magos smiled and clinked her glass to his. Her
shoulders relaxed, back in control of the table. "I'm happy for
you." Then in Spanish, "Flaqui, did you know?"

"Joseph mentioned."

"And you didn't tell me?"

"I asked her not to," I said, returning us to English. "We wanted
to tell you in person."

"Congratulations," M said. Peter's smile broke at M's flat tone.
He knew him well enough to know that this was just the way M
spoke, but he may have hoped for some previously unheard note of
excitement.

"Thank you, M," I said.

The food arrived, and M ordered another beer.

"Are you sure?" I asked him.

"It's Germany, Joseph," Lena said. "Babies drink beer here."

"I don't think that's true," Peter said.

"I'll have one more too then," I told the waiter. When the new
beers came, they toasted to Peter and me once more. We kissed. I
pushed Peter back down to his seat.

THOMAS AND M OFFERED TO show us around and met us at our hotel the next day. Thomas was a broad man with a kind face and a mess of hair sticking out in light-brown tufts. They moved together in an easy unison, the top of M's head barely reaching Thomas's chest. Magos and Lena joined us too. Thomas attempted to explain Berlin to us, and though some of the things he mentioned sounded made-up, Peter kept nodding and taking pictures.

After lunch, close to the Tiergarten, Magos and Lena split from the group and went off on their own. Lena told me that Magos had made some sort of declaration to her earlier and asked if she'd stay in Berlin for longer. Lena had agreed to extend her stay but had rejected the rest. Nevertheless, or maybe because of Lena's rejection, Magos was being her most flirtatious self.

Thomas led us to Checkpoint Charlie, where Peter, solemn, kept repeating how hard it must've been to be trapped in your own city. We strolled through narrow streets filled with boutiques and Berliners enjoying the warm day. Thomas went silent here, tired, or perhaps these streets were self-explanatory. Peter tried to engage M by making comments about the architecture, graffiti, dogs, art, history, the weather—"Does it rain often?"—failing to find a topic that would elicit more than a single-word answer. They walked side by side in silence until M turned to Peter and, in his characteristic loud straightforwardness, said, "I like Ampelmann."

"Who's Ampelmann?"

"The man at the light. He wears a hat. You haven't seen him?"

Peter shook his head.

"I'll show you when I see one."

We came to a crossing where M stopped. "There." He pointed to a pedestrian light.

"Ampelmann?"

M smiled, without his dentures.

He'd let his fangs grow longer and the blunted tips of them showed, giving the impression that his teeth were too narrow and too far apart from one another. Peter's eyes, though he tried not to, darted toward M's mouth again and again. I realized how much like a regular young man M looked despite the oddness of his teeth. M's fangs were charming, if one knew how to look at them. From that moment on, Peter called out every Ampelmann he saw.

We arrived at the Holocaust Memorial. M said he'd wait for us as we wandered among the concrete slabs. I stayed behind with him as Thomas led Peter toward the center of the esplanade, watching until they disappeared.

"I got lost in there," M said.

"Really?" From the outside it seemed like it'd be hard to get lost inside.

"Not lost like I didn't know where I was. More like, how did I get here? For a minute. They are taller inside, Papi. And the ground dips. Very unsettling."

"Unsettling."

"Like feeling odd, but not knowing why."

"I know the feeling."

M smiled.

"You like Berlin, don't you?" I said.

"Yes. Do you?"

"So far, I love it. I'd visit you so much, if you guys decided to stay here."

"Are we going to?"

"Wouldn't you want to?"

M cocked his head. "I don't know. Maybe. Yes. It's hard to think of future things. Isn't it?"

"Sometimes. But we must do it. Plan ahead, think about how we want our lives to be."

"Like you and Peter? Marrying?"

"Yes."

"It makes you happy? Thinking of marrying?"

"It does, actually."

M hugged me at my waist. I put my arm around his shoulders and squeezed. Peter and Thomas appeared at the other end of the esplanade. They waved. We waved back.

We sat at a shaded four-person table on a terrace. Peter turned his gaze up and said, "Delightful afternoon, just marvelous."

We ordered beers but as the waiter walked away, Peter changed his order to a gin and tonic. Thomas changed his order too. A gin and tonic did sound perfect for a sunny, warm afternoon, but because M didn't change his order I stuck with beer too.

Thomas spoke about his town in Bavaria, a small town Peter likened to his own in Michigan.

"City boys," Peter said, pointing to M and me. He snickered as if he had committed the funniest mischief.

I asked M about work at the gallery. They had just finished putting up the newest show. Thomas explained that it had been a long process of constructing the pieces.

"Doesn't artwork already come assembled?" Peter asked.

"Not in this case." The artist, Qi, Thomas explained—who was either a person or a collective, no one knew—sent the materials and instructions. "The instructions were confusing, but Santiago here understood and constructed it all."

"Not all. You did some parts," M said. Thomas rubbed his back.

"Aren't you two adorable," Peter said.

This version of M fit comfortably in Peter's imagination. Perhaps this sanitized version of M would become the default, but I wasn't sure I liked it better.

A fat, hairy bumblebee landed at the edge of M's beer. Without a moment's hesitation, M grabbed the glass and gulped down the bumblebee. He chewed quickly, then stopped, closed his eyes, and savored the moment before swallowing and downing the rest of his beer. When M opened his eyes and saw me staring, he blushed, embarrassed I'd caught him or maybe afraid I might scold him. Neither Peter nor Thomas seemed to have noticed. I smiled to set him at ease, and M smiled back.

Peter and Thomas continued talking. M stood up. I thought he needed to pee, but he walked away down the street.

"Is everything okay?" Peter asked.

"He does this sometimes," Thomas said.

I rose, jealous Thomas knew something about M that I didn't. M strolled without purpose, stopping to inspect chained bikes and patches of earth from where trees grew.

"I got bored," M said when I sidled next to him. "Do you think Peter will stop liking you?"

"I hope not."

M picked up a cigarette butt from the ground.

"M, don't. It's dirty."

He chucked it. "Do you have a cigarette?"

"You smoke?"

"Thomas taught me."

M walked to a corner and stopped, unsure if he wanted to cross or turn.

"Should we go back?" I asked.

"How do you make sure people don't stop liking you?"

"I don't know. I guess you can't be absolutely sure. But I suppose if you like them and are kind to them and don't hurt them, there's no reason why they should stop liking you."

"Not eating them. For example?"

Though M's tone was flat, his eyes glimmered. It was a joke. I laughed. He scratched at his thin stubble of fur, a spot in the shape of a pumpkin on his forehead. M turned back toward the restaurant and walked right through a crowd of tourists like it was his street.

eter and I met Lena, M, and Thomas outside the warehouse where Magos's performance was about to take place. We stood next to one of the shrubby weeds that flecked the rocky ground.

"Is there time for a smoke?" Thomas asked, tapping a carton of cigarettes.

It was almost nine and the sun had yet to set. He handed one to M and lit both M's and his own. M puffed out smoke with unvarnished gusto. I could've channeled the extravagant concern of a father seeing his child smoke, but he looked so at peace, so in tune with the flick of his thumb, the sucking of his cheeks, the way one leg crossed in front of the other, so at home within his body, that I could do nothing but enjoy.

"Magos is a big deal," Thomas said, blowing smoke into a cloud of tiny flies who didn't seem to mind. Other smokers stood in groups under the teal banners that announced *Magos de la Mora* in massive white letters. "Do you like her work?"

His question hovered without any of us picking it up.

"I don't know what she's doing tonight," I said. "I don't think any of us know. It's a new thing, isn't it?"

"Yes, new," Lena said.

"I'm excited." Thomas flicked his cigarette away. M flicked his too. "Lass uns reingehen," Thomas said with a hand flourish. Lena and Peter followed him to the entrance. M stared at the spot where his cigarette had landed.

"Ready?" I asked him.

He looked up at me. "You still miss him?"

"Who?"

"Santiago."

Every now and again M spoke of Santiago as a person totally independent from himself, and every time it hurt.

"Yes," I said.

"Mami misses him too."

THE SPACE WAS EMPTY except for a spotlight illuminating a folded piece of cloth at the center. The audience was ushered to stand along the walls. Thomas and M stood at the far end of the space. Lena, Peter, and I stayed against a wall to their left. People spoke in hushed voices. The ceilings were high, and, unlike a regular warehouse, the floor was polished hardwood.

A loud drum banged us into silence. Magos walked into the center of the space, barefoot, wearing a flowy teal dress which, after a moment, I realized was a nightgown. Her hair was slicked back into a long ponytail. She knelt with her butt resting on her heels. Her nightgown parachuted down, covering her legs. There was considerable rustling as people shifted positions; some cleared their throats. Peter squeezed my shoulder.

Magos picked up the cloth from the floor at the same time bright white fluorescent lights flooded the space. The walls of the warehouse were painted white, producing a glare so intense we were forced to squint. We looked up at the ceiling from where this light blazed, wondering if this brightness was a mistake. The warehouse filled with whispers but because Magos remained unfazed, we realized that the light was part of the performance. When there was silence again, Magos unfolded the cloth.

She revealed a set of pajamas decorated with huge cartoon dinosaurs in bright purple, orange, green, and pink. Santiago's pajamas, the ones he died in. Magos draped the pajamas over her lap and held them as if she were holding a body. Her face contorted, and she began to cry. She wept loud and unabashed. I had seen Magos cry before, rebel tears that fought against her will to contain them, that made her turn away, but never this open weeping. Her face was unrecognizable to me.

She was the Magos I had wished for during those months in Firgesan, when I was drowning and all she could do was follow me around like a kid playing, unable to show any emotion but silliness. I had wanted someone to drown with together, but now that I was seeing this Magos, I realized she would've pulled me down faster.

She sucked in air, trembling as if shaking away a sudden coldness, and her weeping lessened. Tears flowed down. Dull tears without theatrics, ones that dripped uncontrolled, ones that emptied, the scary ones that might leave her a husk. She gazed down on the pajamas, her head tilted, tender, and dejected. Her face broke into a scowl, the scowl that usually fought her tears away. But she battled it, eased it, and willed it away. Her tears rolled fat, and snot gathered on her upper lip.

The audience wept along with Magos, drying their tears with discreet swipes of their fingers. Magos remained alone at the center of that huge white space as she caressed the empty pajamas with the tips of her fingers, tracing the edges of an invisible body. How alone she seemed. Her mouth opened wide as if in a scream, but no sound came out, only a gurgle. Magos didn't care how disheveled she became, how ugly or red or snotty, how wisps of her hair came loose around her face, her ponytail unraveling, how her dress bunched unflatteringly, how her face was loose and limp and her tears dripped. Dripped. Dripped. Her body seemed unable to contain her anymore. She had let herself fall into despair.

People in the audience covered their faces and shook. They knelt, like she did; some squatted; some turned away as if being tortured. Even the most reluctant ones wiped tears from their cheeks, looking up at the ceiling to quell their flow. Lena had one arm crossed over her chest, the other rested on it, a hand extended to cover her mouth. I expected Peter to be weeping most dramatically of all, but he was a respite, befuddled rather than sad. Thomas wept openly as he held M's hand.

M stared ahead. His face showed no sadness or anger or fear, but it wasn't neutral either. It twitched as if unable to decide which gesture was most appropriate, which gesture could possibly communicate whatever mess of emotions were bubbling up as he watched his mother mourn the child she had been grooming him to replace. M kept rubbing the stump on his left hip, the remains of his arm-tail. Magos kept caressing a body that was not there.

I stood very still, tears pooling on the bottom of my chin. I wouldn't wipe them. I had earned these tears. I held my arms by my sides, my hands balled into fists. I wanted Magos to stop.

M disappeared from Thomas's side. I scanned the audience and found him shoving his way toward the exit. His head was low, his neck twisted and his movements fast and jerky as if he'd forgotten how to walk. I moved toward the exit too, shuffling among the mourners who wept for a child that wasn't theirs while I hoped to catch the child I still had left. M vanished behind the audience, but I could tell where he was by the wave of shifting people around him. He was much closer to the exit than I was. I sped up.

"Sorry." "Entschuldigung." "Sorry." "Sorry."

I tripped and fell on my hands and knees. A man grabbed my arm to help me up, but I couldn't untwist myself enough to stand upright. I was just a few yards from the door.

Fwoomp.

The fluorescent lights switched off and the spotlight came back on. Magos breathed in, shook out her last sobs, wiped her face with open hands, and cleaned them on her nightgown. The smear of her tears appeared dark on the fabric. She folded the pajamas, set them on the floor before her, and walked out of the space.

The spotlight faded out.

I ran outside to find M. The area around the warehouse was empty but soon started filling up with groups of audience members talking excitedly, joyous after going through something so dreadful and making it out unscathed.

M was gone.

Thomas sauntered out, puffy and red, a cigarette already between his fingers.

"Where's M?" I asked.

"He's not with you? I thought—"

Lena and Peter found us outside.

"M's gone," I said.

"Maybe he needed the bathroom," Peter said.

"He was . . . I don't know. I mean, this show . . . What was Magos thinking?"

"He must be around."

"No! He—"

Lena grabbed my arm. She dragged me away to an area where the warehouse floodlights didn't reach.

"What's going on?" she asked.

"M was upset. He was . . . skulky. Is that a word? Like he couldn't move properly, but also fast, like he might do something."

"Like what?"

"I don't know. He was upset, Lena!"

"You're upset." Lena reached up to put her hands on my shoulders. My forehead touched hers. "Listen. M's been in Berlin for months, leading a pretty ordinary life. He's found his own way around plenty of times. He'll be fine. This shit was insane. He needs a minute. We all do."

"Are you sure?"

Lena waved Thomas over, and Peter followed. "Thomas, do you have any idea where M might have gone?"

"Maybe Görli? We go there after work."

"Could you go and try to find him?"

"Is something wrong?"

"No," Lena said. "We just want him with us."

"Okay. Call me if you find him first?" Thomas walked away, took a bike from a makeshift rack near a stack of used tires, and rode away.

"What's happening, Joe?" Peter asked.

I stood up straighter. "Nothing. I'm being crazy. This—whoo—it was a bit intense."

Lena grabbed Peter's elbow and dragged him toward the reception.

"You're coming, Joe?" he asked.

The reception was held in an annex to the warehouse set up with wine and canapés. People reached their palms to their hearts as Magos strode in. A few tried clapping, but seeing that not many did, they stopped. Clapping seemed too celebratory a response to this performance. Lena and I stood in a corner as Peter waited in line to get us drinks. Magos came directly to us, ignoring the compliments and hands that reached out to her. I thought she was still barefoot until she came closer and I realized she wore sandals.

"What did you think?"

Lena waited for me to say something, perhaps go on a tirade, but when I didn't speak, she said, "Good."

"Good?"

"I don't know, Magos. Honestly? It was fucking horrible."

"Joseph?" Magos asked.

"Why didn't you warn us?"

"About what?"

"This!" A few people turned to look at us. "Our son, Magos. What . . . ." I stopped before I burst into tears.

"The piece is named *Son*, Joseph. What did you expect?"

"Why now? It's been—"

"Seven years," Magos said. "You cried then. I didn't."

Peter joined us holding three glasses of wine, which he handed to us.

"Wonderful piece." He brought his open palm to his chest like everyone else had done before. "Such honesty. My goodness. I . . . May I hug you?" He hugged Magos. Magos looked at me playfully, as if I should be enjoying this alongside her, as if Peter were a joke between us. She let go of their hug. "Mesmerizing, truly. Consider me a fan. Again."

"At least I have one. Neither of these two enjoyed it."

"Really?" Peter's excitement dropped from his face. "What's wrong? Are you worried about Santiago?"

"What's wrong with Santiago?" Magos looked around the room.

"He left," I said. "Before it ended."

Magos's peaceful demeanor, the smug brightness she'd been carrying as if just enlightened, evaporated. "Where did he go?"

"We don't know," Lena said. "Thomas is looking for him."

"Was he upset? I hope not. This had nothing to do with him."

"Nothing to do with him?" I shouted. "What world do you live in, Magos?"

"I don't understand," Peter said.

"Joseph," Magos said. "Out of all of us, you're the one who always said they weren't the same. You've been telling me for years! I wept for the one who died."

"You're the one who's been calling him Santiago. How do you think he feels? Suddenly he's not—"

A short woman with long dangling earrings put her hand on Magos's shoulder. She stared at me. "Sorry to interrupt."

Magos turned around ready to shove whoever it was who had touched her, but, registering the woman's identity, she smoothed the waist of her dress and smiled. "Sorry, we were . . . Samara, this is my family. Family, this is Samara."

Samara shook hands with each of us. "I'm really very sorry to barge in, but I have some people dying to meet our performer."

"One moment, please, Samara." Samara stood a few steps away. Magos turned to me. "Will you stay? Please, Joseph. You will wait for me, yes? Half an hour. Forty-five minutes max. Joseph, yes?"

"Okay," I said.

Magos walked away with Samara holding her by the elbow. I handed my wine glass to Peter and told him and Lena I'd be back. I walked out into the warm night. A few smokers stood scattered throughout. I scanned the groups, but M wasn't there, no one I could've even confused with him to give me a second of relief. I wished I smoked so that I would have something to do besides pace. I kicked a rock. The ground underneath was dark, as if the rock had bled, or pissed.

"Joe," Peter appeared in front of me. "You've got to tell me what's going on."

"Nothing."

"Stop." He used a tone of forced sternness I'd never heard before. "Tell me. For goodness sake! I've been respectful, haven't I, Joe? Or is it Joseph? Everyone here calls you Joseph. Is that what you prefer? I don't even know that. We're getting married and I don't even know what to call you. What is it that you're so afraid to tell me? I love you, but I can't deal with this . . . ." He twirled his arms around like trying to form a tornado with them. "It's always around you. Don't you think I notice? Tell me."

"I can't."

"Why?"

"Because it's mine, Peter. This—" I twirled my arms like he had, "—is mine. I can't explain more than that. Peter, please, can we go inside?" I walked toward the reception but didn't hear Peter's footsteps following along the gravel behind me. "Are you coming?"

"I'm going to the hotel, Joe. I'm not sure what to do here."

"I love you," I said, but he was already too far away to hear me.

We waited for M, but he never reappeared. Magos called Thomas to see if he'd found him. He'd tried Görlitzer Park, the gallery, his own home where M stayed overnight on occasion, and even Magos's apartment, but no one answered the buzzer. He said he was back at his place waiting in case M came there.

"Thank you, Thomas. He'll appear. Let me know if he shows up, yes?"

Magos, like Lena, seemed to believe M only needed a breather and he'd soon turn up back home or at Thomas's. She suggested we go have a drink. I could've said no, sulked, and gone back to Peter, but I reasoned that he too needed a breather, and I desperately needed a drink.

Magos took us to a dive bar with peeling red leather booths, '80s pop music, and people who were at least fifteen years younger than us. A group of young women who'd been at the performance walked up to Magos and invited her to drink with them. Magos thanked them, said she was already with friends, and pushed Lena and me into a corner booth where the bar was emptiest.

"We won't speak of the performance," Magos said.

"Ever?" Lena asked. "Is that a promise?"

"At least not for the rest of the night."

We drank whisky and beer. Lena got us shots and we forgot we were all in our forties, pretending to be the twenty-year-olds we were when the three of us first met. We walked from Neukölln all the way to Magos's apartment in Prenzlauer Berg. It took us more than an hour. We talked and laughed and stumbled along graffitied walls and bridges plump with chained bicycles. Magos hooked each of her arms into ours, and for the last stretch Lena and I walked on either side of her, our steps wobbly but in sync. Magos shouted "Guten Abend" at a young man passing us by. He jumped back at the sheer loudness of Magos's voice but mumbled "Guten Abend" in return. Magos ranted about how friendly Berliners were, much more than she had imagined, and how fantastic Berlin was, and how everyone loved art. Lena and I agreed because the wind was full of oxygen and it was crisp and the city was dark and the ground firm and we were together.

Magos led us into a courtyard that she announced as "unser Hof," through a door she took several minutes to unlock, and then up four flights of chipped stairs that smelled of the years packed in, layers of feet walking up and down, of sweaty hands holding the banister. We turned right, past a door that was half-open.

"Elias?" Magos said and peered inside. "Elias?"

"Who's Elias?" I whispered to Lena.

"Neighbor."

Magos walked in.

WE FOUND M IN Magos's neighbor's apartment, drawn up into a ball in the far corner of the hallway. He was naked and bloody. The neighbor, too, was naked and bloody, but unlike M, he lay sprawled in the middle of the space.

"Shit. Shit. Shit." The word spilled out of me unrestrained.

"Fuck me," Lena said, and she shoved her way in between Magos and me. She knelt by the mauled man and pressed two fingers to his neck. "He's alive."

Where M sat there was almost no light. Next to him stood a doorway to an even darker part of the apartment. I wanted to save M but couldn't move. The room next to M emitted an uncanny darkness. I would have thought it beautiful if I didn't have the sense it would swallow us all.

"Hey." Lena stood up. "Hey!" She snapped her fingers at our faces.

"What?" Magos said in a quiet voice. Or maybe I only heard her that way.

There was a solidity to the apartment's air that muffled sounds. Lena spoke more words, but I couldn't understand their meaning. I glued my eyes to Magos's face because it was the only thing in the apartment that didn't seem to be twirling.

Lena grabbed my arm. There was blood on her hand. She was getting it on my shirt. She tried to drag me farther into the apartment, but my body wouldn't budge. Lena's knees were bloody too. She gave up pulling me, stepped over the naked man, and reached M. He had hidden his face between his folded knees. Lena spoke to him, but he didn't react. She shook him. His head remained buried.

Is he alive? I asked but no sound came out. I stepped forward in reflex, my body moving until it reached M. I knelt by his side.

"M?" I asked.

Whimpers. They could have been coming from inside the walls. Or the dark room next to us.

"M?" I shook him.

His skin felt warm, though I wasn't certain if the warmth was him or the blood that covered him. I scanned the parts of his body I could see—his arms that hugged his knees, his calves, his feet, his neck, his head. It was difficult to determine if M was wounded, if any of the blood was his or if it was all the neighbor's. I tried prying his arms apart, but he wouldn't let me.

"What happened?" Such a stupid question, but I asked it again. M remained folded. "Lena," I said, but she wasn't by our side anymore.

She had gone back to the sprawled man and was now pressing a towel to the side of his stomach.

"Lena!" I shouted.

"What?"

I forgot why I was calling her.

"What?"

I shook my head. She pressed the towel with both arms.

"He needs a hospital," Lena said.

"Should I call an ambulance?" Magos asked. Her voice seemed to have bypassed Lena because she didn't turn around. "An ambulance, yes?"

Magos pulled her phone from a large bag she carried.

"What about M?" Lena asked.

"He's here," I said.

"He attacked this man."

"We don't know that."

"They'll arrest him."

"They can't say it was him," Magos said. "They were both attacked."

"M is pretty much intact," Lena said.

"He's covered in blood." I rubbed M's naked back. Something burbled inside him. "Why are they naked?"

Lena looked at me as if I were speaking an alien language. Her arms remained rigid against the dying man's body, her hands bloodier, and the pale towel now a dark, wet color.

"This man will bleed out," Lena said. "We need to call an ambulance. Magos!"

"They'll take him away," Magos said.

"M," I said, tugging at him. "Come on. Stand up."

M wouldn't move. I stood up, tried to pull him with me. I slipped. Fell on my knees.

"There's blood everywhere. Do we clean it?"

"Magos!" Lena shouted. "Make a decision!"

The dying man coughed. Magos jumped back.

"He's alive," M said.

"M!"

He didn't turn to me. His eyes were fixed on the man. His fangs sparkled. Magos walked toward us but stopped right before she had to step over the man's body.

"Joseph, take Santiago to my place." I tried to remember if I had stepped over the man myself. I didn't want to have stepped on him. "Get him out of here!"

"I stopped," M said.

"Joseph, get going!"

M got on all fours and crawled toward the man. "He's very tasty."

"Go!"

I stood holding the doorframe. I offered M my hand. "Let's go, M."

He crawled closer to the neighbor.

"Santiago, get away," Magos said.

"Santiago is dead," M said.

"Come on, M. We have to go."

"We need the ambulance now!"

"Joseph, take him!"

I grabbed M's arm, but he snapped it away.

"Elias?" M asked. The man emitted something close to a wail, low and brief. "Will he live?"

"Not if you don't fucking get out of here," Lena said. "Now!"

M sat back on his heels. I squatted, slid my arms under his body, and lifted him. M put his arms around my neck and his body went limp, his head buried against my chest.

"M? M?"

"What is it?" Magos asked.

"I think he's fainted."

"Santiago?"

M tugged at my neck and growled. I hurried, stepped over the neighbor, and made for the door.

"Wait."

Magos tiptoed through the hallway, picked up what looked like M's clothes, and placed them on top of him.

I laid M on Magos's bathroom floor. He curled in a fetal posi- tion, his body a patchwork of skin, blood, and hair. I drew a bath and dipped M in the water. The water turned red. As I cleaned him, M followed my darting, washclothed hand with his stare, curious, as if he didn't know where it came from. I confirmed what Lena had said, that he was pretty much intact, except for a few nasty scratches and a bite on his shoulder. He closed his eyes, and I washed his face. He kept them closed as I shampooed his hair.

"I'm sorry," M said when I unplugged the drain. He said it so quietly I wasn't sure if he'd said it at all. I handed him a towel. He dried himself off.

"Get dressed."

He stood in his bedroom by the side of a pile of sheets and clothes. His nest. He opened a drawer and took out two socks. Mismatched. He put his socks on before anything else. Then he looked around as if he didn't know what was next. He seemed fragile in his nakedness, but also solid. Hairy like me. Hairy like Monstrilio. I found a pair of underwear, pants, and a T-shirt and handed them to him. While he dressed, I packed a bag with more of his clothes.

Once dressed, he looked at me and said, "You're dirty." My shirt and pants had blood all over them. I stupidly tried brushing them clean. "Your face too."

I didn't know if there was time to clean up before the ambulance and police came and all the mayhem descended. But I couldn't stay covered in blood. I showered with one of those hand-held contraptions I couldn't quite figure out how to manage until I discovered I could push up a handle where the thing could rest and make it into a regular shower. I soaped and scrubbed with a focus that had eluded me most of my life. I kept straining to hear sirens. Clean and wrapped in a towel, I called for M. He wasn't in his room.

"M?" I darted through the apartment, into a living room so cluttered I mistook a low chair for a crouched M. "M?" I went into Magos's room. "M?"

On her nightstand there was a picture of Santiago with Magos and me at the Zoológico de Chapultepec. Santiago must have been eight or nine. I hadn't seen a picture of him in years. My legs gave out and I sat on the bed. M looked much more like him than I remembered.

A sharp metallic bang woke me up.

"M?" I ran down the hall and found M in the kitchen. He was shoving our clothes in the washer. "We don't have time for that."

But it wasn't a bad idea; better for the police to find suspiciously washed clothes than bloody ones. We ran the wash. We couldn't wait for the wash to be done. M and I looked for clothes I could fit in. We found a pair of M's shorts that were oversized for him and one of Magos's sweatshirts, a neon-peach number that hung wide but barely reached my waist.

Sirens sounded. I shushed M even though he wasn't making any noise. He walked to the window, where the ambulance illuminated the street blue. I pulled M a few steps away from the window.

"Do we go?" M asked.

I squeezed him tight. We couldn't escape now.

Voices came from the hallway. Lena spoke. A man spoke too. They went quiet. The washing machine was too loud. I waited for them to burst in. To wrench M away from me as I fought like I had never fought before and probably would never fight again. I'd kick and punch and scratch until they were so distracted by my wildness that M would escape. We heard voices again. Louder. More urgent. This was it. M and I stood in the living room. I held him behind me. I didn't know how to fight. But I didn't need to. Adrenaline would take over. That was its whole purpose.

The voices went quiet again.

A dash of blue light swept the ceiling round and round.

M slid out of my grip and walked to the window.

"Don't," I whispered.

He pointed outside. The paramedics were carrying the neighbor on a stretcher and putting him in the ambulance. Magos and Lena followed.

"Let's go," I said to M.

I didn't know if the police would come by right after. We had minutes, maybe only seconds. I snagged the bag with M's things. I opened the door a crack first to make sure the hall was empty. We walked out. We couldn't run. We couldn't make ourselves suspicious. The stairs were unending, flights and flights. I didn't remember having climbed so many flights on the way in. We walked down, step by step, trying to make the least amount of noise.

Voices. People coming in.

M and I froze. I held his hand. We waited. The voices echoed up. Then a door closed, and the voices vanished. We ran down the rest of the stairs. I didn't let go of M's hand until we arrived outside. I hoped to find Magos and Lena in the courtyard, but they weren't there. We couldn't try to find them. We ran down the street opposite the way the ambulance had driven, hoping we were headed toward the general direction of my hotel.

followed M, his strides short and purposeful while mine, though longer, struggled to keep up. Unlike New York, Berlin felt roomy, a city in which the wind could blow and not get trapped. But that night there was no wind. Maybe Berlin wasn't windy, I didn't know, so I whistled instead. I wasn't whistling a tune, only a pretense of wind. M looked up at me. I stopped whistling. M asked me to please continue. I resumed and we walked on. I had no clue where we were. I hoped we were heading in the direction of my hotel even though Peter was there. A rush of overlapping scenarios cluttered my brain: Peter helping us escape; Peter shouting, "Murderer!" and calling the police; Peter trying to kill M; M eating Peter. At this last image, I turned my gaze to my feet and focused on my steps instead. My sneakers had blood on them. I looked up.

We came to an intersection where a massive boulevard opened up and we finally encountered real wind rushing through it. A perk of having shoulder-length hair is that it ripples in the wind. But the wind wasn't strong enough to make my hair ripple, more like a slight quivering. I kept pushing it back anyway so I could have something to tend to apart from the horror of that night. I gave up on whistling. I was getting dizzy.

We walked past stores, restaurants, and cafés closed for the night. I seesawed between wanting the city to be bustling and feeling gratitude that we were practically alone. It was hard to focus on one feeling. We stopped at a corner and waited for the walk signal, the green Ampelmann. I touched M's head, caressed the thickness of his hair, almost bristly. He didn't acknowledge my touch. A car drove by. I gently squeezed the back of his neck, let my hand linger on his back for a moment, and then we went on.

When Santiago was alive, I used to have visions of what he would become. Not visions like mystical forebodings; more like wishes. In these he would be thirty, my age back then, and I'd be old, older than math and logic would account for. I would be sitting at the head of a great picnic table with Magos and Santiago by my side. Lena would be there and Uncle too. Though, again, math and logic couldn't account for how he would still be alive. Also, other shapeless friends and well-wishers. We'd sit under the shade of a humongous tree, most likely in Firgesan but not conclusively. Santiago spoke at the event, which alternated from birthday to anniversary to unprompted celebration. "Best dad," he would say, and he'd tell our dear ones how they only knew one part of me, how he was lucky to know all of me. I'd cry imagining this because, beyond all of the self-indulgent details of this moment, Santiago was alive and happy. It was an amorphous happiness because I wasn't able to imagine the specifics of what made him happy, but he was happy.

I never imagined being on the run in Berlin with M, divorced from Magos, with another fiancé waiting for me. I never imagined needing to escape a murder—was murder the right term? Man-slaughter? I could have never imagined M.

And yet here we were, in Berlin, me in borrowed shorts and a neon sweatshirt, fugitives. Despite images of the mangled neighbor blazing in my thoughts and a constant tide of nausea, I felt a richness that I'd never felt before, as if I'd finally moved from a member of the audience to the main player onstage.

M stopped.

"We're here," he said.

Peter chose the hotel after reading dozens of reviews. Its looming brick facade reminded me of a '60s mental institution, broad and squat, with windows framed in symmetrical white squares through which I imagined patients pining for freedom. Inside, the hotel was modern, bright, in pale earth-toned furniture and yolk-yellow accents. We slipped to our room as inconspicuously as we could. I didn't want anyone to remember us.

The room was dark. I stopped M at the short entrance hallway, letting my eyes adjust so we wouldn't have to turn on any lights. Slowly, the darkness gave way to edges that sketched out the room: the credenza, a chair underneath it, the night lights outside framing the curtains, the bed with Peter's bulk rising on top, all the boundaries we needed to navigate through.

Peter shifted. "You're here," he said.

I walked over to the bed and sat down. "M's staying over."

"Santiago?" Peter tried to sit up, but I pushed him down. "You found him."

"Sleep," I said, but Peter pushed himself back up. He turned on the bedside lamp and squinted. "Hi, Santiago," he said. M stayed by the entrance. Peter looked at the one bed. "Where will you sleep?"

"The floor is fine," M said.

"Okay." Peter looked at him with one eye open. "Are you sure? There should be extra blankets in the closet. Pillows." Peter swung in bed so that his feet found the floor.

"It's okay," M said. "I'll get it."

Peter mm-hmm'ed, his head hung down. Then he yawned, looked up, and scanned me, still using only one eye. "What are you wearing?"

"Clothes." I kissed his head and told him to get back into bed.

He obeyed. I helped M build a nest at the foot of our bed with towels, sheets, blankets, and a couple of pillows we found in the closet. The nest, a circular structure in which M lay curled up at the center, would seem weird to Peter when he saw it. But I couldn't bring myself to push M into a more normal bedding arrangement. Not tonight. The nest was the least of my worries.

I slept in fits, startled awake by imagined sirens and nightmares, the specifics of which I couldn't remember but whose terror lingered. M whimpered, the way he used to when we first removed his arm-tail. I wanted to lie with him and comfort him, but I was stuck in the bed, anchored by the memory of the time I prayed his arm-tail would grow back, promising that if it did I would accept him for what he was. I wouldn't judge his hunger. I'd bring him pets myself if that's what he wanted. But his arm-tail didn't grow back although his hunger had clearly remained. What end of the bargain was I responsible for?

Dawn came. M snored lightly, and Peter's snores bounced loud and raspy in the small room. I was grateful for both, which gave me something to concentrate on apart from the horrifying images of the eaten man. Scenes of us wading through ankle-deep blood haunted me, though there couldn't have been that much. Peter and I had a flight out of Berlin that afternoon. M couldn't stay here waiting until the neighbor healed and accused him. I wouldn't abandon him again. I'd buy him a ticket and bring him back to New York with us.

I texted Magos to let her know of my plan. I saw the *typing* message from her end, but for a while nothing came through.

That would be best, she texted finally. *Today?*

Yes.

How is he?

Sleeping. How's the man?

Elias. Alive. Barely. They have him at the ICU.

You're in the hospital?

We've been here all night.

Do they, I typed, but I decided it was best not to ask. I put my phone down.

Peter woke up. He tried to smooth down the poof of his hair as he stared at M curled in the middle of his nest.

"Is he okay?" He pointed to four long scratches on M's arm.

"It's nothing," I said.

"How can it be nothing?" Peter said too loudly.

"Let's go outside."

We walked out into the hallway. I shut the door behind me. Peter crossed his arms, waiting for me to explain.

"M's coming back with us to New York."

"Why?"

I could've told him everything, about Magos taking Santiago's lung, about Monstrilio and the playground I built for him, how he swung and we played at wrestling, how Monstrilio was easier to love because he was something completely different, how I still couldn't understand M but would fight for him, how I would protect him.

"M just needs some time away from Berlin," I said.

"Is it serious?" Peter asked.

"No." I smiled. "Everything's okay."

"Everything is not okay, Joe. Are you really not going to tell me what's going on?"

"There's nothing going on, Peter. Please understand."

PETER LEFT THE HOTEL ROOM with the excuse of revisiting a few stores that sold local artists' wares and designer trinkets. I was scared he would take his bags and break up with me right then and there, even if we had the same flight back home. But he left his bags behind, and though he could still break up with me later, I saw this as a sign of hope.

M woke up soon after. I told him I'd get us lunch, and I found a café nearby where I bought a sandwich for me and sausages for him. We sat on the carpeted floor, the food by our feet. He eyed the thick sausages wearily.

"Not hungry?" I asked.

He nodded, but I wasn't sure if this meant that he was hungry or not. I realized he might be feeling apprehensive about eating, considering the meal he'd had the night before.

"It's okay. You can eat."

He took a few demure bites out of the sausages. His fangs sliced right through the food. I told him he was coming back with us to New York. M chewed and swallowed the last of his sausages.

"I can't leave," he said.

"You have to."

He stared at me with those big, black eyes of his, so much like Magos's, like Santiago's, and then drew his knees up to his chin.

"I want to apologize to Elias."

"You can't apologize."

"Why not? That's what you told me to do after I've done something wrong."

"You've committed a crime, M."

He scraped leftover purple nail polish from his big toenail. Santiago loved when Magos painted his nails. Magos and M had evidently reignited the tradition. M took a napkin and cleaned the bit of scraped nail polish from his finger. As M transformed and grew, I kept trying to find Santiago in his eyes, his voice, his mannerisms, in the way his hair grew wild, but it was in the tenderness with which he cared for himself, like the way he was tending to the nail polish now, that I found Santiago most evident.

"You could go to jail for what you did."

"I didn't mean to. I'm lying. I did mean to, Papi. I was hungry. Super hungry. I tried not to kill him, but he was very delicious. I stopped. And he didn't die. Lena said he was alive. The ambulance took him." He looked up at me. "I have a job here. Do I quit? And Qi's opening is soon. Thomas is here."

"Maybe you can come back later. When all of this passes. But for now, you'll come to New York with me."

"Is Peter mad?"

"He's a little upset."

"Because of me?"

"No, not you. He's upset with me."

"Did you tell him? The Monstrilio part?"

I shook my head. "He wouldn't understand."

"Do you?"

His eyes glimmered, and I saw Monstrilio staring back at me, wild and confused. His question was not an accusation but rather a plea. I wished I knew how to answer, but the best I could do was to hug him and let him rest on me. The weight of his head on my chest made my heartbeat stronger, not faster, but more pronounced. I told him to get ready.

MAGOS
LENA
JOSEPH
M

passport is a booklet with your name and picture on it. Mine says Santiago Jansen de la Mora. Capitalized letters. It doesn't say human because only humans get a passport. Mine comforts me like an alibi.

IT'S LIKE A TRICK, the way I unhinge my jaw and stretch my lips all the way to my earlobes. My head split halfway through. But it's not a trick. I'm not trying to fool anyone. It feels good. Letting my fangs air out. I do this when I'm alone, preferably outside. At night. People would freak out if they saw. Except Uncle Luke. He gave me a thumbs-up when he saw.

PURPOSE OF VISIT? The passport-control man asks.
I live here now.
He flips through my passport. Looks at his computer.
What were you doing in Germany?
I lived there before.

The man types fast. He could be writing: Access denied, not human. I stand taller. Smile. Lips closed. Easy. I can be very human, though for a while I refused to. I wouldn't even go out. The world was scary. Worse. I was scary in it. In a body I had no clue how to handle. More parts than I knew what to do with. But I had Santiago's memories. His frailty and unwieldy kindness.

All set, the man says. He returns my passport. Waves the next person forward.

I'm hungry.

Uncle Luke waits for us in Arrivals. Pulls me into a hug. Pats my cheek. Grunts to ask how I'm doing.

I'm fine, Uncle Luke, I say.

Uncle Luke and Papi have the same large nose and freckles. There's a photo where Uncle Luke is just as tall as Papi. Now he's crooked. His back bends. His fingers curl like claws. He grunts again. Prods. But I can't tell him why I'm in New York. Not yet. Not in front of Peter.

Hello, Luke, Peter says.

Uncle Luke grunts.

Peter doesn't understand his grunts. When people don't understand you, you can say anything you want. Fuck off, for instance.

During the flight, I sat in between Papi and Peter. For all eight hours they didn't speak. Held their stomachs so tight they smelled rancid. They need to fight. In movies people fight in taxis. Especially in New York. But Peter doesn't get in the taxi with us. Says he's going home on his own. Papi gets out. Leaves Uncle Luke and me to wait inside. I can't hear what Papi and Peter say. They don't seem to be fighting. Uncle Luke brushes his hair back. What's left of it is long. Like Papi's. But it has lost its color. Papi and Peter hug. A hug with pats and a lot of distance. Papi gets in.

Uncle Luke grunts.

It's fine, Papi says.

The taxi starts. I like saying, It's fine. It's a lie that seems smaller.

THE HOUSE IN COBBLE HILL is bloodred with white trim. Skinny in a row of more skinny houses. Stairs lead to the door. Bushy plants grow from planters. I don't know their names. Except *fern*. Above Uncle Luke's window, a wooden mermaid peers down. She's painted red too. Camouflaged. Uncle Luke put her there to keep the house safe. Mermaids are vicious if they don't like you, he told me once. But this mermaid likes me. And Uncle Luke.

We walk into the living room, where I usually read the books Uncle Luke gives me. We leave the suitcases in the foyer. Mine is a small bag. The one Papi packed for me in Berlin. It's enough. Clothes are too much work anyway. And I like my outfit. I wear the same one almost every day. We sit. I don't have a book. Doesn't seem like the moment to read anyway.

Uncle Luke grunts.

Give us a minute, Papi says. He collapses on the couch. We just got here.

I ate our neighbor, I say.

Bit him.

I swallowed parts.

He's still alive.

He may die.

We want him to live, of course, Papi says. What you did was a mistake, M, a bad moment.

Uncle Luke picks up one of his yellow pads. I read aloud: No mistake. This is M.

Papi says, I know this is M.

Telling me I'm M does not afford the clarity they think it does.

PAPI IS NAPPING.

A mistake is something you wish you hadn't done. I ask Uncle Luke if this is true.

He shrugs.

I say that I don't like that Elias is hurt but that I don't wish I hadn't done it. I still keep tasting him. Very delicious.

Uncle Luke grunts but not an answer. He hands me a note: Beef tartare just for you.

We go to the kitchen. Uncle Luke doesn't mind how enthusiastically I eat. He drinks red wine. Pats my hand. I lick my plate.

More? Uncle Luke writes.

I'm still hungry but I say I'm fine.

I take our dirty plates to the sink. A sliver of pink sunset light shines on the wall in front of me. So pretty a dread grows right in my chest. Monstrilio loved this light the best. Night is when we're hungriest. And hunger can be magnificent. I stare at the half-washed dishes. I fight to push the dread out. I pretend my time as Monstrilio is hazy. Muffled sounds and blurred colors. I say I remember warmth. But I don't say I miss my fur. I don't say I'm hungry because my hunger is what makes everyone scared. They are happy to believe I forgot how they maimed me.

My lung struggles and I fight to breathe. A lingering struggle from Santiago. I remember Santiago the least. But he's the one I summon most often. Maybe I'm imagining my lung's failure because I want to be Santiago. I breathed just fine as Monstrilio. I close my eyes. Warm water slides from my wrists to the tips of my fingers. Tickles all the way down. I try to inhale but my lung blocks the air. Is it possible to take everything else from Santiago but leave this part behind? Or is drowning every so often essential to being Santiago? I try again. A wisp of air goes in. I breathe again. Again. And again. More air each time. My lung is fine. The pink light disappears. I continue washing.

Papi doesn't go back to Peter in Williamsburg. Stays in Cobble Hill with us. When Uncle Luke and I read, he doesn't know what to do with himself. He forgets how to stay seated and not talk. I braid his hair. Chunky braids that calm him. I teach him to knit, but his fingers can't hold the needles right.

Peter hasn't called.

Uncle Luke grunts. He dislikes Peter but not enough to see Papi this unhappy. He writes: call.

Papi calls Lena instead. She says Elias is alive. Still unconscious. But alive.

Good, Papi says.

Aside from this, he doesn't mention Elias. We don't talk about what will happen when he wakes up. I keep knitting. Uncle Luke reads. Papi vacuums for the second time.

My knitting project is a scarf. Mami said I should hang it across trees. Make it outdoor art. But I like it better purposeless.

The skein of yarn I'm working with reaches its end. I take a new one. This one is lime-green. I work it into my scarf. I love

this part, knitting in a new skein without any knots required. It
holds by merely following the same pattern of loops. Some sort
of magic. Uncle Luke puts his book down. Watches me as if I
were TV.

THE WALLS AT THE PIER are concrete. Unfinished. Papi says it's on
purpose. An aesthetic. In Berlin, they would've been covered in
graffiti. Papi throws a blanket on the lawn. We've had lunch at the
piers three days in a row. Uncle Luke complains. Too much sun.
Papi says picnics give us something to do. We can't stay in the
house all day. But Uncle Luke and I could.

Today we have noodles with chicken and vegetables. I'm able to
eat the vegetables only because the sauce is spicy. I had mastered
vegetables. Even used to find some tasty. But I've forgotten how to
like them now.

Pigeons waddle a few feet away from us. If I were by myself, no
people walking their dogs, no sunbathers, no joggers, no Papi,
maybe only Uncle Luke, I'd pounce on those pigeons. Have a feast.

I scrape the plastic bowl for all that remains of my noodles.

Once, in Berlin, a pigeon snatched a french fry from Thomas's
plate. We were having lunch close to the gallery. As we used to. The
pigeon flew off. French fry in its beak. Thomas laughed.

I have eaten pigeons. I've eaten crows and sparrows and a fat
green bird I don't know the name of. The green bird was the tasti-
est. All kinds of insects too. Monstrilio ate cats and dogs and bit
Grandma Lucía's leg. There's no adequate vocabulary to describe
taste. Perflousita. A little aplesude. Coming up with words and
then remembering what they mean is harder than the task merits.

TONIGHT PETER IS AT THE DOOR. He smiles like he doesn't know what else to do with his mouth. I ask him to come in. Our foyer is very inviting. Warm-lighted. He tells me I look well.

Thank you. Are you looking for Papi?

Papi appears.

Hello, he says. Blushes.

They shut themselves inside Uncle Luke's old study. Uncle Luke and I stand outside. We listen for key words, *M*, *Santiago*, *prison*, *monster*. Their voices are not loud enough for us to understand.

He won't tell, Uncle Luke writes.

Papi comes out. Still red but happy. He's going back to Peter's. Wedding is still on.

It was never off, Peter says.

MY STUMP THROBS. Not all the time but more often lately. When they first chopped it off, I couldn't feel anything there.

I get naked. The mirror in my room shows all of me. I'm short. Hairy. My stump juts out like an extra hip.

Santiago once saw a werewolf on TV that scared him. Hairy. Eyes red. Long crooked arms and legs. Lots of snarling. Santiago howled at the moon to fool the werewolves into thinking he was one of them. Werewolves don't hurt their own kind, he believed.

I massage my stump.

I had an arm-tail once, I tell Santiago. This is where it was. I think you would've liked it.

THERE'S A STORY IN WHICH a man vomits bunnies. Lots of bunnies. He's in Buenos Aires looking after a woman's apartment. Keeping it until she returns from Paris. He feels bad that the bunnies are destroying her apartment. Uncle Luke loves this story. I like the bunnies part. But I don't get why, at the end, the man throws himself off the balcony.

MAMI AND LENA ARRIVE FROM BERLIN. They meet us in Cobble Hill. Papi cooks steaks. Mami hugs me. Lena carries a suitcase.

Got some of your stuff, M.

I take the suitcase from her and leave it in the foyer.

Peter, Mami says, I didn't realize you'd be joining us.

She walks past him. Peter brushes a corner of the grandfather clock as if it needs cleaning. We sit in the formal dining room. Uncle Luke has set the long table with hydrangeas and candles. Ceremonial. Lots of shadows. Peter asks what Mami and Lena have been up to since we left. Mami and Lena speak over each other, museums, a cocktail party, strolls, restaurants, the Spree. Only a week has passed. They don't mention Elias. Or the hospital. They can't with Peter here. Papi, Mami, and Lena smile a lot. I cut tiny bites out of my steak. I would chomp on it if we weren't pretending.

Thomas asked about you, Mami says. I told him you were spending time with your father in New York. You should write to him. Say goodbye.

I finish my steak. I rationed it out, so I didn't finish first. Peter and Uncle Luke finished before me. I'm still hungry, but I won't ask for more.

I think about what I'll write to distract myself from the hunger. Goodbye, Thomas, on a nice sheet of paper. I liked kissing you. I liked having sex with you. Your body is excellent. Beautiful and yummy. Thank you for sharing it with me. Thank you for being kind. I didn't expect it. Also, I enjoyed talking and working with you. Very much.

More wine? Papi asks, and he walks to the kitchen.

Mami follows. They will talk. I remember this move. Do you remember, Santiago? They'd go into the kitchen when they didn't want you to hear their conversation.

I need the bathroom, I say.

Uncle Luke grunts.

I go into the backyard through Uncle Luke's old study. The door to the kitchen is open. Papi likes to air it out, but the smell of steak lingers. My mouth waters. It's okay to remain hungry, I tell myself. I sit by the door where Mami and Papi can't see me.

Dead, Papi says. Why didn't you tell me?

Mami doesn't answer. The moon is almost full. There are leaves on the garden table. One of them walks down one of the table's iron legs.

We met his parents at the hospital.

Mami's words are slower than usual.

Elias's mother had a charm bracelet. One of those silver ones. She rubbed each of the charms with her fingers like she was trying to commit them to memory. She pinched them. One was one of those metal stovetop coffee makers, you know the ones. She lingered on that one the longest. She pressed on it so hard, the edges of her thumb became white. That one represented her son. A coffee maker. His mother thanked us for trying to save her son, Joseph.

Mami's words now find their speed.

She thanked us. His father kept repeating it was impossible their son had died, that there had been some mix-up, some clerical error. There has to be a mistake, he told the nurses and the doctors. He was desperate. I don't remember thinking Santiago's death was a mistake. Do you? We knew Santiago would die. We always knew. I wanted to slap this man, show him his mangled son, and make sure he knew he was dead. I needed him to understand there was no way to come back from this. That this wasn't a mistake.

He'll control it, Papi says. He controlled it before, and he can do it again.

He ate the cat too.

What cat?

Elias's cat. We loved that cat, Joseph, and he ate her. We didn't even notice at first because she was . . . she was bones. Only the head—

I crawl to where the leaves are walking down the legs of the table. Ants are carrying them. I put one finger across their path. An ant tries to go around. Finds my hand. Tries the other way. Spins in place. I don't understand why it won't just go over my finger. Or bite it. Make me take my hand away. Maybe the ant's afraid I'll squish it. It finds a way around the tip of my finger and returns to its path. Free.

I wish I had a cigarette. I haven't bought my own. I always had Thomas to share.

Papi asks about the police. If I'm a suspect. Mami says no. The German police think I'm a shark. My bite is too wide. My teeth unlike any they've seen on a mammal. They issued a warning: Wild animal loose in Prenzlauer Berg. They didn't say *shark*, of course. Not on land. They couldn't say *monster* either. Ein wildes Tier.

THE MAN IN THE BUNNY STORY repairs all the damage the bunnies caused to his friend's apartment. Still, he jumps off the balcony. Takes all eleven bunnies with him. ·

ncle Luke finds me a job. Assistant at a used bookstore a few blocks from the house. Books brim the shelves. Chipped pale-wood shelves reach the ceiling. More books pile on the floor. I like the chaos. The owner is a white-haired man. Loves talking with Uncle Luke.

I was a conscientious objector, the man tells me.

His name is Keith. I arrange books that come in. Make space for them. Dust. Put books on shelves. More books come in than go out. I make more space. Dust. Rearrange. A week in, I realize there won't be a day when I'm done. Endlessness works for me.

Romy comes in on Tuesday and Thursday afternoons. Every other Saturday too. She's a student at NYU. Literature. Has her hair buzzed short. She spends her time in the Fiction section. Keeps it pristine. History is mayhem and one of my territories. I can't decide if biographies should be separate. Which countries merit their own sections. Or why there are so many books on the British.

Have you read this? Romy asks, luring me to Fiction. This? This?

Most times I say no.

She tells me I need to read more.

I thought I read enough. I put pink Post-its on all the novels she tells me to read. At the end of the month, I'll buy them. If they haven't already been sold.

Three blocks down from the bookstore there's a kebab place.

Extra meat, please, I tell the man. Skip the veggies.

He seems to enjoy how much I eat. I ask for another. The man laughs. Slices more meat. More than he gives other customers. Thomas called them döner in Berlin. In Mexico City, taquitos al pastor. Wherever I am, it is comforting to find vertical meat to eat.

PAPI'S WEDDING IS IN THREE MONTHS. Mami hasn't gone back to Berlin. She stays with Lena. Sometimes she shows up at the bookstore. Flips through books. Never buys anything. Follows me around, talking about helping Papi and Peter with wedding preparations.

Your father has impeccable taste, she says.

I re-alphabetize the philosophers.

Peter not so much, but he can be nudged, she continues.

I step off from the stool.

Does anyone buy any of these books? she asks.

Some people do, I reply.

This place is a bit magical, isn't it? She pulls a book out. Puts it back where it doesn't belong.

I move on to Science, carry my stepping stool with me, and wait for Mami to catch up. Mami and I have the same cheeks, high, the same eyes, large and a tad wide-set. My nose is long like Papi's, but its shape is wider, like Mami's. I've surveyed my face a thousand times to make sure these traits are real. Not details I invented to be their son.

I take extra copies down to the basement. A rat lives there.

Shoo!

It wiggles its nose.

Do you want me to eat you?

It scurries away.

I LEFT MY DENTURES IN BERLIN. Filing my fangs to fit inside them hurt. Romy thinks my fangs are rad. The bits she can see. She thinks I'm rad all over. Très rad.

I'm having a party, she says.

Have fun.

I'm inviting you, you idiot.

Thanks.

Everyone is dying to meet you. We're so over NYU people.

Okay.

You have to come.

I will.

Give me your number. I'll text you deets.

I don't have a phone.

She says something in Korean. She enjoys being exasperated in Korean.

You have to have a phone. Don't get me wrong, it's très cool you don't, but you have to have one for emergencies. It'll be a secret phone. Only I'll have the number.

Okay.

Okay you'll get a phone?

Maybe.

———

THOMAS TOOK ME TO A house party in Friedrichshain once. Not far from Kreuzberg, where he lived. People asked where I was from. My mother, I told them. They laughed and waited for another answer, so I said Mexico City. Many told me they'd been to Mexico City before. Great city. Conversations lulled. People tried hard to find other things to talk about. Thomas spoke with his own group of people. The German words that filled the apartment were somewhat familiar but carried little meaning. I drank beer. After my fourth, I was talking with a woman about a horror novel we both loved. We weren't trying so hard anymore.

LENA, MAMI, PAPI, UNCLE LUKE, and I have dinner at a Peruvian restaurant. Peter is not here. Busy at work. I've had two ceviches. I won't order a third even though I want to. I tell Papi and Mami I'm thinking of getting a phone. Papi says it's not a good idea.

Why not? Mami asks.

It's too soon.

Too soon to have friends? Lena asks.

Too soon to be in social situations, Papi says. Wouldn't it be tempting?

I work at a bookstore, I say.

But that's not really—I don't know.

I'm not going to eat anyone.

Right.

Silence. I smile at Papi. I wish he wasn't scared. I'm trying. Lena pours herself more wine. Mami asks for another pisco sour. Uncle Luke grunts.

Eme will be fine, Mami says.

Papi and Lena turn to Mami, eyebrows raised, but say nothing. This is the first time Mami has called me M. But instead of saying it *em*, like Papi, she says *eme*. I like *eme*.

UNCLE LUKE TAKES ME TO BUY a phone. I can afford a cheap one with my bookstore money. In my contacts, I add Uncle Luke, Mami, Papi, Lena, and Romy.

THE PEOPLE AT ROMY'S PARTY are younger than Thomas's friends. They stand and talk. Christmas lights hang around the room. Lamps are covered with thin scarves.

M, I repeat when asked, I work with Romy.

I drink my beer. Try to make it seem like standing by myself is a choice. I squeeze into the kitchen to get another beer. Narrow. Cramped.

A man with a side part pokes my shoulder. He asks to see my teeth.

I smile.

Whoa! He turns away. You gotta see this.

He fetches two people. Then three more join us. They all stare at me.

Smile, side-part man says.

I smile.

They open their eyes really wide. What the fuck! They hoot. They laugh. Side-part man points at me. I keep smiling. Frozen. Like an exhibit. I smell side-part man's smugness. If I ate him, he'd taste tart. Like zest-infused alcohol. I keep smiling. They keep laughing. They don't even know my name. And they haven't seen my full fangs. I smile wider than should be possible. His friends take a step back. Side-part man's laugh sputters dead. The realization of imminent death tastes the most delicious. Now. There it is.

You're such an asshole! Romy pushes her way through.

I close my mouth.

Come. She pulls me away. He's . . . I'm sorry . . . I don't know why he's here. We broke up like a week ago.

There's an attempt to start a dance party, but only Romy and two friends wiggle. I try wiggling too. No one else joins. Side-part man and friends have forgotten about me. They laugh in a corner. I sit on a couch. A man is sitting at the other end looking at his phone. He's tall and meaty. Like Thomas.

Hello, I say. I'm M.

He scoots closer. He's also not from NYU. He graduated. I get close to him to hear what he's saying.

Wanna get out of here? he asks.

It takes two trains to get to his apartment. His roommates are not home.

Wine? Beer? He rummages in his cupboards. I may have some tequila.

Beer is good.

He puts on music. Electronicky. Like aliens wailing. He turns off the lights. Only a lamp stays on. We sit on his couch. Three empty Chinese take-out boxes sit on the coffee table. I smell his horniness. We kiss. He grabs my ass.

May I see you naked? I ask.

Right now?

I nod.

Here?

I can get naked first, if you want.

Okay, he says.

He takes a gulp of his beer. Unbuttons the first buttons of his shirt. Slips it off. Unlike Thomas, his chest and belly are hairless. He undoes his jeans. Takes his sneakers off. Pushes his pants down. Stands looking at me in his underwear.

You're very pretty, I say.

He pulls down his underwear. His penis dangles. Plump. I stand up. Step on his toes. His breaths are loud.

May I touch you? I ask.

My face reaches his chest. I touch his cheeks first. Move my hand down to his Adam's apple. I play with his nipples. Pinch them.

Ow.

Sorry.

I pinch again. He's fully erect. I place both my hands on his belly. He shudders. I twirl my finger around his belly button. Paying close attention to the edges. I swivel him around. His ass is flat. I squeeze it. Find its flesh. I turn him around to face me again.

Do you want to see me naked now? I ask.

When Thomas saw my stump, he touched it. Ugly? I asked. No, he said. He kissed it and we had sex. After I bit him, he didn't kick me out. But he asked me why I had done it. I told him he could bite me anywhere he wanted. He didn't want to. He said there was no need for anyone biting anyone.

This man avoids my stump. Doesn't answer me when I ask him if he thinks it's ugly. He won't touch it. Let alone kiss it. He steps away. I ask if I may bite him.

I'm not into that. He pulls his pants up. Says it's late. Says his roommates will come home soon. Says I better go.

I dress and leave.

ELIAS'S CAT WOULD WALK ON a narrow ledge five flights up. From his window to ours. Minna, the cat, spent many afternoons with us. While I knitted and Mami read noirs or watched movies on her laptop, Minna curled on an empty chair. Sleeping or licking herself. Elias would come knocking at night. Mami let me answer. For a while, he was my one human interaction besides Mami. I'd hand him Minna back. He'd thank me, pushing his glasses back up his nose. He didn't blink much. Gracias, he'd say. As if I'd like him more in Spanish. I'd reply, Bitte, and he'd smile. Like there was something else he wanted to say.

When I ate him, and Minna, none of this came to mind.

UNCLE LUKE IS SLEEPING WHEN I get back home. I wade through the shadows of our living room, hoping to find monsters. Chat with them. Laugh. But there are no monsters in these shadows. Only me.

Romy sits on a shaky pile of books. I sit on the floor. She suggests dating apps. Sets two up for me. Keith walks past. He doesn't care what we do. Romy says he hired us for company. On my profile, Romy writes that I like to bite. She calls biting a kink. Says it's a good thing to have.

Probably a million dudes waiting to be bitten, she says. She takes a picture of me against a background of full shelves. People will think you're an intellectual. Books and biting. What more could they want!

I ask her how hard I'm allowed to bite.

Dunno. Ask them.

Some customers spend hours browsing. Quiet. Slow. The more regular ones sit on the floor going through the piles of books I have yet to arrange. Their fingertips barely touch the covers. Like they're not allowed to touch. Only graze. As if they could hurt the books.

The rat in the basement sits on a short stool. I feed it a piece of my kebab. The rat holds it with its paws and eats. It's getting fat.

———

UNCLE LUKE SCROLLS THROUGH the apps with me. Two gnarled fingers going up and down. I eat a hot dog.

All these men want bites? he writes on his yellow pad.

No. The ones that do will contact me. So far no one has.

Uncle Luke grunts. Sips his tea. He writes: don't get caught.

I'm not going to eat them.

Uncle Luke points at his writing, leaving black dots with his marker.

I won't get caught.

He pats my hand. Goes back to reading a novel Romy recommended. Now I'm the one telling him what to read. I swallow the last of my hot dog.

You like biting?
Yes.
Playful biting, right?
I guess so.
Sounds fun. I can host. Park Slope, ok?

THE MAN HAS HUNG many things on his walls. Paintings, masks, prints, photographs, mirrors. There's lots of furniture too. And plants. Makes me think of loneliness. The man is barefoot. Bare chested. Wears shorts and a flowy lilac robe. Outside it's chilly and raining. My umbrella drips. He points to a mat by his shoes. I prop my umbrella against the wall. My backpack next to it. He asks if I want water. I tell him I'm fine. He stares at my mouth then looks away. I've filed down my fangs' sharpness. They still look weird but less threatening.

He smells of chemical fruits and flowers. Probably just showered. He takes me to his bedroom. We have to walk sideways between a dresser and an armchair to get to his bed. We sit among mountains of pillows and cushions and folded blankets. He fiddles with his robe. I put a hand on his shoulder. He kisses me. Pulls my sweatshirt and T-shirt off. Kisses me more.

May I bite you now? I ask.

He gets naked. Lies facedown on his bed. I'm so excited I can't decide where to begin. His body is skinny. Lots of moles and freckles. Like a chart. I kneel on the bed. Like I'm about to impart a sacrament. I lick his thigh. Tastes like soap. I wipe my tongue with one of his blankets. Keep licking until I find the taste of his flesh. I place my teeth on his thigh. He says he doesn't want it to hurt too much.

I bite down. Little by little. My stomach expands, ready to welcome meat. I tell my stomach eating him is not part of the deal. My stomach, mouth, fangs, and intestines tell me to forget the deal. I bite down harder. The more his flesh resists, the more his taste lures me. I bite even harder. He tenses. I'm about to break skin. I pause. If I taste blood, I don't know if I'll be able to stop. My mouth holds his flesh. My tongue plays with it. He moans.

Clamp down, my body says. Eat him! My mouth waters.

I can't.

Come on. One small bite. Chew and swallow. Not a big deal. Bite!

I shove myself away from him. Fall off the bed. He coils. Inspects the back of his thigh. I scramble to dress.

Is that it? he asks.

I grab my sneakers and my umbrella and my backpack and run out of his apartment. I leave him uneaten.

A man sings a sad song on the subway. His voice is hoarse. The rest of the car doesn't pay attention. He keeps singing. His voice gets sadder. The saddest. People look up now. We look at each other. We don't usually do that. Instead of letting his voice out, it seems as if the man is reeling it back in. Like it was stolen. He seals it back inside his bones. The last word comes out a whisper. The man stands with his eyes closed. The train rattles. Some people clap. I wonder what his marrow would taste like with his voice trapped in it.

Papi is home when I get back. I haven't seen him in two weeks.

Uncle tells me you were out on a date, he says. How was it? I plop on the sofa next to him. Was it not good?

He was okay.

Just okay?

I nod.

Are you going to see him again?

I don't think so. I put my hands on my belly. Has Uncle Luke gone to bed?

Yes.

I'm hungry.

I got you some pork chops. You guys had no food in the house.

We manage, I say. I find the pork chops and bite one.

You're not going to cook them?

I'm making Papi uncomfortable. But I'm too hungry to care. I eat all of them raw. Papi points to a box.

Fruti Lupis, I say. You bought this?

Got some milk too.

Thanks, Papi.

I pour myself a bowlful. This is the one food craving Santiago and I have in common. Milk drips from my chin. Papi hands me a napkin. I eat another bowlful. Papi watches me, and I can tell he's pleased by how much I enjoy it. How I slurp the dregs of milk out of the bowl. Fruti Lupis make me feel 100 percent human. I burp.

Monstrilio was hungry all the time. The difference is he didn't know he shouldn't be.

Papi plans to stay the night. Peter is away for work. They both need a break from wedding stuff. Papi makes his bed on the pullout sofa in Uncle Luke's old studio. I go upstairs. Brush my fangs. Swipe their blunted tips with my tongue. I sit on the bed. My stump aches. Pulsates. Itches. I prod it. I can't feel my own touch. I squeeze it harder. Nothing.

Does it bother you? Papi asks from the doorway.

I can't feel myself touching it, I say. But it hurts. I wave him over. Can you try?

I take his hand and place it on my stump. Papi squeezes.

Harder, I say.

Papi squeezes harder. I feel something faint. Like a touch remembered. Papi sits on the bed next to me.

When we removed your arm-tail, a horrible sadness came over you. You were so joyful before. Jumping and playing and swinging all over that patio. Do you remember?

We played a lot together, I say. Papi doesn't usually talk to me about Monstrilio.

We did. Papi smiles. You never let me win. He scoots farther into the bed. You know why I never called you Santiago, even after your transformation?

Because I'm not Santiago?

Right. Santiago is dead. He died.

Papi's voice becomes thin. It always does when he talks about Santiago.

I don't want you to be carrying his death with you. You're someone else. Not Santiago or Monstrilio. Someone new.

M?

M.

I'm hungry all the time.

Your hunger will lessen. You'll see.

I want to eat people, Papi. I ate Elias.

Papi's face tightens. He struggles to soften it.

You won't eat anyone else.

And if I do?

Papi doesn't answer. He pulls me to him. Kisses the top of my head. I nestle my head on his lap.

DO YOU REMEMBER THE ZOO, SANTIAGO? You were eight or nine. Mami and Papi took you. Your first time. Zoológico de Chapultepec. Mami's cousin and her children came too. Two were teenagers, and a third was a boy around your age. You saw a hippopotamus and a giraffe. Papi got you ice cream. The older cousins teased the youngest one. Told him they were going to feed him to the wolf. Then they ignored him. They ignored you too. The youngest one waited behind to walk alongside you. You matched his pace. You thought that made you friends. But with everyone else far ahead, he smooshed your ice cream on your chest and ran. Left you dripping. He went right up to his siblings. They laughed. Called you a sissy. Papi ran to you. Kissed your head. Made sure you were okay. You couldn't speak, you were so angry. So angry you worried your lung would conk out, but it didn't. Papi got napkins to clean you up. Mami looked at the broken cone on the floor, snapped right up, and walked over to your cousins. Papi whispered, Magos. He knew what was coming. Mami knocked the youngest kid's cone to the floor. One swoop. The boy froze, then cried. Mami's cousin screamed at her. Mami pretended to have no idea what she was talking about. Mami's cousin screamed at Papi too. Told him his wife was insane. Kids are clumsy, Papi said and smiled like Mami. The cousin looked at you. At your T-shirt drenched in strawberry ice cream. Let's go! She snapped her fingers and dragged her three children out of the zoo. Papi held your hand. Mami held his.

I often steal this memory from you, Santiago. Right before I go to sleep.

We receive a huge donation at the bookstore. Keith, Romy, and I stare at the boxes. Rare books on biology. Very valuable, we're told. But not one of us has any clue how much they're worth.

Hire an expert, Romy says.

We can't afford an expert, Keith says.

Dust puffs from the books. Keith decides not to price them. If a customer shows interest, he will ask them what they think they're worth. Take their word for it. Keith tells us to stack the books. Romy disappears in Fiction. We don't have a Biology section. We only have Science. I stare at the three shelves brimming with glossy picture books, scientific paperbacks, and leather-bound tomes. I grab one of the new books. It's filled with etchings. All manners of creatures. Plants, mainly. I linger on a page titled "A Carnivorous Wonder: Drosera." It's a plant with slender tentacles dotted in dewdrops. Like a spindly splayed hairbrush. The plant curls down at its topmost tip, trapping a fly in it. Digestive juices will do the rest. I close the book. Make space for it in the middle shelf. Where it's easiest to reach.

That week, I go on three dates. They let me bite, but when I ask if I can eat them, they laugh. I learn to laugh too. Like I was joking. I bite as hard as I can without ripping flesh. I allow myself to break skin. Draw drops of blood. Tasty but not enough. Teasing. I control myself. Respect our deal. Still, my dates seem thrilled. As if we've crossed over into naughtiness. We have sex. They say I'm good at it. Wild. Fun. They are satisfied. I'm left hungry.

How hard do you bite?
I could eat you, I write back.
His name is Sam. His photo shows wild straw-colored hair. Bags under his eyes. A smile that tries to compensate. I like him. He doesn't respond. Maybe he thinks I'm joking. Maybe I freaked him out.
Interested?
Possibly, Sam writes back.
The app shows him go offline.

THOMAS TOOK ME TO A club once and gave me tiny crystals to swallow. He swallowed some too. People danced, jumped, and twirled to gypsy punk. Hot. Sweating. Thomas carried me on his shoulders so I could see the sea of heads. Their musk drifting up. Like offerings. I wanted to eat them all. But I didn't. I licked Thomas's sweat right off his chest. He kissed me right after. Wanting to taste himself too. He made me really hungry. But I had promised I wouldn't bite him again. I kept my promise.

Free?

My heart pounds thinking it's Sam, but it's just some generic well-coiffed man.

I bite, I write back.

I read.

Hard.

Good. In Hell's Kitchen. Free tonight?

Yes. Around 8.

THE MAN WEARS A GRAY SUIT. Tie and all.

Sit.

He points to a stool by his kitchen island. Pours me whisky without asking. His apartment has no rooms. Only areas. Bedroom area, living room area, kitchen area. Even the shower is only separated by clear glass. I can't find a toilet. His furniture is arranged like a magazine. Stylish. Spotless.

I wear my customary sweatshirt, khakis, and dirty white sneakers. Chipped purple nail polish. I unbalance his whole setting. I drink my whisky. He's done with his already. Now he flicks a little plastic bag. Taps powder on the marble countertop. A card appears in his hand. Mesmerizing how straight he draws the lines. Almost lovingly. He rolls a dollar bill like in the movies.

Want some?

I'm curious. He waves me over to stand next to him. Points at the thinnest line. Instructs me to hold one of my nostrils shut while I inhale with the other. One sweeping motion. My nose tingles. My mouth tastes bitter.

I don't kiss, the man says.

I don't need to kiss, I say.

He sits on a wide chair. His hair stays coiffed. Makes it seem like it's naturally shaped like that, but it's not. I smell oil in it. Chemicals I have no name for. And mint. An acid smell of aftershave. His forehead is smooth. Unnaturally. His eyebrows too defined. His jaw precise. Pockmarks scatter under his chin, hiding from the rest of his polished skin. His nails are manicured. His knuckles slightly hairy. His fingers squat. He hasn't taken his suit jacket off yet. Still wears his shoes. Socks. Tie. Only the tiniest sliver of his shin shows. I sniff and receive the combined smell of recently dry-cleaned fabric, sweat stewing inside his tight pants, and a day's worth of his feet inside his shoes. His apartment's cleanliness makes his human smells stand out. Smells he tries to hide underneath cologne, soaps, and deodorant. Every smell defines itself. Delicious. It's the cocaine. But it's also Monstrilio.

What now? I ask.

You're the biter. You tell me.

Get naked, I say.

Make me.

I'm not sure how to make him. Take your jacket off, I say.

He stares.

Please, I say.

He takes a sip of whisky. I stand right in front of him. The floor feels sturdy. I grab his tie. He lets me. The knot is tight. I struggle to undo it. He doesn't offer help. I finally slip one end loose and throw the tie. He looks over to where it lands. I grab his jacket's lapels. Try to push his jacket down off him, but he won't budge. I pull his shirt out of his pants. Unbutton it. Hairless chest. Waxed,

I think. I kneel. Slip off his shoes easily. I throw one to the left. The
other to the right, where his bed is. He tries to hide his displeasure.
Challenging his pristine order thrills me. Socks off next. He shifts
back. Sits taller. Looks down at me. I undo his pants. Pull them off.
Underwear too. He drinks his whisky. Smiles. I swipe my tongue
over my fangs. Pointy. I haven't filed them in a week.

Fuck!

Sorry.

Don't apologize.

He pushes my head down.

I bite. And bite.

There's blood on his left thigh. An open wound near the top.
More on his right thigh, almost at the knee. I taste skin. Blood.
Meat. I haven't bitten off anything big enough to chew. But still,
yum. I lick my fangs. I bite again. Deeper. His fists are clenched.
His eyes closed. I wait for him to say enough. Kick me out. He
doesn't. I lick his blood. Suck on it.

Bite! he says.

I obey. The world turns dark. The pleasure of biting drowns the
rest of my senses. Tasting flesh again. People flesh. Worried, inse-
cure, joyous, loving flesh.

Then, I taste my own blood.

He's hit me. Slapped me away. The world lightens and refocuses.
He's standing above me now. His open shirt and jacket hanging on
his naked body. Blood slithers down his legs.

Stand up, he says.

I get on all fours. Try to stand. My head booms. Dizzy. I kneel.
Lift my head up. He slaps me again. I fall over.

Don't, I say.

I thought this was what we were playing at, he says.

He steps toward me. I scoot away. Backward on my ass. I can't remember if the door is in front of or behind me. I stand up. My head whirls. He's in front of me. Punches me in the stomach. Chuckles. I can't breathe. I put my hand up.

Wait, I say.

Did I flinch when you bit me? Ask you to wait?

I dodge his next punch. Pure reflex. He laughs.

Good, he says.

I step back. The apartment organizes itself again. The door is behind him. Windows behind me. He steps forward. I smell his thrill. Prickly like pepper. I step back. Step back. Step back. Hit a wall. I turn to see. It's a column. He punches me in the face. The back of my head bounces off the column. He punches me again. I bend over. Hands on knees. I hear only heavy breathing. Mine. He waits for me to stand upright. I don't. Blood drips from my nose and mouth. Mostly mine, but I savor the remains of his. He will hit again. Until he's full. Like eating.

I open my eyes. My pupils dilate. Light rushes in. The hardwood floor is bright. I can see its pores. I open my mouth. Feel the click of my jaw unhinging. The stretch of my mouth all the way to my ears. My fangs breathe. I uncurl.

What the fuck!

I growl.

He steps back. Just one step. He's still not sure if he has lost the upper hand. I growl again. Smile my huge monster smile. I hope my fangs are gleaming. They must be bloody. I extend my arms, curl my fingers as if they were claws. I perform for him. He runs. There's really nowhere to hide. No rooms. Only areas. He backs himself into a nook created by a wall and wardrobe. I walk toward him. Prowl on my tiptoes. Feline. Menacing. I relish the smell of his fear. Lick it in the air.

His eyes narrow. He coils and jumps toward me, swinging a metal bat at my back. I collapse. He strikes me again. Stand up! my body orders. I scramble to run but I stumble back down. I crawl away, digging my nails in the wood's grain. But they're too short. Too human. I turn to face him. He swings his bat again and misses.

This time, I roar. So loud it freezes him. I get on my feet. Find the door. And run.

MONSTRILIO ONCE FELL FROM the roof in the garden Papi built for him. Splat, all the way down to the tiled floor. Three stories. He hit himself on a platform's edge coming down too. The pain was sharp. But brief. He was squishy. Filled with dark goo. Nothing in him could break.

I HIDE IN CENTRAL PARK, on a hill among the trees. Away from the paths. I'm alone. He won't come chasing. I think. My fangs are still out. I hinge my jaw back to human form. My face throbs, but the dirt is cool on my butt. The silence calming. I breathe. There's rustling behind me. I swivel. Too brusquely. Pain shoots through my back. My legs are going numb sitting like this. I stand and try to shake the whole night away. I can't. My head pulsates dizzily. I can't take the subway home. People will ask. Call the police. I walk. Everything hurts.

WHAT THE FUCK HAPPENED TO YOU?

Lena squints in orange pajama bottoms and a tank top. She lets me in. Pulls out a chair from her dining table. Wooden with a cushion tied to its seat. Her hair has white flyaways. We sit.

What happened?

I tell her a guy beat me up. Lena walks behind me.

I'm going to lift your shirt, she says.

She presses different parts of my back. I tell her the spot that hurts the most. Toward the bottom of my ribs. She touches my stump.

Wait, I say.

What?

I felt it.

What?

My stump.

She sits back down. Pushes my hair back with both hands.

I think you'll live, but I'd much rather take you to the hospital.

Eme? Mami asks. What's going on?

She rushes to me. Doesn't believe me when I tell her I'm fine. She makes us tea. Lena drinks coffee. I repeat the story. Mami agrees with Lena about taking me to the hospital. But says we have to come up with a different story.

Robbery! You were knocked down and couldn't see anything. It was horrible but quick, and there's no need for the police to get involved.

And if the man tells on me?

He won't. He attacked you.

I attacked him.

You technically didn't, Lena says. Biting him was something he wanted you to do.

I was going to eat him.

Because he attacked you! Mami says.

Mami and Lena wait with me in the ER. Lena talks to busy nurses and doctors. They tell her I'll be looked after. Then disappear. Lena paces. Mami says Lena isn't used to not being in control. A nurse takes me into a screened area, tells me to strip down to my underwear, put on a gown, and sit on the bed. The nurse cleans my face with cotton gauze. He's gentle. Tells me it'll be just a minute.

I wait.

Voices. Voices. The voice in the speakers pages this and that doctor. The nurse shows up again. Takes me to radiology. I bite down on a plastic guard for face X-rays. I try not to bite it off. I lie on my stomach for my back X-ray. The nurse returns me to my little enclosure and gives me a pill. I sit on the bed.

I wait.

Back hurts. Head hurts. But less now. Maybe the pill makes me care less. Lena appears and asks what they've said, what they've done. X-rays, I tell her. She goes away. After a few minutes, she reappears with Mami. Lena holds my X-rays up to the light. Mami peers too, as if she knows what she's looking at. I find my stump on the X-ray. Only darkness. Gooey darkness.

Nothing's broken, Lena says. I would love an MRI, though.

I tell her I want to go home.

Lena drives us to Cobble Hill. Uncle Luke doesn't ask what happened.

He writes: I'll take it from here.

Mami hesitates. Tells us to call if anything feels wrong. Even slightly. Lena says to rest. I nod. I'm tired. They leave. Uncle Luke walks me to bed. I ask him to loosen the bandages around my torso. He unwraps me. Spooling the gauze in his hands. He grunts. Runs his fingers down my back.

Is it bad?

He grunts a yes.

He wraps me again, looser this time.

Can I have a hot dog? I ask.

Uncle Luke grunts and brings up four. I eat them almost without chewing. Uncle Luke tucks me into bed but watches me from the armchair in my room.

Go back to your room, I tell him.

He lifts a finger to his mouth. Turns off the lamp next to him and pretends to sleep.

Papi wakes me up the next morning. Draws my curtains open. Sunshine. He sits on my bed and inspects my face. Peter's in the room too.

How awful! he says. I can't believe they would do all this just to get what? Your phone?

I have my phone, I say.

Peter turns even more bewildered. What on earth did they want then?

Papi stares at me. Opens his eyes wide.

My wallet, I say. And my watch.

The only watch I own is a calculator one. Santiago's. It's in Berlin. Or Mexico. I don't remember. Peter paces the room.

Could you fetch M some water? Papi asks. Please, Peter?

Peter goes out. I get ready to retell the story a third time, but Mami has already told Papi. He takes my hand. Rubs my nails with his thumb.

Want me to do them?

I stretch to my bedside table. Hand him a jar of blue nail polish.

You didn't eat him, Papi says. I'm proud of you.

I would've.

But you didn't.

Papi paints my left pinky.

I could argue. The truth is I would've eaten him. If it were not for the bat. But Papi looks so happy. He thinks I'm getting better. Less hungry. More capable of being human. He says our family is back together. All of us. Plus Peter. He takes my other hand. Very precise in his brushstrokes.

Done, he says.

My nails are pretty in blue. I take his hand and paint his next.

WHOA, KILLER, Romy says at the bookstore.

I still have purple around my eye. Some cuts. But I look less swollen than a few days ago. I debate which story to tell her. Robbery or biting. I decide on biting. Without the monster parts. She holds a pile of novels under her elbow. Doesn't seem to want to part with them.

Why do you like biting so much? she asks.

Feels like something I have to do.

Huh.

She slides the next novel in place. I walk away and stand outside the bookstore. Tap a cigarette out. My first self-bought cigarettes. I suck smoke in, but it doesn't taste the same alone. Romy comes out.

You smoke?

Want one?

Nah.

I puff out smoke.

You're so hairy, she says.

She stares at the patch of fur on my forehead. It shouldn't be noticeable. I shaved in the morning. But the stubble has already grown in. Romy touches it.

Soft, she says.

PAPI MADE ME PROMISE no more dates. For a while. But I open the app as I finish my cigarette to see if Sam has written. The same four text bubbles show on-screen.

Hello? I write.

Sam's not online. Maybe tomorrow.

MAMI SITS ON THE ONLY CHAIR at the bookstore. Old leather. Comfy. Keith's chair. I arrange the Fantasy & Sci-Fi section. It didn't need arranging, but Mami is talking and seems reluctant to follow me around. She tells me she suggested Firgesan for Papi and Peter's wedding. Papi was opposed. Peter excited. But they convinced Papi together. The house needs a fresh start. Joy, she explains. She crosses her legs and leans toward me.

Eme, she says. A Spanish arts organization has asked me to perform at a festival in Valencia. I can't say no. And I need to get back to work.

You're leaving?

I've been thinking about it. I can't figure out what else to do in New York but tag along with your father. Or visit you. Lena is too busy at the hospital. She's made a life without me. Would you come with me, if I went back?

The book cover I'm holding shows a woman holding a gun made of two baubles stuck together. She is facing head-on. A gargantuan robot looms behind her. Square head. Metal jaws. Panel of lights on its chest. A sole purple shrub grows on their planet. I can't tell if the robot is about to attack her. Or if it is her guardian.

I tell Mami I won't go and ask her to stay instead.

She uncoils her legs. Says she'll think about it.

I WALK BACK HOME FROM WORK. It's dusk. Many colors in the sky. A boy and his mother walk on the sidewalk. His mother holds his hand. The boy stops and cries. He won't walk anymore. The mother tugs. Tells the boy she will leave him. He keeps crying. The mother lets go of his hand. Steps a few feet away. Just enough that if he needs her, she can jump back to him. The boy slurps his snot and sees me standing behind him.

Hello, I say.

He runs back to his mother and grabs her hand. They go on walking.

THE HOUSE IS DARK WHEN I ENTER. It's getting darker earlier. I scratch my stump.

Uncle Luke?

No answer.

Uncle Luke? I say louder.

All over my body my hair stands up. Scared. Electric.

Uncle Luke?

I unhinge my jaw and walk to the kitchen. I kick the door open for the element of surprise.

Uncle Luke stands on the other side. In front of him, on the table, is a bloody carcass. He grunts. Extends his arms. Surprise, he means. The table is covered in plastic.

What's this? I ask.

Uncle Luke lifts up an index card. Half cow, it reads, all for you.

I whiff. Meat. Dead for a while. Still yum. I strip down to my underwear. Like I don't want to get my clothes dirty. But really, a feast calls to be enjoyed flesh to flesh.

My jaw is already unhinged. I only have to stretch my mouth back. Let my fangs out. I wish I had claws. Something to fork the half cow in place while I bite. I use my knee instead. Gnaw and rip with my mouth. It tastes good. Not great. The taste of fear has gone. Also, it tastes like cow. Nothing wrong with cow. But a cow doesn't dream. Not really. And if it does, it dreams of grass. Maybe open skies. A human dreams crazy dreams. Horrible dreams. Great dreams. Like flying. Or teeth falling. Or people long forgotten who pop up as if they never left. They dream of what they were and what they could become. And the dreams seep into their meat. Like a delicious marinade.

Good? Uncle Luke writes.

I'm halfway done. My chest is wet with blood and drool. I give him a thumbs-up. Cow may not be human, but it's still a whole lot of meat.

When only bones are left, Uncle Luke asks if I'm satisfied.

Yes.

My stump itches. I scratch. Uncle Luke wets a rag. Cleans my stump of the dried cow blood. Rubs. Wets the rag and rubs some more. My stump stays red.

Normal? Uncle Luke writes.

No.

Hurts?

Itches.

Uncle Luke takes me to his bedroom. Hands me a green tube of ointment.

For itchy skin, he writes.

Over the next few days, I'm back to pork chops, hot dogs, and lunch kebabs. Uncle Luke can't buy me half a cow every day.

MAMI SHOWS UP AT THE BOOKSTORE. She's leaving for Valencia.

I'll be back for your father's wedding.

To stay? I ask.

I don't know.

We hug goodbye. Her body is just my size. We fit.

I go down to the basement. Basement-rat walks over to me to smell my kebab. I give it a piece. It eats the kebab. I eat the rat.

LATER THAT NIGHT, Sam writes back, *Will you eat me?*

Papi is upset.

She left, again! he says.

She's coming back, Peter says.

He rubs Papi's shoulder. Lena tops off everyone's wine glasses.

More pasta, anyone? Peter asks.

Uncle Luke grunts and lifts his plate. Peter scoops shrimp fettuccine onto it. Papi also cooked garlic toast and salad with walnuts. It's family dinner at their place. Minus Mami.

Is she coming back? Papi asks Lena.

She shrugs.

Did you fight?

No.

I thought you were together.

We tried. I don't think it can work.

Why not?

Why am I responsible for making her stay, Joseph?

You're not. It's just . . . we were all here. The rest of us are still here. What is she leaving for? We're her family.

Uncle Luke grunts.

MAMI WATCHED ME TRANSFORM. I was awkward. Couldn't figure out how to use my legs. Arms. Hands. My eyes couldn't focus. Everything was too dark. Muted. I tripped all the time. I slept a whole lot. Mami moved me into Santiago's old room. Gave me a new bed. Clothes. She talked to me even when I wasn't great at conversation. Got me tutors. Some days she left me with Grandma Lucía and Jackie, who taught me to shave and gave me dentures. They made me a boy. They called me Santiago. They tried. And I tried.

I became less awkward. I followed Mami around like Santiago used to do. She painted my nails. Something else to make me hers. We were alone. Only Mami and I. Papi had moved to New York. Lena too.

Then Mami found her performances.

She wrote a lot in her journal. Ideas, she told me. Things to remember. I practiced writing too. A skill half remembered, half newly learned. Sometimes Mami stopped writing and stared. She stared for thirty, forty minutes. I tried to puzzle it out, but there was nothing to stare at. Mexico City hummed outside. Cars and birds. Inside nothing made a sound. If I asked her what she was staring at, my words never reached her. Like she was too far away. I never found out what she was looking at.

PETER ASKS IF I will give a toast.

Am I supposed to?

It would be nice.

You don't have to, Papi says.

Romy says wedding toasts are supposed to tell the couple how much you love them. Wish them happiness.

Some people tell stories, she says and rolls her eyes.

Stories are not good? I ask.

You'd have to tell a good one.

I have a good one. But I can't tell it.

I'm ready. Please come over, Sam writes.

Is tonight okay?

Now. Please.

I can't.

It's Saturday afternoon, and I'm going suit shopping with Papi. For the wedding.

I don't know if I'll be here again.

SAM'S PLACE IS GREEN. Green walls. Green couch. Green rug. Green table. Green plants. Everything old. Cared for. He dresses in loose white pants. Loose white shirt. His hair sticks out in different directions. Dry. Like he once washed it too much. He bows when he meets me. I bow too. Not sure what else to do.

Master, he says.

I turn around to see who he's talking to. There's no one there.

This way, Master.

He's talking to me. I ask for water. Sam grabs a green glass. Fills it from the tap. The water is fresh.

Thank you, I say.

Master, he whispers. He's barely taller than me. May I?

He extends his arm. Touches my cheek. Men do this. Sometimes. Before they kiss. He doesn't kiss but lifts my upper lip. Caresses my fangs.

Beautiful, he says.

I unhinge and smile wide. Show off. He makes a sound like chuckling. His eyes become red. Tears form. Like happiness. I smile wider. Open my mouth fully. Let my face split in half. He gasps. And bows. Like he wants to touch his toes. He shows me to a bedroom. The walls are green here too. Carpet as well. There's no furniture except a mattress draped in a white sheet. Unlit candles surround it.

Is this good? he asks.

Yes.

I don't care where, as long as I can eat a chunk of him. I ask if he has bandages. Something to cure himself with after I eat.

I won't need it, he says. Like he knows what he's doing.

He lights the candles. One by one. Sunlight shines through gauzy green curtains. Too strong for the candles to produce an effect. He doesn't seem to mind. He undresses. Folds his clothes. Puts them at the top of the bed. Lies on his back. Faceup. Head on his clothes, like a pillow.

I will bite your thigh, I say. Okay?

Yes, Master.

It will hurt.

I know.

No need to attack me or anything.

I won't.

I undress too and leave my clothes outside his room. I step over the candles. I lick. Leg hairs tickle my tongue. No hint of soap.

I like this man. I prick him with my fangs. Let him know the pain is coming. He tenses. I bite. Determined. Fast. He screams. Like a high-pitched roar. He stifles it, biting his clothes. I chew. Exquisite. His neck is red. Tears run down the sides of his face. I've bitten more than I intended. He tries not to squirm. To ease his face.

Okay? I ask. Mouth full.

He attempts a nod. More tears flow. He wipes them. I swallow. You are very delicious.

Thank you, he squeaks.

May I bite again?

He doesn't answer. I wait.

May I?

He wipes tears. Like he shouldn't be crying. But he cries more. Not loud. Ghostlike. Heavy. Like his pain isn't only from the bite. Like it's deeper. Marrow deep.

Eat, he squeaks.

I bite his same leg on the other side of his thigh. His stifled scream screeches louder. More piercing. He weeps. Bubbles form in his mouth. Spit and tear bubbles. Snot. I chew his flesh. My eyes dilate. My mouth waters. My stomach growls. I don't want to swallow. Not yet. The bed is red. Sam grabs the sheets. Pounds his fists. Writhes. I swallow. Try to keep his taste. This is it. End of meal. I can't ask for more. But it feels like I've just started. Maybe I can just lick him. I steady his leg. Lick. He flinches.

Wait, he says. Please.

I pull myself away. Stand up. His smell prevents me from fully walking away. He mumbles. Can't make his voice work. He mumbles again.

I'll go, I say.

Give me a minute, he says.

He calms himself by panting. Like some rite.

Eat.

I lick my fangs. Rediscover his taste.

I eat.

The suit store in Greenpoint is old. Smells of fabric, chalk, and cologne.

What kept you? Papi asks.

Nothing, I say.

Papi doesn't press. The tailor has a suit ready for me to try on. A gray simple cut. I set my backpack down inside the dressing room. Undress. I spot blood on my shin. I cleaned up at Sam's place. Must've missed this part. I wet my finger with saliva and rub away the blood. It smears but doesn't come off. I hike up my socks.

I try the suit on. Jacket is too wide. Pants too long. I step out and stand in front of the three mirrors. The tailor pulls the bottom of my pants up.

Not too high, I say.

The tailor pins the fabric and drops the pant leg.

Jacket is too big, no? Papi says.

The tailor measures shoulder to shoulder.

Let me check, he says and leaves.

He measured you before, Papi says. Why is everything so big?

Maybe I'm shrinking, I say.

The tailor comes back. Says he'll need to take it in. Papi says I look handsome. Regardless.

Papi asks if I want something to eat. I say I'm not hungry. Not hungry? He smiles. Like victory. Papi buys himself ice cream. We walk to McCarren Park. People stroll. Families play. Dogs. Picnics. Music. Like a nice day is all that matters.

Autumn skies you can drown in, Papi says. Peter said that this morning. Who knows where he stole it from.

You like Peter.

I do.

Papi's hair reaches his shoulders. A sun-yellow curtain. It shimmers.

You'll be happy, I say.

He puts his arm around my shoulders.

I'm happy now, he says.

THE DOORBELL RINGS. It's night. Uncle Luke is in his robe about to go to sleep.

He grunts.

I don't know, I say.

The doorbell rings again.

He grunts again.

Ignore it, I say.

Knocking follows.

It can't be Sam. But maybe someone looking for him. Who loved him.

Wrong house, I say.

Uncle Luke peers through the peephole.

Uncle Luke, don't.

He turns to me like he knows I've done something and opens the door. Mami walks in. Rolls a suitcase behind her.

You came back, I say.

I never left.

Mami was at the airport when she decided not to go to Valencia. She didn't want to come back to us either. Not yet. Stayed in a hotel in the Catskills. Hiked. Communed. Tried to understand why so many people love nature.

It's slow, isn't it? Nature, she says.

Uncle Luke grunts in agreement. Offers her cookies.

Why didn't you go? I ask.

I don't want to miss it, my sweet.

Miss what?

Everything! She looks around as if the everything were in this room. Or maybe it's your father wanting all of us together. I can't seem to find it in me to let him down again.

Mami eats a cookie in two bites. Uncle Luke offers Mami his room to sleep in. She says she'll be fine on the sofa bed. Uncle Luke and I arrange it for her.

MY THROBBING STUMP wakes me up in the middle of the night. I massage it, try to soothe it. I feel something protruding. Sharp. I turn on the light to inspect further. A claw is poking out. The very tip. I tug at the claw. Try to coax it out. But I can't grip it properly. The throbbing stops. I lie down. Turn off the light. Stare at shadows until sleep comes.

SANTIAGO, YOU WOKE UP ONE NIGHT. You had peed the bed. You were terrified. Not of the pee. Of the thing that made you pee. Some nightmare. Can't remember what it was exactly. A monster like me, maybe. Or death. You tried not to think too much of death. You believed Papi and Mami when they told you that you would live. You had lived so far. But sometimes death creeped in anyway. Papi! Mami! You called. Both appeared. The lights came on. You calmed down right away. Mami and Papi didn't ask about the mess. Mami helped you change. Papi took your dirty pajamas and sheets down to the washer. No big deal, Papi said. Mami read you a story. You fell asleep and forgot what had scared you so much.

I could write this memory down in my Santiago journal. My record of your memories. Like a house sitter keeping everything in order for when the original inhabitant comes back. Like in the story with the guy who throws up bunnies. He wanted to keep the house ready for his friend too.

But I won't write this memory down. Seems silly. Keeping these. You're not coming back.

Mami invites Lena, Papi, and Peter to Cobble Hill to celebrate her non-departure. Buys fresh flowers. So many she runs out of vases to put them in. The house looks lively. She prepares a taquiza. Picadillo. Rajas. Mole with chicken. Rice. Beans. Avocados. Uncle Luke and I help. Peter brings wine. Lena mezcal. Mami talks loudly. Cheerfully. They make themselves tacos. Peter looks lost. Tries to imitate what Mami and Lena do. I eat spoonfuls of picadillo. Mami raises her glass.

No more running away, she says.

We toast with mezcal. Papi forgets he was angry.

Grizzly scene in Bed-Stuy, Peter says suddenly.

We go silent.

Bones. Bones. Bones! He waves his hands. His eyes widen. You haven't heard? Well, apparently, they found human bones in a Bed-Stuy apartment. A cadaver picked clean. Tabloids were all over it. I confess, they're my guilty pleasure. It all sounded made-up, of course, but now the paper has picked it up too. It's all speculation at the moment, but it seems the victim was part of a cult! Maybe started it. Who knows? Can you imagine? Here in Brooklyn! They found printed texts in his apartment, something about an extraterrestrial god consuming people in order to transport them to a new realm. Bonkers! People will believe anything. What's fascinating, though, is that he was consumed! Actually consumed. Everything but his bones. How they did it, I don't know, but someone had to do it, right? This guy couldn't have possibly done it to himself.

Maybe he died years ago and was just found, Mami says.

Couldn't have been, Peter says. Fresh blood soaked the mattress they found his bones on. Besides, someone would've noticed the smell.

Acid will peel flesh right off, Lena says.

But it would've destroyed the mattress too, right? Possibly the floor.

Someone could've brought the bones from anywhere, Papi says. Then splashed blood on a mattress. It sounds like someone wanted to create a scene, some sick prank.

You're right, Joe. He could've been killed somewhere else. But why? Oh, and they found hair that doesn't match the victim's DNA at the scene. They'll soon know who else was there. People are going bananas over this on Twitter. I can't believe you hadn't heard!

Uncle Luke grunts at me and goes to the kitchen. I follow.

You? he writes.

Yes.

We slip out of the kitchen through the backyard. Past the hall. Upstairs to my room. I fetch my backpack. Sit on the floor and open it. Take out the green glass I drank from, Sam's phone, and the sheet he was lying on. Bloody.

What's this?

Uncle Luke and I jump. Papi appears next to Uncle Luke. Stares at the bloody sheet.

Oh, M, Papi says. It was you.

Of course it was, Lena says from behind him.

Papi leaps to shut the door.

We can't all be up here. Peter will wonder.

Magos is with him, Lena says.

She squats. Doesn't touch anything. She points at the phone.

His?

I nod.

We need to get rid of it. All of this.

Dumpster? Papi asks.

Uncle Luke grunts.

Of course not here, Papi says. Maybe we can drive it to New Jersey.

Will they find anything to connect you to him on his phone? Lena asks. Pictures? Texts?

Texts. That's why I took it.

Uncle Luke grunts.

Fuck, Lena says. Okay. We need a hammer.

Another hammer? Mami asks.

Where's Peter? Papi whispers.

In the bathroom.

He can't come up here!

Go find him then.

I'll go, Lena says. We'll figure this out. Don't be long.

Lena takes Uncle Luke with her. Shuts the door behind them.

Oh, my dear Eme, Mami says.

I tell Mami and Papi that Sam wanted to be eaten. That I only took two bites to start. I was going to leave. But he asked me to go on. I don't tell them that after a few more bites, he asked me to stop. I don't tell them I couldn't stop. Despite his screams, his weeping, his begging, his fighting. I was too hungry.

Papi says he thought I had my hunger under control. Says I can never do this again. Says at least this man wanted to die. Says I must try harder. Says I should . . . He doesn't finish that thought. Like his words crumbled.

I don't say anything. I can't keep saying I'm sorry.

Lena appears again.

We have to go down. Peter is asking about you.

Joe? Peter calls.

Lena shuts the door. Peter is walking up. Papi helps me stuff things back in my backpack.

Joe?

Papi fumbles with the zipper. Can't close it.

Joe? Magos?

Papi struggles. Mami kicks the backpack. It rolls away. Lena opens the door.

What's going on? Peter asks.

Uncle Luke huffs behind him.

M wanted to show us something, Papi says.

What?

This, Mami says. Holds one of the novels Romy recommended.

A book? Peter grabs it. Reads the cover, *We Have Always Lived in the Castle*. I haven't heard of it. Is it good?

Fantastic, Mami says. My mother loved it.

I don't know if this is true. Though it is a book Grandma Lucía would have liked. Mami grabs the book back from Peter. Strokes it. Pretends it's a treasure. No one moves. The house creaks.

I feel like I've interrupted something, Peter says.

Lena clears her throat.

Time for dessert, Mami says.

We move downstairs. Mami serves dessert. Bananas with condensed milk. I push banana slices around on my plate. The only sweet thing I can stand are Fruti Lupis. And I don't even crave them much anymore. Mami talks. Tries to sound cheerful. Like at the beginning of dinner.

THE WALLPAPER IN THE DINING ROOM shows vines crawling upward. Intertwining. There are flowers too. And an owl.

In Firgesan, there was an owl that hooted in the mornings. Santiago, you loved this owl. You woke up early to catch it. You weren't allowed in the woods, but you ran outside anyway. Every morning. Stayed at the edge of the trees but went a little farther in each time. Looking for it. But the owl hid. Once, you thought you were lost. You went too far into the woods. You were scared. Nothing but trees. No hint of the house. You thought of crying, but tears wouldn't come. Like there was no time. You traced one step back. Then another. Found your way back home. The next morning, you went to the woods again. You knew you wouldn't find the owl. But you wanted to tell it not to hide anymore. You wouldn't look for it again.

PETER YAWNS. Says it's time to leave. Early start tomorrow. Papi says Mami and Lena are staying for a bit and he wants to stay too. Peter says he's tired. And that Uncle Luke and I must be tired too. Uncle Luke grunts.

You go, Papi says.

Peter doesn't seem to like this. But he says, Okay. Don't party too much.

Back in my room, I unpack the things I took from Sam.

Can't we just throw everything out? Papi asks.

Let's destroy the phone first, Lena says. We can't risk them finding whatever interactions M had with this man.

Sam, I say.

How well did you know this man? Sam? Papi asks.

I met him on an app. I know his name was Sam. He liked green things.

What did he know about you?

That I like to bite.

Do you know if he told anyone else about you? Mami asks.

I don't know.

We can't really do anything about that, Lena says. We better focus on what we can do.

Uncle Luke grunts in agreement.

Peter said they found hairs, Papi says.

I don't think they can trace them back to Eme, Mami says. Don't you need a record for that? Your DNA in some database?

I don't know, Lena says. But either way, it'd be infinitely better if they don't find these things here.

Should we wash the sheets? Mami asks.

Do you have bleach? Lena asks.

Uncle Luke grunts.

We go downstairs. Uncle Luke finds a hammer in the kitchen. Papi suggests we go outside to smash the phone. Lena says we don't want peeping neighbors. She wraps the phone in a rag. Papi hammers it on the kitchen floor.

Find the chip, Lena says.

What chip?

The card. What is it called? The SIM card.

Papi finds it. Lena bends it in half.

Cut it, Mami says.

Burn it, Papi says.

Uncle Luke grunts. I find my lighter. The chip won't catch fire, and I burn the tips of my fingers trying. Mami finds scissors. Cuts it in half. She walks to the sink. About to throw the pieces in the garbage disposal.

No, Lena says, let's not keep anything here.

I take the cut-up pieces from Mami. Chew them. Make sure they're pulp. And swallow. Lena ties the rag holding the phone pieces. Runs water through it. Adds soap. Rubs. Adds more water.

In case there were prints, Lena says.

What do we do with the pieces? Papi asks.

Wait, I say.

I bring over the green glass. We wash it. Lena unties the rag with the smashed phone in it. Puts the glass in. Papi smashes again. Pound. Pound. Pound. Until Mami has to stop him.

It's broken, Joseph, she says.

WHY DO WE NEED TWO? Papi asks in Lena's car.

I don't know where we're heading. We made two bundles in black garbage bags. One with sheets. Bleached and cut up. Another with the smashed phone and glass.

Because if they find one, Mami says, they won't have the whole story.

Isn't it more likely that they'll find one if there are two to find?

Should we burn it all then?

I vote burn too.

We can't just grill the phone, Lena says. It needs a fucking furnace to be destroyed.

You think throwing it in the river is better, Flaqui?

I'm just trying to do my best here. We got lucky in Berlin. I don't know this time.

Lena parks. No one gets out.

Maybe next time we'll be experts, she says.

There won't be a next time, Papi says. His voice low. Like he knows he's lying.

Lena walks us down a street. I carry one bundle. Papi the other. He wears dishwashing gloves. I wear winter ones. To avoid fingerprints.

Papi says, I think we're close to where Peter proposed to me. He stops. Like he's forgotten what we're doing.

Go home, I say.

What?

I'll do it, Papi. You don't have to worry anymore.

I'll always worry, M.

He walks on. We reach the water but can't walk to the edge. A brick factory stands to our left. Water to our right. Everything barriered by gates.

What now? Mami asks.

I thought there was an opening to the water around here, Lena says.

Uncle Luke walks up to a gate. Chained. He pulls on it. Lights come on when he shakes it. We freeze.

Hey! A shadowed man appears on the other side of the gate. What are you doing here?

Uncle Luke steps back. I growl. Papi grabs my elbow and pulls me away from the light. I coil. Unhinge.

No, Papi whispers, and he restrains me. I squirm against him. Snap my fangs. Dig my heels. Try to break away.

The man shines his flashlight toward us.

What's going on?

Stop, Papi says in my ear. He's strong. Stronger than I thought. He pulls me back. I fall on top of him.

I roar.

What in—

We made it, gang! Mami shouts.

She stumbles toward the man. The man swivels his light to her. Lena steps forward, behind Mami. Papi and I freeze on the ground.

This is Asterisk, isn't it? Mami says. We're on the list. Amanda Lucas.

The man mumbles something in response. His face hidden by bright backlights.

Oops! Mami says. Laughs loudly. Wrong place, everybody.

She puts her arm over Lena's shoulder. Fake stumbles back toward us. Uncle Luke follows. Mami pulls me up. And Papi too.

Go, go, she whispers.

We rush to the corner. The factory's lights go off. We slow down and walk one block in silence.

Good save, Papi says to Mami.

Mami bows.

I want to eat, I say. My jaw remains unhinged.

I may have some snacks in the car, Lena says.

Let's finish this first, Mami says.

I hinge my jaw back in place.

Papi says that we'll figure out a diet that satisfies me. He proposes many things. His words fast. Like the next one will have the answer.

I know what I want to eat, Papi.

Papi shuts up. Mami combs my hair with her fingers.

My darling, we can handle it.

I don't want you to.

Papi snatches the bundles and runs. I run behind him. He makes it to the next pier. To the water. Mami catches up. Then Lena and Uncle Luke. Papi doesn't pay any attention to us. He weighs down both bags with rocks. Heaves the first bundle. Splash. Walks farther up the pier. Heaves the second. Splash.

Let's go home, Papi says.

Mami hooks her arm in Uncle Luke's. They walk away behind Papi.

It seems possible they'll just keep going. Leave me. Forget I was once theirs.

Ready? Lena asks.

No.

She stays but looks away. Like she's also not sure if she wants to catch up with them.

Waves lap. Light wiggles across the dark water. The air smells fishy. Like there should be seagulls screeching overhead, but there aren't any. It's night.

May I show you something, Lena?

I lift my T-shirt and sweatshirt. Thrust my left hip toward her. Lena shines light on my stump with her phone. She touches it.

Does it hurt?

Sometimes.

She squeezes. Grazes the tip with one finger.

It's a claw, she says.

Is my arm-tail growing back?

Is that what you think?

I nod. Pull my T-shirt and sweatshirt down.

Am I going back to being Monstrilio?

I don't know. Lena puts her hands on my shoulders. Finds my eyes. Do you want to?

I smile. She pats my back. We walk toward the others.

Papi's wedding is in three days. Mami is writing in Uncle Luke's study. Ideas for new performances. Uncle Luke checks the papers and tabloids for news on Sam. The case remains a mystery. Results for the hair they found at the scene have not come back. Or they haven't yet reported them. Papi and Peter have gone to Firgesan. Busy with last-minute wedding details. I check my stump. The claw has fully emerged. I take a picture. Send it to Lena. She asked me to keep her updated.

Pain? she writes.

Sometimes.

Unbearable?

No.

I change for work. My largest sweatshirt barely hides the claw. When I get to the bookstore, Romy tells me she's feeling the pressure. She says her last year in college is slipping by though it's only fall.

I can't work here forever, she says. My parents are driving me nuts. I promised them I'd have a plan by the time I graduated. I have nothing. What is a comparative literature degree good for?

Maybe I'll open a bookstore. We can do it together! We could, M. You're so good at organizing. And I have the best taste in books. Something small, curated. A boutique bookshop. With a café. Wouldn't that be très rad?

Romy waits for my enthusiasm. I try to picture the bookstore. Cozy. The smell of ink and paper. Coffee. Stacking books. Working the register. Telling customers to come again. But I can't seem to glue it all together. When I try, the vision falls apart.

ON MY FIRST DAY AT WORK in Berlin, I walked into the gallery. Thomas asked if I was Santiago. I said, Yes. I thought he would laugh. Say, No, you're not. Kick me out. But he smiled. I followed him around all day. He mentioned artists' names, where different artworks were stored, where the tools went, paint. All the while, I waited for the moment he would turn and shout, Impostor! But he kept on explaining, and I kept on waiting. At the end of the day, he said, Hey, Santiago? I tensed for a fight. Swept my dentures with my tongue. It's nice to have you here. See you tomorrow.

SO? ROMY ASKS.

Très rad, I say.

I buy as many of the books with the pink Post-its as I can afford. Keith gives me a discount. And a box to carry them in. Heavy. But I make it home. Mami and Uncle Luke are waiting for me. They seem excited. Uncle Luke grunts. Shoves a newspaper in front of me. I set the box down and grab the paper.

Nonhuman, Mami says before I can read.

What?

Nonhuman. That's what the tests said. The hairs! They're non-human. Probably from a pet, it says, or a raccoon or skunk.

Or me.

Mami touches my face. Rubs my cheek as if I had a smudge on it.

The important thing, my love, is that they have run out of clues. The case is probably going to be closed. Says so right there.

That's good.

Uncle Luke grunts. Happy. He eyes the box.

For you, I say.

He grunts again. Less happy.

THE STUMP KEEPS ME AWAKE. It itches. And when it doesn't itch, it hurts. A second claw begins to show through my skin. I scratch. Pace. Unhinge my jaw. Stretch my mouth. Let my fangs out. Growl like a breathing exercise until I fall asleep. Unhinged.

When I wake up, Uncle Luke is on my bed. He points to my naked stump. To the claws blooming from it.

My arm-tail, I say.

How long? he writes.

Don't know. It was pretty long before.

Uncle Luke grunts and writes, You know what I mean.

WE ARRIVE AT FIRGESAN. Mami, Lena, Uncle Luke, and me. This was the last place you saw, Santiago. This pond you liked to call a lake. You swam in it. Until it froze. That's Mami's favorite tree at the far end. There's the white cube house. Its surrounding woods. You pretended the whole world had turned into these woods. Remember? Pretended you were the last inhabitants of Earth. Just Firgesan, Mami, Papi, and you.

WELCOME, PETER SAYS. Or should I say welcome back?

Maybe you shouldn't say anything, Mami says.

Right. Peter flusters. Says he'll let Papi know we're here and runs back to the house.

Easy, Lena says. He's trying, Magos.

His son didn't die here, Flaqui.

He doesn't know.

He's playing host in a house that isn't his.

You suggested it.

But it's annoying, isn't it? I'm allowed to be annoyed.

Uncle Luke grunts.

We walk away from the car. Mami walks toward the pond. Lena, Uncle Luke, and I follow. Light twinkles on the water's surface. Dragonflies hover.

Eme, the dogwood. You—Santiago loved it. Do you remember?

He thought it was hiding something, I say. The way you cared for it.

We scattered his ashes there. But you can't possibly remember that. You were born after.

Mami walks along the pond's edge. Stops when she reaches the tree and crosses her arms. Lena stands next to Mami. Wraps an arm around her waist. Mami rests her head on Lena's shoulder. I kick a stone. It rolls but doesn't make it into the pond.

People buzz inside the house. Caterers. Florists. Peter shouts instructions at them.

Sorry, Papi says as he leads us upstairs. The tent people haven't come yet. We're losing our minds a bit around here.

Papi and Peter have taken the main bedroom. Mami and Lena are given the guest room. I'm in Santiago's old room, shared with Uncle Luke. He gets the bed. Me, an air mattress.

I hope you don't mind, Papi says, fidgeting. Like nerves. Like joy.

The florists leave first. Then the caterers. They will return tomorrow. The tent is up. Tables and chairs too. Centerpieces. And swarms of light bulbs. Like an enchantment. Peter tears up seeing it lit.

Wow, Papi says.

Even Mami looks pleased. Wedding guests will arrive tomorrow afternoon. Peter's friends and family. We're all of Papi's guests. Already here. Peter gets pizza from the nearest town. Forty-five minutes away. We eat in the sitting room. The cheese and bread get stuck in my throat. Too gooey and processed. I eat it anyway. Outside it's dark and empty. Inside, the light is warm. Like a cocoon filled with their voices. Loving voices.

I fall asleep on the couch. When I wake up, Mami is sleeping on one side of me, Papi on the other. The couch is not that big, but the three of us fit. Papi's hair falls on my face. It tickles, but I don't brush it away. If I move, our breathing might unsync. And it's easier in unison. Like Mami and Papi are breathing for me. My stomach growls. I put my hands over it. I don't want them to wake up. Not yet. But then Mami's stomach growls too. And Papi's. I laugh and sneak away.

Outside, I light my last cigarette. Very human of me. Très M. I puff out the smoke. Watch it swirl into nothing.

Santiago's room is silent except for Uncle Luke's snores. I tiptoe, but he turns on the light as soon as I walk in and grunts.

I freeze by the door.

He starts writing something but stops. Gets up, grabs my hand, and pulls me to him. He hugs me tight. Pats my back several times.

Uncle Luke grunts softly into my ear. It's a placeholder grunt to fill in with any words I want. But I don't need to fill it in. The grunt is enough.

I WAKE LENA UP NEXT. She springs upright. Her hair sticks out from behind.

What's wrong? Is it hurting?

I lift up my T-shirt and sweatshirt.

A little, I say.

Lena holds my stump in her hand. Traces the two claws that have grown from it. Points to a small prick that protrudes.

There's the third, she says.

I'm leaving, Lena.

I push my T-shirt and sweatshirt down.

Going to give the wildlife a try?

Yes.

Good, she says. Leans forward. I'll keep an eye on them. Don't worry.

MAMI RUBS HER FACE AWAKE. She breathes in and looks at me. Tries to smile, but her eyes remain sad. Papi shifts on the couch next to her but doesn't wake up. Mami takes me into the library.

I thought you'd wait until after the wedding.

You know that I'm leaving?

Yes, my darling.

Tonight is better, I say.

Mami pushes her hair back and ties it into a ponytail. I place my hand on her cheek. Like she has done to me many times. I follow the wrinkles near her eyes with my finger. Her cheekbones. Her nose. Down to the dimple above her lip.

We looked alike, I say.

Of course, she says. I made you.

She takes my face in both her hands. Kisses both my cheeks and wraps me in a hug. I sniff her one last time. The same smell Santiago loved. Like nothing could go wrong.

MAMI JOINS ME to wake Papi up.

What's happening?

I wanted to say goodbye.

Where are you going?

I'm leaving.

Papi walks me outside. We sit together with the pond in front of us. The dark outlines of trees beyond. The air is chilly. Like something new. Papi snaps blades of grass with his hands and sprinkles the bits over his feet. Mine too.

I don't want you to leave, he says.

I have to, Papi.

We'll figure out your hunger. You'll see.

I don't want to figure it out.

Wait until after the wedding, then.

I tuck my knees under my elbows. A spider with long legs crawls across my forearm. Papi blows on it. Gentle. The spider pauses. We let it find its way back to the ground.

At least let me help you pack your things, Papi says.

I'll be fine. I promise.

Papi takes my hand. He kisses it and lets it rest on his knee.

I pull him to me. He falls onto my lap. I comb through his hair with my fingers. Clean the tears from his face. Mami sits next to us. Takes my hand in both of hers.

We stay like this until dawn.

I WALK ALONE TO THE DOGWOOD TREE. Leaves crackle under my feet. I fold my pants. My sweatshirt. T-shirt. Underwear and socks. And leave them in a pile by the foot of the tree. My sneakers on top.

Mami, Papi, Lena, and Uncle Luke watch me from the other side of the pond. Lena holds Mami's hand. Papi puts his arm around Mami. Uncle Luke stands behind them.

Mami blows a kiss.

I turn toward the woods.

Ahead of me there's only darkness. It will swallow me. But I don't panic. The panic is not mine to carry anymore. I can let it go. My arm-tail uncramps. I unhinge my jaw. Let my mouth stretch as wide as it will go. Soon I won't feel the cold anymore. My body is already regrowing its patchwork of fur.

The world lightens before me and reveals its edges. Its shapes and in-between spaces.

I step forward.

ACKNOWLEDGMENTS

I set out to write my first novel and this, what you hold in your hands, is what came out. The fact that anything came out and somehow coalesced is due to the support, patience, and all-around good vibes of the following people (and one dog).

Jenni Ferrari-Adler, my awesome agent, who relentlessly championed this book along its many iterations, always trusting it was worth it. My amazing editor, Sareena Kamath, who adopted *Monstrilio* and gave it its truest shape possible. The terrific people at Zando without whose magic this book wouldn't be in your hands.

My intelligent, kind, incisive, talented, fashionable, and great-looking readers (also some of my favorite friends and writers) 'Pemi Aguda, Thea Chacamaty, Wes Holtermann, and Nishanth Injam, who in more ways than one breathed life into this monster. Eileen Pollack, who saw a future to my writing and strove to make it happen. Michael Byers, who read the very first draft and convinced me to stick with it. Everyone who read an incarnation of this book and helped push it forward.

The Helen Zell Writers' Program at the University of Michigan, whose gift of financially supported time not only allowed this novel to be born but gave me the confidence that I might actually be able to finish it. Meagean Dugger, Coleen Herbert, Akil Kumarasamy, Eirill Falck, Elinam Agbo, Peter Ho Davies, and all the beautiful friends and artists who inspired me and made me look at my work more lovingly. The wonderful communities at Tin House and Bread Loaf (Summer '19!) who made me happy to be a writer.

The places that inspired this book, Ciudad de México, Brooklyn, and Berlin; and the ones that gave me shelter, Ann Arbor, Querétaro, and Montréal. The fabulous crews who put me up (and put up with me) in their homes while I attempted to finish the monster: my dazzling sister Paola (Naquis/Pol), Pierre, nieces extraordinaire Valentina and Léonie, and Muffin; my incredible parents and best dog/companion Lola; la prima Christine; Carlos (Rufi); Primooo Daniel and Karla; Irma (Chata) and Carlos; Panchis; Erandika (Butt) and Alberto—I'll forever be grateful.

Butt, you drove me from Brooklyn to Ann Arbor to start this bonkers dream, you helped me set up my life, this book would not exist without you.

To my friends who are family and family who are friends for tirelessly cheering me on.

¡Gracias!

READING GROUP GUIDE

1. Each act is narrated by a different character. Why do you think the author chose to tell this story in this way? Did you like this structure? Did you have a favorite perspective? What made you identify most with your choice?

2. The novel centers a family that is made up of both biologically related and chosen figures. How essential is this unconventional family system to this story and, relatedly, to Monstrilio's development?

3. Magos is a complicated character who makes several surprising, uncomfortable, and even disturbing choices in this novel. Did you feel her actions were justified? Why or why not?

4. Lena's is the only section not narrated by a member of Monstrilio's nuclear family. Why do you think the author included her perspective?

5. A recurring motif in this novel is monstrosity, explored through Monstrilio's arc, Lena's relationship with her mother, and Joseph's attitude toward the tarantula in his apartment. What do you think the author is communicating about the social construction of monstrosity?

6. Monstrilio's perspective is saved for the very end of this novel. How did his voice compare to other characters' descriptions of him? Were you surprised by anything he revealed about his experiences or interior life?

7. Many of the characters in this novel are queer, but the story itself could be analyzed through a queer lens. How does using this framework deepen your understanding of *Monstrilio*'s themes?

8. Similarly, the author pays close attention to the physical bodies of his characters. Crip Theory combines queer theory and critical disability studies to investigate different intersecting social norms and pressures. Are you able to apply Crip Theory principles to this text? What would that look like?

9. What do you think the author is trying to say about love through each character's relationship with Monstrilio?

10. How did you feel about this novel's portrayal of grief? Were there any passages that felt especially impactful or truthful?

11. *Monstrilio* is a work of genre-bending fiction, with elements of horror, folklore, and literary realism, that employs a variety of tones. Did you find this blending effective?

12. Some readers might categorize Monstrilio's proclivities as cannibalism. Do you agree? And if so, what do you make of the recent rise of cannibalism in fiction?

13. Did you enjoy the ending and/or find it cathartic? What do you think happens to Monstrilio after the final page? What do you hope for these characters' futures?